PHANTOMS

PHANTOMS

ROS GOUGH

Published by Rosalind Gough

ISBN (print): 978-1-7393771-0-6

Edited by Aimee Walker aimeewalkerproofreader.com

Cover design by Robin Vuchnich mycustombookcover.com

For my lost little strangers,
Goughling, Sam, Poppy Seed, and Maby,
and yours.
Loved. Always.

PART ONE

PRESENT DAY

NOVEMBER 2015

Paige

IT STARTED WITH A livid streak of horror. Or maybe that was what it felt like afterwards, Paige's mind twisting the rusty smear into something far more lurid, jamming everything through the lens of informed fear.

Blood in her underwear was normal. A regular, unremarkable experience for the bulk of Paige's adult life. But now it had become something panic inducing. If there was one thing everyone knew, it was that you weren't meant to bleed if you were pregnant.

Dashing to the bathroom, she dabbed at herself, desperate and gentle and shaking all at once. She had to see how much blood there was. Not a lot, as far as she could tell. Much less than an ordinary period. More than there ought to be a mere seven weeks into pregnancy though. *Unless it's spotting? How much is reasonable? Why don't I know?*

Alone on the toilet, Paige felt glued to that moment, stuck in it like a rat in a trap. Paths and possibilities unspooled in front of her feet, clad in their fuzzy socks. All that potential ran across the tiled floor and disappeared into the grouting. Was there still a chance this would all be okay? Was it already too late to do anything? Could she be spinning nothing into blind panic?

Tears prickling in her eyes, scrambling to search for reassuring information on her phone, Paige became aware of another presence on the other side of the bathroom door, a shadow blocking the light spilling from underneath. Luke was used to her hurried trips to the toilet, pregnancy making itself unmistakeable even at this point, but this was the wrong time of day for one of her urgent wees. It was easy for Paige to picture him standing on the landing, confused and uneasy, hair tousled.

"Everything alright, love?"

Confessing to him would make it real. Paige made a non-committal noise and took her time finishing up in the bathroom, washing her hands twice, smoothing her hair with shaking fingertips as she watched herself in the mirror, stringing out the inevitable. As soon as she crept out to face her husband, Paige saw the heartbreaking concern in his eyes. She couldn't keep this to herself.

"There's blood." She pitched forward into Luke's arms, tears trickling down her cheeks. The hopes Paige carried were too heavy to bear under the weight of the moment. She couldn't help but leap to all the worst possible outcomes.

He understood right away. "What do you want to do? Should we go to A & E?"

Maybe it was the wrong choice, but Paige shook her head. It was too late in the day for a dash to the hospital. They both had work in the morning. If she didn't make a big deal out of this, perhaps there'd be nothing to worry about at all. "It's not much. Could be spotting, maybe. We'll see what it's like by tomorrow." She sighed and shuddered. "I'll call the doctor first thing."

"Sounds like a plan."

It wasn't much but making a decision about what to do helped a little. It wasn't as if there was anything they could do if it wasn't spotting, not at this stage. They both knew that. Luke kept Paige close as they went through the motions of going to bed like any other night, tucking her under his arm like a lost duckling. She nuzzled close to him, breathing in his reassuring heady scent.

As they both tried to go to sleep, bracing for a restless night, Luke stroked Paige's hair. He probably felt as lost as she did. And as powerless. Maybe more so. It wasn't even his body things were happening to. As dark minutes slid on into hours, a damp patch spread across the fabric of her pillowcase, silent tears trickling down her cheeks.

The toilet paper came away pink in the morning, impossible to explain away as a trick of bad evening light. Was it heavier than last night? Pleading a fictional plumbing emergency, Paige arranged a last-minute work-from-home day. A sympathetic GP on the phone gave Paige a different number to call and started to make plans about next steps. Assuming this pregnancy was continuing.

There was some reassurance in that, still some slim chance that this whole mess was nothing to worry about. BMI check, midwife booking-in appointment, Paige scribbled down all the things to sort out for if… *when* things could move forwards. One short week ago, she'd been counting the days until she could start making these appointments, not sure when she was meant to tell her doctor about it, ticking off the first few items of pregnancy admin. Now it all felt further away than ever.

Nerves thrumming, Paige called the number she'd been given: the early pregnancy assessment unit. A woman with a gentle Scottish lilt answered. Yet again, Paige had to explain what was happening. Most of the answers were at her fingertips, the date of her last period, how long her cycles usually were, when she'd first noticed this bleeding, how much there was. Medical professionals always appreciated Paige's penchant for data collection. Her diligent tracking had to count for something.

One question brought Paige up short: when was the positive pregnancy test result? How long had she been allowed to experience the carefree joy of a wanted and uncomplicated first pregnancy? She wasn't sure. A fortnight or so, Paige supposed. Why on earth had she failed to log it?

SEVENTEEN DAYS AGO

OCTOBER

Paige

"**I** THINK I MIGHT BE pregnant." It was a half-truth. The positive test meant that Paige was as sure as it was possible to be at this stage. But somehow it was easier to fling the idea at Luke's feet as if there was some element of doubt about it.

Her periods weren't quite like clockwork, but fell within the normal bounds of variation, a few days here and there. However, it was three days past the estimated start date and something about the tenderness in Paige's chest and the lack of cramping had led her down a particular path of suspicion.

"What?" Luke's eyes were wide as saucers.

Her husband's disbelief made Paige smile. For a moment, she flashed back to the last time they'd been trembling on the brink of something wonderful together – at her father's wedding. Luke's proposal. Now it was time to level up again. "You heard me."

"Were we…" Luke swallowed hard, as if trying to dislodge a block of sand. "Were we trying for this?"

It was hard to gauge his mood. He didn't seem angry. Paige was almost sure of that. Of course, he had no right to be. It took two to tango with this sort of thing, after all. Both parties were responsible for staying on top of the contraceptive situation. He wasn't allowed to be cross about this, but Paige couldn't quite work out whether he was flushed with excitement over the prospect of impending parenthood or just caught off guard by her unexpected declaration.

"Bit late for that question, don't you think? Does that matter? I'm already pregnant." Paige was hoping that she didn't have to wonder whether they both wanted the baby she was almost sure she was carrying.

"Well?" He wasn't giving anything away. The ghost of a smile clung to Luke's lips, his eyebrows flat and inscrutable. "I asked you first, didn't I? Were we trying?"

Sighing, Paige gave in. "I don't think we were trying, no." She chose her words with care, watching for every micro-expression that refused to cross his sphinx-like face. "But it's not as if we were doing anything to prevent it, were we? Sort of like passive trying?"

It was what married people did. Sometimes. Once the ring was on the finger, you didn't have to be quite so careful. And since Paige had never got on that well with her IUD, it had been a relief not to feel the need to replace it in a hurry once it expired. After a conversation about if they ought to stock up on condoms that never reached a satisfying conclusion, neither Luke nor Paige had revisited the subject of birth control.

They'd been flirting with this exact situation ever since, a matter of time until a baby or odd lack thereof reared its head. And now here they were.

"And I don't hate the idea of it," Paige continued. "What d'you think?" She was desperate to get Luke's true opinion on this development.

To Paige's heart-pounding relief, her husband grinned. "We're having a baby."

They were laughing together, a happy bundle of family. And love. Luke's hand found its way to rest on Paige's stomach, which was still flat – ish – and a long way away from growing into any sort of bump. There was no outward sign of the life that had taken root. But Paige understood Luke's impulse. Ever since she'd had that positive result, she couldn't stop touching her belly either. Knowledge of what was in there drew the hand like a magnet.

PRESENT DAY

NOVEMBER

Paige

THE FIRST APPOINTMENT THEY could offer her at the pregnancy assessment unit was Tuesday. Four endless days away. Like an idiot, Paige heard herself asking if they could do it in the afternoon. Why wasn't she getting in there at the earliest opportunity? But Tuesday mornings were always so jammed with meetings. It would be difficult to wriggle out of them without calling attention to the situation. And there was still a chance there was no situation at all. It was supposed to be weeks before she needed to tell Pippa about the pregnancy, start planning maternity leave.

It would be much more straightforward for Paige to slip away saying she had to go to the dentist or something. Easier than admitting what was going on. Would a handful of hours make that much of a difference?

What was the alternative? Storming into the clinic and demanding a scan there and then? Paige couldn't do something like that. She was practical, so very sensible indeed. Responsible. Everyone said so. Over time, she'd discovered that practicalities had limits.

Her preference for low-maintenance hairstyles was trumped by her friend Kelly's unwelcome but accurate observation that the beloved pixie cut made Paige's head look odd... kind of pointy? Ever since, the neat helmet of a bob was the next best alternative. These were the sorts of functional compromise Paige's days were built around. There were plenty of factors outside the influence of these decisions, like biology, but you couldn't sweat that sort of thing too much, right?

Every now and then, Paige felt stifled by the sensible face of relentless organisation, the one she presented a little too often, to the point that it was all the world ever seemed to notice about her. A rebellion would dart to the surface, breaking out like a dolphin bursting forth from the rolling surface of the ocean. That sort of momentary madness was responsible for the lighthouse tattoo on Paige's right shoulder. It was tasteful, at least, dinky, and monochromatic. She'd managed to hide it from her mother for the best part of a decade.

The tattoo had been the insurgent twitch Paige regretted the least though. Trying so hard to convince Luke that they ought to buy that refurbished church, somewhere far quirkier than either of them wanted or could live up to, had been a wasted effort. And the less said about signing up to volunteer for Greenpeace on a remote Scandinavian island to protest offshore oil rigs the better. Paige's pledge was soon downgraded to several hours of working the phone banks for fundraising efforts and a large guilty cheque of her own. Which was probably more appreciated in the long run than her initial fervour anyway.

*

Watch and wait. That was the meat of the advice the kind Scottish nurse could offer Paige between now and Tuesday. If it got heavier or the pain got worse, call back. By the small hours of the next morning, before it was bright enough to inspect the loo roll without snapping all the lights on, Paige couldn't fool herself into believing that the bleeding was getting any lighter. She'd almost been able to convince herself that there was less blood, that the blip of a baby wasn't disintegrating into nothing and leaking out between her legs. But even in the pre-dawn gloom, Paige could see the bright red of it. Freshness wasn't a good sign.

Dialling the pregnancy unit in the small hours of Sunday morning didn't yield quite the same sensitivity as it had the first time. *Keep watching, keep waiting, take it easy, treat yourself to some paracetamol to manage the pain, no point putting yourself through needless discomfort, try not to think about it.* As if there was anything else Paige could focus on.

While she waited for the ultrasound appointment where they'd be able to figure out what was going on, Paige exercised outright denial. Her pregnant-lady behaviour was impeccable. Nothing she wasn't meant to eat or drink, no matter how much Paige might have been craving a heaping platter of sushi and a glittering glass of ruby-red Merlot. She swallowed her daily dose of folic acid as soon as her phone pinged with the reminder, and she went without a scalding bath to soothe her increasingly achy abdomen. What was the point of a soak if you didn't emerge from it as red as a cooked lobster?

The pain wasn't as bad as a period, not really. She went for a walk in a doomed attempt to clear her mind, blow away the cobwebs that were looking more sinister with each passing hour, dripping with macabre implications. When Paige had to stop and sit on a park bench to ride out a wave of cramping, she was being kind to herself, nothing more serious than that, giving her pregnant body a break from the exertion of the stroll. There was still reason to hope.

She didn't want to know how slim the chances of survival were for the baby.

Every time she went to the toilet, it was harder to cling to any sense of optimism. The paper always came away red, or pink. Sometimes light, but then darker too, rusty, and brown. Tuesday stayed forever far away, a dot on the horizon.

*

Paige was wittering to the ultrasound technician. Anxiety wound tight after too many hours of waiting for this moment had triggered a wave of verbal diarrhoea. The patient woman with her stoic expression must have done this thousands of times. She'd be used to delivering news both good and awful. And yet Paige was desperate to prepare the professional for what was about to happen, trying to impart as much information as possible before the wand was inserted. As if it would make any sort of difference to the outcome.

"I'm hopeful, but not that optimistic," Paige said in a strangled voice. She'd been bleeding for days. In her heart, she knew this story wasn't going to have a happy ending.

The probe inside her was far from comfortable. Paige gritted her teeth, keen to prove herself equal to it, and rode out the alien feeling of prodding deep inside her. It was more intimate than a smear test, far more clinical than sex. A necessary invasion.

She lay there and tried to imagine the technician telling her what she wanted to hear: that Paige was worrying about nothing. That there was the heartbeat, pumping away, even though it was early. Even with all the bleeding, it was alright. That she had a little fighter on her hands.

But Paige didn't have the imagination for happy endings. She knew. The bleeding hadn't let up. When she arrived at the clinic, she'd managed to produce a urine sample but had been too horrified to hand it in. There was too much red floating in the container. Instead, she gave them the paler one she'd brought from home. As if it had any power to change the outcome.

The technician knew too. But the hammer blow wasn't any easier to bear even though Paige sensed it coming. How could you brace for the impact? The three of them, the technician, Paige, and Luke, were all holding their breath. Husband and wife clutched hands as the probe examined every corner of Paige's womb, due diligence at work.

"I'm so sorry. I can't see anything here. And the lining of the uterus is thin."

A keening howl burst out of Paige's mouth. She crumpled into Luke's embrace, incapable of speech.

"I'm so sorry," the technician said again, backing out of the room to give the bereft parents some time alone with their grief.

The few short weeks of secret smiles and tender breasts evaporated as if they'd never been. By the time the clinical staff concluded that it wasn't an ectopic pregnancy, just a straight-forward miscarriage – though they were diplomatic enough not to emphasise the lack of more serious consequences as a blessing – Paige wasn't even bleeding that much anymore.

She didn't know how to grieve. All her grandparents were still alive. There'd been a certain giddiness for Paige that she was going to be able to introduce Nana Dot and Grandad Alan to their first great-grandchild. Paige hadn't even ever had a pet to educate her tiny tot self about the finality of existence. The blood in her knickers was the worst thing to have ever happened to her, no contest.

But she knew she owed it to the people in her life to tell them what had happened. Sweeping the mess under the carpet felt more wrong, somehow, a disservice to the baby. The twelve-week taboo loomed large in Paige's brain. This was why you weren't supposed to tell so soon. These sorts of circumstances were what bound up mouths before the end of the first trimester, when things got safer for all involved.

Dutiful as ever when it came to the rules, Paige hadn't breathed a word about the pregnancy and now it was too late. Who should she choose to break the seal with? Luke could have the responsibility for telling his lot. By all rights, Paige's mother should have been the obvious answer to the question of who she ought to tell first. But there was that gulf that stretched all the way to Dorset. Even so, Margaret wouldn't forgive her if Paige managed to let the news spread to her father and his new wife before her own mother got wind of it.

Her sister. Annie was a neat, elegant solution that stood a decent chance of making Paige feel the tiniest bit better. Sucking in a shuddering gasp at the idea of pushing the actual words out into the world, she picked up the phone.

"I was pregnant."

Dark spots appeared on the fabric of her top.

TWELVE YEARS AGO

APRIL

Paige

"**M**UM'S ACTING WEIRD."

That was Annie's conversational opener. No preamble, no context. Home from university for the Easter holidays for all of about five minutes, and Annie flopped onto Paige's bed brandishing a champion non-sequitur.

Paige blinked at her big sister. "Huh?"

"Have you noticed anything?"

What was there to notice? Mum was just Mum. "Why? What've *you* spotted?"

Annie rolled her eyes at Paige's cluelessness. "Nothing really. She keeps asking me funny questions. And she wanted me to set up Facebook for her, but she banished me from the room as soon as I finished her profile."

The sickening pull from the pit of Paige's stomach warned her that maybe her sister had a point, even if she didn't want Annie to be right. She tried to ignore it. "Disturbing as it is for parents to pop up on the socials, it's not as if we can ban her. Or can we? Maybe get her kicked off?"

"No. Well, I guess it's too late for that now anyway." Annie's worried expression didn't shift, her eyes still squinting and suspicious, as if she thought that Paige was holding out on revealing information. "Maybe I'm making a big deal out of nothing."

The ominous mood that Annie had ushered in hung around over the next few days. It felt as if all four of them, Annie, Paige, Margaret, and Russell, were waiting. However, Margaret was the only one who knew what they were waiting for. On Annie's last night at home, Margaret asked them all to come and sit with her in the front room. If it weren't for the prickling sense of dread, one or other of them might have joked about being summoned for an audience with the Queen.

"I don't," Margaret gulped, "I'm not sure how to put this."

"What's going on, Mum?"

"Yeah, you're not dying or something are you?" It was clear from Annie's immediate wide-eyed expression that she regretted her attempt at humour. Something serious was about to go down and, for all either of the sisters knew, they were about to learn that it *was* cancer or something equally scary. Then again, if that was the case, why did their dad look as bemused as Annie and Paige?

"I'm sorry that it's come to this, but I'm leaving your father." When her declaration was met with nothing but a wall of stunned silence, Margaret ploughed on, still not looking at her husband. As she spoke, the pitch of her voice rose, giddy with nerves. "I haven't been happy for quite some time, I hate to say. And while it's a recipe for disaster to depend on one's life partner for fulfilment, I've come to the realisation that I can't get what I need while I'm still living under this roof. I… I have to soar, to spread my wings and see what I can find out there for myself, out in the wider world."

Parts of the speech sounded rehearsed, as if they'd been repeated many times in the mirror. Points for Margaret to aim at while she made her desperate leaps in the dark to try and make her perspective understood by her bamboozled spectators.

None of it made any sense to Paige. Buried in confusion, her eyes flicked towards her sister. Annie's mouth was hanging wide open. Then Paige glanced over at her father. Russell had better control over his reaction to his wife's announcement. The sole sign of his utter surprise was that his eyebrows had shot upwards, rocketing towards his hairline.

"Margaret dear, why is it that the first *I'm* hearing about this is the same time as the girls?"

His wife stared down and shifted her feet. "I didn't want for there to be any secrets."

"You mean you wanted an audience." The tone he used was mild, but the accusation would have cut through no matter how he said it. Margaret's mouth popped open to protest, but Russell carried on. "Presenting this… this decision as a fait accompli. You wanted to make sure that I was defanged, to minimise any chance that I'd try to make a scene of my own. Not in front of the children."

A petulant impulse prompted Paige to protest that, at a few weeks shy of seventeen, she wasn't a child anymore. Knowing that it wasn't her moment to interject, Paige managed to stop herself. Margaret might have made sure that she and Annie were around to witness what was going on, exactly as Russell had accused, but neither Paige nor her sister were meant to be active participants in this conversation.

"It's my decision, Russell. You can't make me change my mind, force me to stay."

It was like a scene out of a soap – trembling voice, fluttering eyelashes, overwrought lines. The only problem was that there'd been some serious miscasting for the villain of the piece. Russell was about the furthest thing possible from an ogre, or a gatekeeper, mild mannered in his button-up cardigan and faded slippers.

"I never suggested that I'd want to force you to do anything. Not exactly the dream to keep someone else in a marriage against their will. But there are some basic courtesies when it comes to putting an end to any twenty-four-year partnership." He raised an eyebrow. "Break the news to me in private, give me some level of right to reply. Those sorts of things."

The words dropped into the room shrouded in ice. When Paige dared to peep over at her father, she noticed that Russell's eyes were swimming with tears. He was far more hurt than angry about what was happening. "I didn't even know you were unhappy, dearest."

"I..." Margaret wasn't made of stone either. She looked so lost and alone, deflated rather than buoyed up by her surprise declaration of independence. Who knew how long she'd been psyching herself up for this? "It took rather a long time for me to work that out for myself. And then even longer to come to a decision as to what to do about it," she confessed.

As much as Paige wanted to stick around and keep watching the fascinating one-act play unfolding in the front room, she didn't resist when Annie tugged at her hand. The sisters slipped out to sit in the hall, side by side on the bottom stair, confident that their parents wouldn't be following them anytime soon.

"Reckon he'll get her to change her mind?" Paige whispered to Annie. She wasn't sure what she hoped the answer would be.

"Course not. You heard what he said about making her stay. And after she pulled such a stunt, why would he want to? But Dad's right, there was no reason why *we* had to be there to witness that."

25

Staring at her worldly sister, Paige felt her face creasing into a frown. She couldn't make sense of any of it. "Why did she do it then?"

Annie shrugged. "For all we know, she's been building it up for ages. Or maybe she tried to talk to him before and he missed it? She might've been too nervous to say anything *without* us there. I guess it was me shipping off back to Durham that made her take the plunge tonight. Whatever her reasons, it's done now. No going back." She sighed and looked over at Paige. "You going to be alright?"

"Me?"

"You." Snatching up Paige's hand, Annie tucked it under her arm. "*I* get to leave this madhouse. After I go, you'll still be here with these beans spilled all over the table. Stuck between Mum and Dad. Think you're going to cope?"

Paige considered the uncomfortable picture Annie had painted. It wasn't hard to predict the inevitable pinballing back and forth between parties, the freshly drawn battle lines. "Can I come and stay with you for a bit?"

A sympathetic laugh erupted from Annie's chest, and she leaned over to wrap her sister in a hug. "I don't think I can get away with kidnapping you, sorry. I'll get Dad to arrange a proper visit for you. I'm sure guilt money will finance the thing in style, takeaways for days, sneak you out for a night of clubbing. And in the meantime, day or night, ring me if you want to talk."

There was something urgent pressing on Paige's shoulders, forcing her down into the worn carpet. Without even realising it, she *had* been keeping something from Annie when she'd asked.

"It's my fault," Paige whispered.

"Why would you say that?"

"She... well, Mum kept pushing me to think about all these mathsy jobs, apply for accounting or something. Even though it's not what I want to do, even though I don't know what I *do* want to do. So, I agreed. I asked her if there was anything she wanted to do with *her* life that she never got to. I think that's how all this started. She talked about acting and then there was this… faraway look in her eyes. What if that was what got her thinking about leaving Dad?"

For a moment, Annie was quiet. Then Paige felt her sister's arm tighten around her comfortingly. "Oh, P. You didn't do this."

"You don't know that." Paige sniffed. "She said it took her a while to figure it all out. It was me who—"

But Annie wasn't having any of it, cutting in before Paige could indulge further in her impromptu pity party. "Course I do. Think about it, sis. If that's all it took, a few innocuous questions, to send Mum off the deep end, well, something else would have done it before long. It's not like you were trying to break Mum and Dad apart. Stop being a massive cliché. The kids are almost never the total cause of parental divorce."

Even if Annie was right, her words weren't doing much to ease the cloying sense of guilt cluttering up Paige's brain. "But—"

"Don't do this to yourself, doofus. All of this is going to be rough enough on you. No sense in making it any worse. And I mean it, if you ever need me, call me. Sympathetic ear if nothing else."

Paige leaned her head against Annie's shoulder. "Will do."

"Hey," Annie's gaze was fixed on the front room door, "looks like dinner's going to be a bit delayed. I say we raid the freezer. There's ice cream in them thar hills."

Grinning, Paige followed Annie yet again.

SIXTEEN YEARS AGO

FEBRUARY

Celeste

"**A**T LEAST YOU CAN get pregnant."

It took Celeste a few moments to register who was talking. Once the nurse had delivered her devastating news, those dreaded words, "I'm sorry, there's no heartbeat," she'd slipped out to give Celeste and her husband, Stephen, some privacy.

The reprieve was temporary though. The doctor was on the way to discuss what to do about the tiny dead baby in Celeste's womb. Far smaller than they ought to have been at ten weeks. Celeste already felt guilty for missing the moment her child had stopped developing. How could she have carried them around for weeks without noticing they were no longer alive?

"We'll try again."

Mutely, Celeste nodded at Stephen. She clutched the flimsy paper sheet to stop her hands from shaking. The sheet wasn't doing well in its attempts to lend her a little modesty. She should put her trousers back on.

Trying again. It *was* what Celeste wanted to do. But did he have to be quite so clinical, so... unilateral about it?

She knew what people thought about her and Stephen, how they looked. Older man, childless, who'd taken up with a much younger woman while he was still married to someone else. The only thing people were right about was that it was nothing more than a matter of time before they had children – something she and Stephen had joked about, even in the early days of their relationship. Maybe it had ended up happening a little earlier than Celeste had expected, but the joy of that positive pregnancy test had told her everything she needed to know. She longed for motherhood.

The affair with Celeste had been the final straw for Stephen's first marriage. His wife, a practical woman who'd become accustomed to a certain quality of life, had been more than prepared to ignore his frequent indiscretions. Especially when their starts and ends came coupled with jewellery – whenever he wanted to make a more extravagant apology.

But a woman like Celeste was more than an idle flirtation. A little older than his usual conquests, someone readier and more serious about starting up a life, a family. It didn't matter that the relationship had begun like all the others, with whispers in corners and a distinct lack of solid promises about the future. This time it was different.

Whether Stephen had realised it at the time or not, Celeste was a way for him to get something his current wife couldn't provide. Helena would stick around while he hunted down meaningless sex elsewhere, after all, it wasn't as if she wasn't getting some of that outside of her marriage too. But she wasn't going to wait around to be left for someone her husband could have a baby with.

Celeste hadn't blamed her friends for making assumptions. They thought the bun was already in the oven when she walked down the aisle to the discreet altar, that it was the reason they'd decided to have a small register office wedding. Nothing to do with not wanting to rub anything in Helena's face – the fact that the wedding had been three weeks after the decree absolute came through accomplished that already — or that Celeste's parents didn't approve.

There was a tiny kernel of truth in what everyone assumed about Celeste and Stephen though. If Celeste had somehow been able to not notice or avoid it until then, the pride on his face when she told him she was pregnant was unmistakeable. The expression had been tinged with something else, though. She'd struggled to place it.

Relief? She knew there'd been tension between him and Helena. Had it been because of difficulty conceiving? Or maybe she hadn't wanted children at all. In all their time together, Stephen had told Celeste as little as possible about his other marriage. At the time, Celeste had liked to believe that they'd lived totally separate lives and Stephen had done little to dispel that notion.

But the way Stephen had gazed at Celeste with such startled reverence once she'd broken the news made her certain that at least an element of the last marriage's breakdown related to Stephen's lack of children. And he didn't have to wait too long after marrying Celeste to get what he wanted.

Except now it had been snatched away. Celeste couldn't think any more about beginnings. Not with this new little life inside her already snuffed out. This pregnancy had to be finished.

Her broken heart would have to wait until the practicalities had been dealt with. The baby had to come out, one way or another. Through a haze, Celeste struggled to understand what the doctor was trying to tell her. Something about surgical evacuation of... of the products. Or medical management? What were these clinical terms and what did they have to do with Celeste's baby?

How was she supposed to decide what to do? The baby was meant to stay inside and keep cooking for many more months. She didn't *want* to let them go. But if she didn't, she and Stephen couldn't start trying again for another. Not a replacement, but one who stood a chance of going the distance.

When Stephen asked about when they might be able to schedule the surgery, things came into sharper focus in Celeste's eyes. She noticed a tiny frown playing across the doctor's face. The expert in the room didn't think surgery was the right thing to do – the one sign Celeste needed to make her mind up. Though it hardly felt like a choice at all, Celeste knew she didn't want to part ways with this child under sterile lights. She wanted to be in safety, at home. If it happened during surgery, even if Celeste was conscious, the moment would have to be shared with so many people…

She'd take the pills.

As Celeste wandered into the open air, surprised that it was still sunny when she felt so dark and gloomy, she tried not to dwell too much on what was going to happen next. A stack of leaflets she'd blindly accepted would tell her lots of things she didn't want to know. More clinical jargon.

She hadn't told anyone else she was pregnant yet. Perhaps she'd been too quick to tell Stephen. It might have been better to wait, to check and see that it was a sure thing. Since there was no one to un-tell, maybe it would be better for Celeste to keep this sorry business to herself. There was no danger of Stephen telling anyone about it. All his questions had been about when they were safe to try again. He was already focused on the future.

It wasn't that Celeste wanted to pretend it hadn't happened, more that she thought it would be easier to act as if it hadn't. She laid a hand on her stomach, tears rolling down her cheeks, and said a silent goodbye to the little one she knew she'd miss forever but wanted to put behind her as soon as possible.

PRESENT DAY

NOVEMBER

Paige

GRUMPY AND MOROSE, PAIGE almost jumped out of her skin when she spotted one of the neighbourhood cats watching her through the front window. Her scowl soon matched the hostile feline's. As if she didn't have enough to be annoyed about.

Cats hadn't always inspired such feelings in Paige. Once upon a time, she'd been keen to make friends with next door's cat, childish eagerness compensating for the occasional scratch from the stripy creature. But then came the time in the middle of the summer holidays that was enlivened and then dulled by the ultimately fruitless search for him when he went missing.

After hours of combing the neighbourhood for little Wombat, they'd found out that an HGV had squashed the hapless moggy. Mrs Fuller moved out a few months later, replaced by the stern and ill-named Goodmans, keepers of what had to be an extensive collection of errant balls and frisbees. After that, cats had become symbols to Paige of bad tempers and death. No wonder she was seeing one now.

The first confession about the miscarriage had been the hardest. All the ones that came after that conversation with her sister followed the same basic pattern. Getting the words out of her mouth, the devastating use of the past tense when it came to her baby, made it all so stark that the journey just begun was already over.

After the short round of phone calls was done with, Paige crawled into bed. What seemed like days later but would in fact have been a few short hours, she was aware of Luke curling up behind her. He wasn't trying to get her to leave the bedroom. All he wanted was to be close to her after he got home from work.

It had been difficult to convince him to go out in the first place. There was nothing Luke could do for either of them by hanging around the house like a spare part. The glimmer of possibility that he could do something constructive at work was enough to tempt him out the door. As soon as he got in from his commute, Luke must have peeled off his shoes and climbed under the covers to spoon his grieving wife.

"Would it be weird if we named them?" Paige whispered to her pillow. After a moment of silence, she was almost prepared to let it go. But then she rolled over to get a good look at Luke's reaction, wanting to try and work out if he'd heard her in the first place. "Something else, I mean?"

He frowned. Maybe she shouldn't have asked. If the idea didn't make sense to Luke, Paige wasn't sure she wanted to take the time to unpack her thinking. Was she being ridiculous? The clump of cells that had nestled inside her until it had disappeared, it hadn't been a baby. An embryo, not even a foetus yet. Who named an embryo? Why waste a perfectly usable name on a child that never developed?

Paige let the idea go. It felt like too much effort to coax an answer out of Luke. All she wanted to do was sleep, craving the oblivion of unconsciousness. She had the office to face in the morning. Without a proper explanation for what was going on, Paige couldn't expect Pippa to be any more accommodating about her string of absences.

TWO WEEKS AGO

OCTOBER

Paige

"**I** WAS THINKING."

Luke looked up at Paige with an indulgent smile. It had become his default expression recently. Regarding Paige through the rose-tinted glasses of the future, already seeing her as a mother, his partner in parenthood. Every little interaction between them was bathed in the hazy golden glow of this secretive time. Before it was safe to announce.

"Always dangerous."

Swatting at him, Paige giggled. "Thank you for that. I was wondering what we were going to call it, them, you know." With her hand resting on a spot below her navel, they both knew who Paige was referring to. There was no real need to grapple with indistinct pronouns.

"It's way too soon for us to be thinking about names, isn't it? Pregnancy test's not even dry yet."

"Sure." Paige dragged out the syllable. When would it be the right time for Paige to admit that her brain had been teeming with name suggestions from the moment that second line faded into view? Her current front runners were Eric and Amelia, although the latter was a bit too trendy for Paige's liking. She was already counting down the weeks until they could find out the gender, cut out some of the mystery in picking names. "But it'd be helpful to have a way to refer to the baby while they're still in there, wouldn't it?"

Luke frowned. "Not just 'Baby?'"

Where was his imagination? Paige didn't want to be quite that boring. She shook her head. "Kind of gives the game away, doesn't it? Anyway, we're not supposed to tell anyone before, what, twelve weeks? Just in case." Though it seemed mad to hold back because of a slim chance of something horrible happening. That sort of thinking was a thing of the past, surely? It wasn't worth considering, as far as Paige was concerned. This little thing was staying put.

"End of the first trimester's still a couple of months away," Paige pointed out. "Besides, people might start thinking you call me that." She shot Luke a significant glance. "Do we want to run the risk of coming off as one of *those* couples?"

Shrugging, Luke didn't seem to be too fussed about what other people might think of him. Oh, to have that level of self-assurance. But if there was a time for Luke to indulge his wife, then this was it. Paige almost wondered if she was wasting her opportunity to ask for something way more ridiculous. Plenty of time for that further down the line, midnight ice cream feasts and foot rubs on tap.

"Did you have something in mind for a pregnancy nickname, then? If Baby won't do?"

Paige's lips twisted in contemplation for a moment, not wanting to admit that she didn't have any suggestions for nicknames locked and loaded before she brought this idea up. She glanced down at her shirt, trying to picture the baby swimming around under the layers of material and a smile spread over her face at the flash of inspiration. "Button."

"I like that. Button it is. May all future parenting decisions be this easy."

"Amen."

Luke wandered over, giving Paige a hearty kiss before he crouched down in front of her abdomen. Planting his hands on Paige's hips to steady himself, Luke nuzzled her stomach with his nose. "Hello, young Button, it's Daddy."

"They can't hear you, not yet." But Paige could feel her grin stretching from ear to ear. Her heart was melting into marshmallow goo at the sight of Luke already being so silly yet so tender with their child. He was going to be such an amazing father.

"Doesn't hurt to get the practice in though, does it? Otherwise, it might feel weird when the time comes for me to start talking to your bits in the hope that they can hear me. Got to give our little Button as good a chance as possible to recognise me too when they make their grand entrance. Can't have Mama stealing all the glory."

"Mama?"

"Mummy then." They smiled at each other, revelling in what was going to happen. When the baby came, everyone would be getting new names. It wasn't just Paige and Luke making the shift to Mummy and Daddy. There would be at least four new grandparents, depending on who was counting. Paige still wasn't sure how she felt about her stepmother's pending status.

It was much too soon to tell anyone though, no matter how much Paige wanted to tell Annie. Two people in the world knew that Paige was pregnant: her and Luke. It was a glorious secret to be held close to the heart. In so many ways, it felt as if Paige were holding her breath, steeped in a heady disbelief that this was happening.

Because, for all her bravado about sailing towards twelve weeks, Paige had doubts. She was almost half-convinced that every time she sat down on the loo there would be blood in her knickers, that it would turn out she'd made a mistake and wasn't pregnant after all. Late periods for other reasons were a thing. And a positive could get explained away.

Certainty would come later, Paige had to hope. In the coming months, there would be more signs, like the bump and the sensations of something alive squirming around in her belly. She couldn't wait. For the time being, Paige wasn't even plagued with morning sickness. What a relief to have been spared.

SIXTEEN YEARS AGO

FEBRUARY

Celeste

AFTER IT WAS ALL over, but before Celeste's pregnancy tests were coming up negative, it wasn't quite *unfeeling* for Stephen to do what he did. If you were prepared to grant him the benefit of the doubt, the way he packed Celeste off to her mother's house could be regarded as the most loving of gestures.

Stephen wanted her to feel looked after, she knew that much. The fact that he wasn't prepared to dispense said care himself was a little bit regressive, sure, but you couldn't argue too much with a bit of outsourcing when he was grieving too. A man like that was afraid of anyone having the chance to see past the stiff upper lip exterior, even his own wife.

It would have been much easier if Stephen had gone to the trouble of telling his mother-in-law what was going on before he deposited his wife on Gail's doorstep as if observing a teenager's curfew. The mystery of it all had piqued her curiosity in an unhelpful way.

It took less than half a cup of tea for Celeste's shaky defences to come crumbling down. Even with her father in the room, Celeste found it impossible to keep holding things back. She wanted to talk about her lost baby, the experience of the birth and what it all meant for the future.

The words came out in a tumble. "I had a miscarriage."

Gail raised her eyebrows for a moment. Expectations had been confounded. Then her face sank into a careful expression of sympathy. "Oh, sweetie. What did you do?"

"What?"

Celeste's father, John, shook his head. "It's not an accusation, little star. Just, something to bear in mind for the future. That's what Mum's saying, right, dear?"

Gail nodded. "Were you trying to do too much? Heavy lifting, I mean? Stephen should have known better than to make you manage... Or was it, my goodness, sex?" She mouthed the last word.

It all sounded a lot like an accusation.

When Celeste was still too stunned to speak, Gail continued talking. "I remember being pregnant with you and feeling as if I were made of glass, so anxious that something would go wrong. It's such a stressful time, but, well, it's so important to look after yourself properly. If you take the proper care... things shouldn't..."

She sighed and shot her daughter a sideways glance. "Oh, I'm sure it wouldn't have been anything like that. They're not so easy to dislodge, no matter what it feels like. Unless you were doing something silly." A small, scandalised gasp fired out as something awful occurred to her. "You weren't drinking, were you?"

"Of course I wasn't!" The indignance was helping Celeste, holding her together when she wanted to disintegrate. Neither of her parents were saying anything she hadn't thought of already, but it was beyond unsettling to hear such things coming out of someone else's mouth.

This was going to be what everyone assumed, wasn't it? Even though it was the opposite of the gentle reassurances from all the medical staff, the assertions that there was nothing Celeste could have done, no method at her disposal to detect what had happened. Maybe it was another generation operating Gail like a puppet. Celeste couldn't bear the thought of everyone deciding she was such a terrible mother that the universe had to deny her the baby to keep them safe.

"But she must have done something to make it fall out, surely?"

That was the last straw. The not-so-quiet mutter out of the corner of his mouth served as confirmation that her dad didn't have a clue what he was talking about. A flare of jealousy ricocheted through Celeste. It was clear that he and Gail had never been through loss like this. Suddenly, Celeste found herself resenting her own birth and its relative easiness compared to her more recent experiences.

What had Gail done to earn a straightforward pregnancy that Celeste hadn't? There was no point in asking her mother. Gail would make some reference to the affair. To "poor" Helena. Celeste had brought this little tragedy on herself.

"Fall... I mean... Dad." Eyes wet, Celeste turned to Gail. "Mum. It was a missed... " She scrambled to find a way to make sense of the conversation, force them to understand what they were being told. "I had to give birth to the baby."

"Oh."

Seconds stretched on into awkward minutes while neither John nor Gail said anything else. They didn't even offer a hug. If either of them could ask the right questions, any questions, that weren't trying to pin the blame for the lost baby on their daughter, they might be able to reach a place of sensitivity together.

It didn't take much more conversation for the bar to lower all the way down to the ground. This wasn't a safe place for Celeste to share the details of her miscarriage. All she could do was stuff everything down. If she didn't, she'd end up exploding at her parents and give them the satisfaction that her emotions stemmed from guilt or something just as awful.

Getting through this visit with all three of them still alive would be enough for Celeste to consider it a win. She might not be getting anything resembling the kind of care Stephen wanted for her, but the fire Gail had ignited, the righteous fury coursing through Celeste's veins, was giving her more of a reason to live than Celeste could have expected.

PRESENT DAY

NOVEMBER

Paige

I N THE END, PAIGE couldn't be too sure what tipped her over the edge. At first, it was almost too easy, too natural, to waltz back into the office as if nothing had happened. She strode through the front doors, head high, shoulders back, and laughed off the concerns of her colleagues. It seemed that they were all buying into the lie she'd fed them about a brief spell of something nasty but run of the mill. No, it wasn't contagious, she didn't think. Probably something she ate. Much better now thanks, ready to get back to it.

Paige didn't know how she felt about the fact that the prospect of spreadsheets was a welcome distraction from staring at the walls, trying not to picture the bloody mess that was all that remained of the life she'd housed so briefly. It was reassuring, more than anything else, to come back in and get down to something she was good at. There were plenty of women out there in the wider world who could produce babies without incident, but how many were there who could whip financial reports into working order?

Her shoulders slumped. It didn't matter that she'd been out for a handful of days. Truth was, Paige could have taken longer, and no one would have been too bent out of shape over it. Who was she trying to impress with her show of soldiering on? No one even knew what she'd been through. The giddy rush of normality hadn't lasted long at all. Paige hadn't even managed to check out the maternity leave policy while it was still relevant.

Something about the pointlessness, the grinding endlessness of her work made something inside Paige snap. As much as she couldn't bear the idea of sitting around at home, the stale air of the office around her was compressing her lungs, squeezing the energy out of her. Numbers swam in front of Paige's eyes, a chorus line of insignificance.

Lurching to her feet, she snatched up her coffee mug. Caffeine might not be the answer to all her problems but having something warm to clutch between her hands was a comforting notion. She'd feel more human with something in her to jolt the system into normality.

When Paige reached the kitchen area, she almost turned on her heel and ran away. Nothing against Kwame or Jia, of course. It was more that conversation of any kind, let alone something light and breezy so as not to give anything away, felt downright impossible. But Paige knew she'd draw more attention to herself if she fled now. If she dashed to the loo, they'd get the wrong end of the stick.

Maybe Paige would be lucky, and they'd carry on with their chat without involving her, sounded like it was something about films. What was out? Paige had no idea. On her way to the kettle, she smiled and nodded at the others, but kept moving in what she hoped was a purposeful way rather than anything too rude.

Her heart pounded, pulsing in her ears so much that it almost drowned out the cheerful query Jia lobbed her way. They were being so nice to her, even though they didn't know why they needed to be. Not that they weren't nice people. Maybe something about Paige's face was giving her away, fragility peeking through to the surface. Even though she'd lied about the root cause, she *had* been ill.

Don't be kind, Paige thought, panicked. She'd never get through the day with all these gentle smiles and soft words. Could Jia sense what had happened? Was it possible? For all his general sensitivity, Kwame would be none the wiser, being a man.

Would it make it all easier to cope with if Paige told Jia what was going on? It would make the need to pretend go away. The acknowledgement of the loss would make it real, transform it into something that had definitely happened. But if she told someone, Paige wouldn't have to wonder if the fact of it was written across her forehead in indelible ink.

She'd always be an example, Paige realised with a shock. If they all knew, whenever any of them encountered someone else who'd been through pregnancy loss, Paige would be introduced into the conversation whether she liked it or not, their pet reference. Paige was now someone who'd had a miscarriage. Nothing would wash away that new ingrained part of her identity. Who had she been trying to fool? There was no going back to normal.

Full of hesitancy, concern pouring out of her eyes, Jia broke through Paige's cluttered concentration. "Paige? You alright? Maybe you came back too soon, there's no shame in some more time away. You look a bit—"

"I... I'm fine. S'nothing." Paige gulped, panic rising in her gullet. The harder she tried to rein in her feelings, to stop the tears before they got into full flow, the more unquenchable they became. There was no choice, she'd have to tell the truth. It was the only way to explain. She'd look out of her mind otherwise.

"I... I lost..." But the words wouldn't come.

Before, the idea of breaking into noisy sobs in front of everyone would have been the height of embarrassment. But Paige was well beyond caring. She couldn't hold the torrent back. It didn't matter how desperate she was to reassure Jia that she hadn't done anything wrong, that the utterly disproportionate reaction had a lot more behind it than anything she might have said, Paige couldn't get the confession out.

A few cups of tea in her line manager's office and a raid of the deluxe biscuit stash later, Paige left the building. The truth was out, to be dispensed to the others at Pippa's discretion. With any luck, Jia would be called in to see Pippa for a "little chat" as soon as Paige was well out of earshot. As she hurried out towards the car park, Paige kept her gaze fixed to the ground in front of her feet, unable to bear the idea of eye contact with those who'd seen her weeping.

DECEMBER

SIGNED OFF FROM WORK, Paige found it easiest to stay in bed for most of the day. Rather than thinking about anything, allowing the flashes to intrude, she stared at the TV screen. She watched people with unrealistic budgets and outsized dreams make hashes out of the simple tasks of finding somewhere to live or doing their houses up to the standards of their stupid grandiose plans.

Watching strangers fail made Paige feel a little bit better for not meeting her own modest goals of basic hygiene or stepping outside the house. It was all too gargantuan, well beyond her capacity, after the meltdown at the office. Even the post made Paige cry. A card that didn't reference the miscarriage but contained an entreaty for Paige to "look after herself" and a voucher for a massage was her mother's version of long-distance caring.

On the fourth day of Paige's new hermit existence, she was graced by a visitor. There was a knock at the bedroom door. It couldn't be Luke then. He'd been coming and going with food that Paige couldn't muster much interest in, barging in and out of the room as he pleased.

"Yeah?" Paige called out.

Annie marched into the room. Arms folded, she stopped and surveyed the scene before her. Paige didn't want to know what her sister thought of the state of her. After a loaded pause with no recognition of anyone's overpowering BO, Annie darted forward and reached out a hand, dragging Paige out of bed.

It was sheer luck for both of them that Paige was wearing pyjama bottoms as well as a top. Then again, the notion of Annie clapping eyes on the knickers Paige had been wearing until that morning was nothing like as excruciating as it might have been a week or so ago. Torture wore a different face these days.

Before Paige could protest at being manhandled, Annie slipped down the side of the bed, sitting them both on the carpet with their backs wedged against the wall. "Get your feet on the floor, little P, and tell me anything you'd like to about your baby."

With a surge of relief, Paige broke into a fresh wave of tears. Her head dropped down to meet Annie's shoulder, something of a natural resting place over the years. Annie wouldn't have said something like that if she hadn't meant it.

It was odd, how pushing her feet into the floor helped to make Paige feel better. With her toes sinking into the carpet fibres, she was rooted to the ground, stepping down from the cloud of bed she'd been languishing on for days.

"We were saving the news for Christmas. I'd have been just out of the first trimester by then. Felt like the ideal present for everyone. Seemed to make sense, since you're meant to wait until then anyway." Paige sniffed, hating the gag of the twelve-week taboo. The way you were supposed to hold back, *just in case*. "First grandchild on both sides."

Annie's smile was wan. "So, they would've been a summer baby?"

Accurate pregnancy calculus. Impressive. The way Paige had raced ahead, letting the months melt away before their time, picturing the moment she'd have an actual baby in her arms, felt like an age ago already.

"Yeah. And…" Paige took a moment to get a handle on her breath as tears trickled down her cheeks. "When I was still bleeding, but hadn't given up on the pregnancy, it made me think of how much mischief the baby was going to get into. If they were prepared to give us that much trouble before they were even born, I could only imagine what they were going to get up to once they were outside the womb."

"They'd have run amok."

Another surge of tears welling up, Paige nodded. It was a relief that Annie seemed to understand what she was trying to say. "They would."

After that, Paige couldn't stop talking. She shared details she'd already told Luke, taking Annie on a guided tour of those dark days of interminable bleeding, and before that. The sore boobs, the thrill of the secret she shouldn't share with anyone beyond her husband, the horror of the streaky redness, the way it refused to stop, how it did. And then Paige went further. She began to spill secrets, the need to share spurring her towards deeper confessions.

"I missed the baby. When they came out of me, I mean." Her cheeks were wet, salty droplets silently sliding down to splash on her grubby top. "I… I must have flushed it down the toilet, thinking it was another one of the clots because… because it, they, must have been so small when they d-died inside me."

Annie's arms circled tight around Paige as she made the same sorts of crooning noises that had become Luke's primary method of communication. It was tricky to pick the right sorts of words to tamp down the torrent of Paige's hopelessness in full flow, but Annie was doing her level best to comfort her.

Not having to look Annie in the eye made it easier for Paige to keep talking to the open air, knowing that what she said was being heard without having to observe the reaction to her words. "This… it's with me forever now. How can I spend the rest of my life grieving someone I never got to meet?"

When Annie seemed to have nothing to say in response, no easy reassurance to combat Paige's bleakness, Paige scrambled for something to make Annie feel better instead. Her sister had to understand what this meant. Free rein to talk about her lost child was the most precious of commodities.

"How did you know? I mean that the feet on the floor thing would help? And that… that I'd want to talk about the baby? Can't help but feel like everyone's impulse is to avoid all mention, makes it easier to move on or so they see it, especially since I was pregnant for such a brief time."

Annie smiled. "I asked my friend Mara for advice. She had a miscarriage in between her two children. I knew that about her and, well, I hope it's not a problem that I told her about yours. She'll keep it to herself, of course. Anyway, she told me that the best thing anyone can do to help is come and sit in the hole with you, let you say whatever you need to. And that anything to try and make you feel a bit more grounded can work wonders."

With a sigh, Paige added another entry to her mental rolodex of women who'd shared a version of her own experience, some form of pregnancy loss. Paige had met Mara a handful of times and hadn't had a clue of the woman's sorrow. "Yeah, don't worry. It's fine you told her. I mean, why does no one talk about these things? Why do you have to go through it all on your own?"

Annie cocked an eyebrow. "I'm going to go with something to do with the patriarchy?"

"Probably." It was such a relief to Paige that Annie didn't have children. Not just that, but she wasn't in a long-term relationship and there didn't seem much chance of her being in one anytime soon, given her track record. Even though being the married one carried its own kind of pressure for Paige when it came to Margaret and Russell's empty grandparental arms, her sister's continued thirty-something childlessness did help Paige to feel that little bit less alone.

Once Annie had taken her leave, Paige allowed herself to do something she hadn't felt strong enough to do before. She pictured the baby for the first time. What, who, that lost life might have become. It was as if Annie had given Paige permission to imagine her child as a person. The way their eyes would have crinkled with mirth, splashing through puddles on unsteady legs to test out a brand-new pair of bright yellow wellies, sleeping on their stomach, head half buried in the mattress.

No, they should be sleeping on their back. That was the safe position, helped to decrease the risk of SIDS. Paige could almost picture looking down into the cot, seeing the downy hair wisping around their ears.

Her ears. The bundle of cells never had the chance to develop a gender. It would have been there, coded into the cells, but as far as Paige and Luke were concerned, the coin had still been spinning in the air. And thanks to her thoughtless flushing it wasn't as if there was any tissue left to investigate. Right then though, Paige knew in her bones that the baby was a girl. Could have been. Since there would never be a way to know one way or the other, Paige had the luxury of making the choice for herself, determining who her child might have become.

SIXTEEN YEARS AGO

OCTOBER

Celeste

TWO LINES. IT FELT like such a long time since there'd been two lines. A lifetime. For the first couple of months, Stephen had been the model supportive partner: kind, patient, understanding. It wasn't so surprising that he'd started to wear a little thin after that. Even so, even though Stephen didn't want to talk about any of it, the reasons Celeste was struggling, he held her while she cried. He could do that much for his wife, be gentle and tender. He gave as much of himself as he could.

It was pointless to wish that Stephen would morph into the sort of man who could be open and honest about what he was feeling. At least part of the problem was that his focus was on his wife's reproductive failings. Or what he regarded as Celeste's deficiencies, rather than his. It might have been far more joyless this time around, but it had taken them fewer cycles to conceive again. Celeste was more fertile than she'd thought.

A happy bubble popped in the back of her throat. It was all about to change again. It was going to be better this time. Without any hope or reason to suspect that it would be the least bit different to her first pregnancy, Celeste found herself smiling.

She'd never taken the time to ponder if she'd been ready to try again. It was one of those immovable facts of the universe, that she and Stephen were heading back into the trenches together. Even if he was the general at the back of the lines barking out orders and she was the one taking actual fire. There was also a small possibility that, yet again, Celeste wanted to prove her parents wrong. Her marriage was going to be as much of a success as her motherhood.

It *was* different this time. Celeste had more fight. If she'd felt like she had a choice in the matter, if she could have decided *not* to try, how would she have ever been ready to put herself through it all again? Ready or not, they were taking another spin on the rollercoaster.

Which meant Celeste had decisions to make. Last time, she'd told Stephen right away. Would it be better to hold back for a while now, make sure it was going to stick? This time, the joy of that positive test was adulterated. Doubt swirled in Celeste's belly. Despite all her rising misgivings, a smile spread across her face. Savour the moment. There was nothing else she could do. That and hug this brand-new secret to herself for a little while longer. It was her and this tiny seedling against the world. No need to let the battle cries rip yet.

PRESENT DAY

DECEMBER

Paige

PAIGE WISHED SHE HAD the energy to appreciate her best friend, Kelly. As soon as she'd heard about the miscarriage, Kelly insisted she had to take Paige out for coffee. Or something stronger if she wanted? Paige didn't want to have to get gussied up, a café would be fine. Getting out and about was difficult, of course Kelly was here to give Paige the not-so-gentle nudge she needed to brave the big bad world.

It was hard to know where to start. In a way, it was a relief that they didn't get straight into Paige's sad news. Kelly was practically oozing enthusiasm for her latest venture. "I've been setting up an Etsy store for all these cards I've been making. John said I've got to value my own time more, see if I couldn't find my way towards a revenue stream. I'd been doing it as a hobby until then. It's so sweet that he has such faith in my talents."

Paige attempted to reflect some of Kelly's smile. It was nice to be able to indulge her friend in this new endeavour. The last thing Paige wanted was to let Kelly know how much it was costing her to maintain a happy expression.

"Look at these designs, some of them are so sweet." Kelly was off, flashing up one card after another. Graduation, birthday, wedding, Christmas. New baby.

Paige's breath hitched. Something at her core wound tighter and tighter, cutting off the blood flow, starving her brain of all rational thought. Gripping the table so hard her knuckles went white, she waited for Kelly to cop on to her staggering faux pas.

The job of a friend was to understand. Paige knew Kelly hadn't done it on purpose. Somewhere, tucked away in a rational corner of Paige's mind, an area that was taking the day off, she knew her friend was a good person. A matchmaker, a shoulder to cry on, a bolsterer of broken hearts.

Kelly would be mortified when she noticed the smoking gun in her hands, the trigger she'd pulled. Excitement about her creative efforts had carried her away to a fairyland inhabited by only good news, bows and babies and heralds of triumph. Any sorrows were expressed through the medium of pastel shades and dew-brushed flowers alongside trite euphemisms.

But she kept wittering on, oblivious, it seemed, to the sheer thoughtlessness of a normal action. How could she not understand that there was nothing in the world to think about other than the baby Paige had lost? It ripped Paige's wounds open, her flesh raw and tender, heart bloody and exposed to the caustic open air.

She couldn't breathe with it. Her pain wasn't a reasonable entity. It was a sprawling monster, pushing its way into all the corners of her mind, blotting out the sun and swamping her neurons in black tar.

Somehow, she managed to find her way to the end of the conversation, to employ a neutral voice to say her good-byes to Kelly, to overrule her confusion that Paige was cutting things short, even to thank Kelly for her concern at a difficult time. Only when the front door stood between Paige and the rest of the world at last did the bubble burst, its thick skin splattering her back with the force of a bull-whip's lash.

It was the most that Paige had cried, howling into the empty air, since the awful day of the ultrasound. It wouldn't be the last time she'd have to stuff her feelings down until she could unleash them in the privacy of her own home.

You felt the weight of a decent cry for the rest of the day. Screw that, the week.

EIGHT YEARS AGO

JANUARY

Paige

"**O**WEN BLOWING COLD ON you again?"

Paige's head whipped up from the banner she was working on. It was proving to be more difficult than she'd thought to remove the ill-judged streaks of glitter paint. Didn't do much to help convey the seriousness of the message. She supposed it served her right for unfurling it all over the communal space in the lounge, inviting feedback she didn't want. There hadn't been enough space for Paige to work on it in her room though.

Her cheeks flaring, Paige peeped up at Kelly. From the way her friend's hands were planted on her hips, Kelly's question felt a lot more like the kick-off of a confrontation than an innocent inquiry.

Maybe Paige would get away with playing dumb. "What? Why would you say that?"

Kelly's eyes glittered. "You always go a bit more… strident with the environmental stuff when you're not getting any."

It was a struggle to contain the urge to groan. Kelly liked to believe she was such a Samantha, delivering delicious one-liners about bedroom activities, a knowing gleam in her eye. Just because she was right, this one time, didn't make what Kelly had to say any pithier.

"Are you trying to make out that this isn't important?" Easier to lean into indignance. After all, Paige had right-eousness on her side. And not everything *had* to be about boys.

Sighing theatrically at her friend's cluelessness, Kelly flopped down onto the floor next to Paige. "I'm saying that you wouldn't be quite so fixated on this stuff if Owen were a more attentive boyfriend."

Paige ducked her head to try and hide that the tell-tale bloom of her cheeks had darkened beyond tomato-red. It wasn't Kelly's fault that she'd got it wrong when it came to Owen. "My libido has nothing to do with the uncontrolled melt of the Arctic ice caps, thank you very much. We're pumping noxious shit into the atmosphere and even though there's overwhelming scientific consensus that such activi-ties cannot end well, no one seems bothered enough to *do* anything about it. Doesn't exactly put me in the mood when I could be doing my bit to combat this stuff."

"You're going to start banging on about whales next, aren't you? Or the poor ickle polar bears?"

How narrow-minded was Kelly? A flare of anger fired through Paige's veins. "Just because you've got no environ-mental conscience—"

"What makes you think I haven't?"

Better than ire, a sense of triumph now warmed the bat-tered cockles of Paige's heart. The moral high ground was all hers. "For one, the way you insist on cranking the heating. It's tropical in here. The agreement we all signed says noth-ing above twenty-two degrees." Even that figure had been a painful compromise.

Kelly's mouth twitched to one side. "Don't think I haven't noticed that you've changed the subject."

Damn. Paige's stomach flipped over. She'd been hoping she was getting away with it. "Did I?"

"When I said something about Owen being a terrible boy-friend." Kelly prompted.

It was too much to expect for her to let this go. "He's not."

"Oh, don't defend him." But then something in Kelly's expression shifted. The concern was almost too much to bear. "Or do you mean you've split up? You never said anything."

"He's never been my boyfriend," Paige mumbled to her mournful-looking banner. The nightmarish seal she'd tried to draw regarded her with derision. No less than what she deserved thanks to her terrible artistic skills.

"What?"

Raising her head, Paige shifted to face Kelly. Her attempt at a shrug turned into a jerky half twitch. "We didn't want to put labels on anything. There was never any reason for it to go beyond anything casual."

"I get the feeling that the 'we' in question is somewhat one-sided. You're being a good little parrot, repeating all the party lines. And I note that you're using the past tense."

Paige winced. "Don't miss anything, do you?"

"P, talk to me."

There was something in the way Kelly was looking at her, or maybe it was that she'd used Annie's favourite form of address for her little sister, which nudged against the flood-gates in Paige's brain. Some of the truth had been let loose already, there was almost nothing stopping her from deluging Kelly with the rest of it. And if you couldn't share this sort of thing with your best friend, who could you tell?

"I... I wanted something more. I thought we were ready for something... well, not serious but something a bit more established. Exclusive."

The sympathy on Kelly's face killed Paige the most. She hated feeling like some tragic scrap, an object of pity. But they both knew there wasn't going to be a happy conclusion to events. She had to tell Kelly everything. "And then he said that he agreed with me. Well, that he was ready for something like that. Which was why it was only fair to Vicky that he and I stopped sleeping together. *She's* the one he wants to get serious with."

"Right." Kelly's mouth settled into a determined line. "Hang the polar bears. Oh, not like that, don't give me the face. But put that sad little banner down this minute. It'll still be there for you in the morning. I'll even help you display it somewhere when you've made it a bit more presentable. Never let it be said that I don't do anything for the cause. In the meantime, though, we're going to get wasted and do lots of stupid things. Anything to stop you thinking about that total *waste* of space."

Kelly was as good as her word. That night included a date in the tattoo artist's chair. No matter how many powers of persuasion Paige attempted to apply to her friend in later years, she never did find out what Kelly had chosen to rival Paige's minimalist lighthouse. For all she knew, Kelly never got inked at all.

In the morning, along with her sore shoulder, Paige had a fistful of phone numbers attached to names she couldn't remember meeting. While she didn't think it was at all wise to follow through on the promise any of them held, they were going to make excellent additions to her growing petition. The banner was never going to see the light of day, she'd decided, so Paige had to do *something* to contribute to the environmentalist cause.

SIXTEEN YEARS AGO

DECEMBER

Celeste

*D*ON'T BE DEAD THIS *time. Please don't be dead. I won't be able to keep going if you're dead. Not again.* Celeste couldn't bear to say any of it out loud as she scooted into position. Again. The words had been playing on a loop in her head all morning, throughout the pale hours of the long night as she'd counted down the minutes until this appointment, unable to sleep. She couldn't even move in case she woke Stephen. He wouldn't understand her fears if she tried to explain them.

After all, there was no reason to suspect anything was wrong. No bleeding this time and only light cramping, which the midwife had assured her was normal. A sign that her womb was growing.

Now Celeste was here, in a different room, another building altogether, she couldn't stop herself from reliving the experience of her last ultrasound. In so many ways, it was the exact same oppressive environment as that terrible moment. The low, dingy lighting, the faint hum of machinery.

Her heart had to be thundering at least as fast as the baby's was meant to be. If they were still alive. But it was impossible to focus on anything other than the sensations of dread firing around her nervous system.

Even if he was prepared to try, Stephen wouldn't understand. That being said, there was a certain tension to him. His rigidity was difficult to interpret as he sat in the chair next to the couch Celeste was lying on. Was he scared of repetition too? Or something else? Celeste wished she could find the courage to ask.

Before she could worry too much about what her husband was thinking, the technician began her task. And that was when it became clear that this wouldn't be the same as last time at all. Rather than the necessary invasion of the probe slipping inside her, Celeste was directed to lift her top up for the cold gel. The screen wasn't angled away from her apprehensive eyes. Rather than carry on repeating her prayerful mantra, Celeste couldn't do anything other than watch.

There they were. There was a baby. A baby who could *move*. They were swimming around in that cavernous space. Doing their level best to be reassuring, staging a performance for the benefit of the camera, making the most of their short window of time with an audience.

Show off, Celeste thought to her baby, heart brimming with pride.

"Are you alright there?" The technician's words broke into Celeste's newfound happy place. "You seem ever so tense."

"I..." Was it safe now? For Celeste to confess why she'd felt like glass on the verge of splintering into a thousand jagged pieces? "I lost one before. Earlier this year, I mean. But it was before we got this far. So... well, I mean. My last ultrasound didn't go well."

"Oh, I see. You poor thing. Well, you can relax now, can't you?" The woman's voice was full of warmth. Her eyes crinkled in the low light as she smiled and gave Celeste's arm a reassuring pat. "Mummy," she added.

While the technician clicked through the rest of the measurements she needed, Celeste watched her baby, enraptured.

She didn't even need to look at Stephen to gauge his reaction. It was like a dream, the same kind of floatiness that a just-right bath granted. Celeste emerged into the bright wintriness of the world outside the warren of hospital corridors, clutching the scan photo, her first one, to her chest. Her beacon of hope, her shield.

This sense of reassurance would be temporary, Celeste knew that much. Babies still died. Making it this far was no guarantee. If only Celeste could have a direct line to that fluttering heartbeat, pipe it into her ears, maintain the knowledge that her baby was still thriving. That might help. She just had to find a way to keep hope, and the baby, alive.

Celeste knew to keep these sorts of thoughts to herself. If Stephen's relieved smile was anything to go by, he wouldn't want to entertain such negativity. It was going well this time, which was all he needed to know. Take it as read, check back in when necessary, consider no adverse outcomes. She'd noticed the disapproving glances he shot her way every time he had caught her slipping off to the bathroom to check her knickers for blood. Women had babies every day, Celeste would be the same. It was going to be fine.

Besides, Celeste knew she was being foolish, altogether far too cautious for no reason. Why couldn't she accept the evidence she was holding in her hands? Everything was great. This baby was growing. This baby was alive. One loss was a blip. It couldn't be anything more than that. Celeste's luck had turned and now she had the proof.

It wouldn't be too much longer until the next scan. The leap from twelve to twenty weeks was nothing. She could do this. Count the days. Keep this little one alive until the doctors wanted to see her again. Everyone else managed it. Celeste had failed to take one baby into the next millennium with her. She owed it to this one to do better this time around.

EIGHT YEARS AGO

JANUARY

Paige

BEER AND PIZZA WITH a friend, balm for a battered heart. Paige had been wondering what to do with herself since Kelly was out that night with her course mates. They were pretending that they were going to discuss their dissertations when it was obvious it would develop into a night of heavy drinking before they got past the introductions.

Two episodes into a mindless reality TV marathon and Paige had been over the moon when her phone pinged with Luke's garlic bread-accompanied suggestion.

"I'm surprised you're not out with Owen."

Was he being sweet, pretending not to know what had happened? Letting Paige choose whether she told him? Or was Luke genuinely in the dark, striking lucky with his hang out plans that evening?

"Owen and I… we're, I mean, we've never…" Admitting the Owen situation to Kelly when her friend had already guessed half the truth was one thing. Saying the words out loud to Luke now meant that whatever she and Owen had was well and truly over. *Nut up, woman. Admit the truth.*

"He's out of the picture now."

"Yeah, Kell said something about it." The half-hearted subterfuge was over, heralded by Luke's guilty smile. "I'm sorry."

"You don't have to... um." Paige stopped and groaned. She hadn't the faintest clue what she wanted from Owen, let alone what she needed from her friends during this time when she was supposed to be getting over her not-boyfriend. "This doesn't have to be what we talk about."

"But you're hurting. I'd be a pretty rubbish mate if I didn't want to listen to what was getting you down." Kind, practical Luke. A dependable Labrador of a guy. Such a good friend.

"That's sweet of you, Ook. But it'll take less than five minutes to get super depressing. If I start moaning about the miserable nature of my opposite of a love-life, next thing we know I'll fire up Google to hunt for any nearby nunneries. Check if they've got any openings for heartsick agnostics."

"Owen's got a hell of a lot to answer for if he's put you off men forever." While Paige had been talking, Luke had shredded the pizza box lid. He frowned at the pile of cardboard scraps.

Paige gave a bitter little laugh. "Reverse situation, my friend. My stunning lack of sex appeal was what sent him running for the hills. Not to go all Meredith Grey, but he didn't pick me even after I went all gooey-eyed. Probably because of that. So, I might as well be the one to make a change before a pattern of fleeing men sets in."

But Luke didn't seem to appreciate Paige's attempt at humour. If anything, his face was even more serious, a scowl settling across it. "Don't talk yourself down like that. If Owen couldn't appreciate you, that's his loss. Not yours. Better to know that now than later."

"That's kind of you, Luke. Really." Paige meant it. She was beyond touched by Luke's words. Not that they did much to lift her mood. "It doesn't do a fat lot of good though. Since he was much more tempted by what, who, else was on offer.

Why would anyone pick me when there're other options on the table?"

She was the disappointing salad of the Indian takeaway, wilting and superfluous, and she'd tried to take on a tandoori thigh. How else could she have expected things to shake out? It wasn't an attempt to fish for compliments. Her question had been rhetorical, but Luke held up a hand to stop Paige from talking.

"I've always thought you were the most beautiful woman I've ever met. Anyone who could choose someone else over you would have to be at least half mad, and all blind. Utterly clueless."

And before Paige could challenge such a ridiculous statement, Luke's lips were right there in front of her. For a heartbeat, he waited. Until she nodded. And then his mouth covered hers. He claimed her, cherishing Paige in a way that felt reverent and alien to her at the same time. He was tentative enough to make it clear that, should she want to, Paige could still pull away. She was the one with the power. Even so, for the first time in her life, Paige understood the meaning of the phrase "weak at the knees".

It was so different to how things had ever been with Owen. Not that Paige thought Luke would appreciate that she was drawing comparisons while she was meant to be in the throes of passion. Even though he came out of the evaluation very well indeed. With him, there was none of Paige's usual self-consciousness, wondering if the other person in the room was really enjoying himself, whether there was someone else he'd rather be with.

Unable to shut her thoughts off, Paige tried to work out which of them, her or Luke, was taking advantage that night. Once Luke had said such things to her, she was helpless. Paige was ready and willing to use his sweetness as a salve to dull the ache of the wounds Owen had left behind. But it felt as if there'd been something pent up in Luke that he was having the opportunity to unleash at long last. Wonderful as it was, it was beginning to become clear that they were both in this for all the wrong reasons.

PRESENT DAY

DECEMBER

Paige

"**A**T LEAST YOU CAN get pregnant?"

The fact he'd said it as a question rather than an assured statement, the sheer hesitation in his voice that it was the right thing to say, was all that saved Russell in the moment. At least he wouldn't notice Paige's wince from the other end of the phone line. Or maybe the involuntary response would have been the best thing to help Russell understand that it wasn't the most helpful line to pursue in his attempt to comfort his daughter.

But I wanted this *baby, Dad. I wasn't running a test on the system for future use. There doesn't always have to be a silver lining. I'm not interested in making lemonade.* Paige wanted to put him right. But even as the words streamed through her head, she knew it would be too much effort to get them out of her mouth. Still, her father deserved some kind of response to his well-meant attempt at reassurance.

With an audible shudder, all Paige could manage was a faint, non-committal "mmm." The small answering sigh sent relief coursing through Paige's veins. Russell understood. "I suppose that's cold comfort though. Sorry, Pidge."

"It's okay, Dad," Paige whispered.

"No, it isn't…" Mid-sentence, Russell caught himself. "I

mean, it doesn't have to be. I want to help. I hope you know that. But I'm sure I've put my foot in it."

"Well, I guess maybe it's better not to try and bright side every situation."

"Roger that. The last thing I'd want to do is bring you any more pain."

"I know."

The conversation needed to move on in a hurry before Russell cracked out the sackcloth and ashes over his blunder. People were so afraid of treading on feelings that they went a bit overboard with apologies when they made you cry.

Paige scrambled for a change in topic. "How's Celeste?"

"Oh."

Why was Russell so thrown by the question? Was it that unexpected for Paige to ask after her stepmother? Paige found herself grimacing again, but this time she was the only one to blame.

It was a shame there was such a gulf between Paige and her mother figures. There were times when you needed to go to someone from the next generation up. Well, someone older, anyway. Not that Paige much enjoyed having to put Celeste into a parental category.

But while Paige knew that Celeste didn't have any children of her own, no personal pregnancy experience to bring to the table, she was bound to know at least one or two women who'd come out the other side of miscarriage. It was basic maths.

Paige was suddenly desperate to hear about women who were even further down the line from the event than Annie's Mara. Light at the end of the tunnel. It was quite the development. For the first time she could remember, Paige was keen to talk about, if not to, her stepmother. Maybe there was an upside Russell would appreciate to the situation after all.

"Dad?" Russell still hadn't said anything.

"She's... Celeste's fine." He spoke as if he were choosing his words with immense delicacy, like he was wedged in an uncomfortable situation. "I mean, she's very upset for you, of course."

"Thank you." It was the reflexive answer. As she processed her thoughts, Paige took her turn to talk carefully. "I was wondering, do you think maybe you could ask her if she knows anyone who..."

Her tongue was tied up by the awkwardness of sending such a request by proxy. Sensitive as he was, as a man, Russell wasn't the right vessel. Paige could wait until she next saw Celeste herself. It wouldn't be the worst thing in the world for the two of them to have something to talk about, good motivation for Paige to visit sooner rather than later.

"Anyone who what?"

"Forget it. Maybe it's not such a good idea."

"Are you sure? I do think you're right – it might be for the best. I really would do anything to help, Pidge. But, if you don't mind too much, good to leave Celeste out of it. Just if you can. She's..." he paused, more meaning loading onto the silence the longer it went on, "she's taken this rather hard."

It was Paige's turn to be stumped. "Oh."

"She sends her love, of course."

"Me too." It was easier to be affectionate towards Celeste when the sentiments were sent via Russell.

The conversation wrapped up after a few more stilted minutes of inconsequential chat. Paige tried to listen to Russell's answer when she asked him about his work, how he felt about being on the verge of retirement after so many years spent at the same company. But it was hard to make the words go in.

It was sweet of Celeste to feel so deeply about Paige's loss, if a little presumptuous. She wasn't related to Button, after all. In fact, where did Celeste get off being so inconsolable about *Paige's* loss that she couldn't be there to help Paige herself when she might have been useful? The one time that Paige wanted to hear from Celeste, she was nowhere to be found. Maybe it was all wrapped up in any regrets Celeste might have for her own childlessness, transplanting extra remorse onto Paige.

Unless Russell was covering for Celeste? Maybe she was disgusted by Paige and the evidence that she hadn't been blessed by Mother Earth or whatever Celeste believed in. Whatever was going on, since it was clear how touchy a subject it was with Celeste, Paige was grateful she hadn't managed to ask about it. She could find women with losses on her own. There'd be forums.

FIVE YEARS AGO

MAY

Paige

IN THE IMMEDIATE AFTERMATH of the divorce, Paige had been worried about her father being alone, that being abandoned by Margaret would leave him bereft of a partner for the rest of his days. They might have sounded like sexist concerns, that Paige was afraid Russell couldn't take care of himself. But it wasn't that. She worried that what Margaret had done would render him unable to trust again. It wasn't his fault in the slightest that he'd been deserted.

So, it was a relief that Russell was more than capable of attracting girlfriends. It seemed Paige hadn't been alone in her thoughts, that others within Russell's various social circles had, subtly or otherwise, nudged him towards assorted fix ups. He didn't get much opportunity to sharpen his bachelor cooking skills as he attended dinner party after dinner party where he was sat next to someone eligible he just so happened to have been briefed on, not in an in-your-face way or anything, beforehand.

Even with such romantic assistance, Russell managed well enough on his own. More than anything else, he was attracted to… projects. As far as Paige saw it, Russell took a woman under his wing – under the guise of a relationship – and she would emerge after a while, a metamorphosed butterfly plunging out of the chrysalis nursing some exciting new direction in life or reconciled with her children or just with a new haircut that suited her better. And then they'd move on and out of each other's lives.

Still, it didn't take Russell long to find a new mission after a break-up. Take the most recent one, Celeste. Head in the clouds, drippy in the extreme, and a month or two into going out with Russell guess whose health food shop had a shiny new range of innovative merchandise? Paige's father was a man of surprising talents.

Such thoughts were enough to make Paige groan. When had she become her mother? Margaret's take on Russell's post-marriage love life would have been fascinating though, if a little problematic to gather. She wouldn't approve of Celeste's tattoo, Paige knew that. No matter how tasteful the dinky deer and bird silhouettes on her wrist happened to be. There was a reason Paige had never revealed the lighthouse to her mother.

Maybe it wouldn't come up if and when Russell's new girlfriend and Margaret ever met, given Celeste's preference for flowing sleeves. It was probably for the best that Paige was in regular touch with one of her parents, rather than both.

As long as Russell was happy. That was the motto. Had to be. Besides, it would be a bit too obvious to ask how long this one would last before Russell put right whatever flaw had brought Celeste into his life.

It would be nice to know if any of them would last, that was all. He couldn't keep cycling through women forever, so Paige wanted to know which one's myriad quirks she was going to have to get used to. After another evening spent enduring Celeste droning on about the health benefits of flax seeds or whatever it was, Russell at least had the grace to acknowledge the strangeness of his girlfriend's choice of discussion topics once she was out of the room.

"Sorry, she's always so keen to make a good impression in front of you or Annie. I think she gets a bit nervous when the conversation's getting away from her."

He could have changed the subject for Celeste in the moment though. Rather than appeal to his daughter to make nice after the fact. But Paige didn't want to pick a fight. "Well, so long as she's not trying to recruit me for the shop floor."

"Don't think you have to worry there. She's got plenty of staff."

"Good." Paige sipped her tea. "It might be helpful to have more, I don't know, neutral topics to discuss. Like TV or whatever. I'm not sure she and I have too much in common there though. You must do things together, hobbies and stuff? Help."

Russell scratched his chin. "We're putting a lot of time into Celeste's business, to be honest."

"I see." Her drink was still too warm to go in for another slurp. Paige shifted back in her chair and crossed her legs. "Don't give me that look."

"What look?"

Russell returned the judgemental glance with a narrowing of his eyes. "Is there something you want to tell me?"

Shrugging, Paige mulled her options. "Sometimes it seems like you spend all your downtime playing the saviour. Crosswords might be a bit less taxing."

"Maybe I want to be helpful."

"What if the two of you end up getting married? There can only be so many things for you to fix in Celeste's life. You won't know what to do with yourself." She couldn't help it. Paige had to ask. Maybe Russell would get bored once Celeste's business was thriving, find someone with a clapped-out houseboat in need of repair.

"Oh, I don't think I'll ever get married again."

Relief and concern warred in Paige's heart. The last thing she wanted was for her dad to be alone in his old age, but it wasn't as if he was there yet. The knowledge that they wouldn't be lumbered with the likes of Celeste in perpetuity was welcome news, lightening Paige's load. "Are you sure?"

"Can you ever be too certain about the future, little Pidge? It would be devious of me to commit to anything definitive. But it gets so messy to untangle things, it would take something very significant indeed to overcome that kind of concern."

The silence afterwards felt like a bit of a dig at Celeste, the implication was clear: she wasn't that special someone to reinstate Russell's faith in matrimony. Paige was almost sorry for her, but somehow not quite.

FIFTEEN YEARS AGO

APRIL

Celeste

WEEK BY WEEK, THE swelling of Celeste's belly delighted her. The baby was the size of a lemon, an avocado, the length of a banana, a mango. It was going well, in a scary, thrilling, tantalising way. At the twenty-week scan, Celeste had wondered whether she should find out if it was a boy or a girl, but that felt far too much like tempting fate. And hitting week twenty-four felt like getting to breathe fresh air. Viability week. It was everything. The only hurdle left before the big finale was getting to the third trimester.

Of course, the world kept turning while Celeste kept her eyes on what was going on inside her, counting every kick, revelling in the progression from uncertain flutters to unmistakeable movements. When her parents had told her they were throwing a garden party for John's sixtieth birthday, it was a shock. The prospect was chilling. All those people? If she got that far, there'd be an obvious bump and nowhere to hide. Everyone would know. They would know what was coming and there'd be so many questions. How would anyone be able to understand her reluctance to celebrate?

She'd just about got her head around the idea of going when Stephen informed her he would be unable to attend.

Work conflict. He'd been so absent through these past few weeks that it had taken Celeste a while to understand what he was doing. Rather than abandoning her, he was piling up his plate at the office, flitting off at every opportunity, to make sure he could be around as much as possible after the baby came.

So, even without her husband as her social shield, Celeste had come. And it was fine. She wasn't denying the baby who'd come before when everyone asked if it was her first. She held the other one in her heart still, but Celeste didn't want to bring the sunny mood down.

Sitting back in her chair, resting a hand on the prominent bump, an irrepressible smile stretched across Celeste's face. The steady thump of kicks from within was the most wonderful sensation she could remember experiencing. Even more precious because she knew how easy it was not to get to this point, that all her little miracle had to do was keep going.

I hope all this activity is a sign you like the food, little one. Just wait until you're born, you'll get to taste all this stuff first-hand. Well, in milk form first. But it's worth the wait.

She knew what she looked like, a glorious cliché of the stereotypical beaming pregnant lady. Celeste really was having a baby. The moment would have been perfect if Stephen had been there to share it, for him to see her relaxing into the reality.

Or maybe Celeste was finding the afternoon that little bit more lovely because her husband wasn't there to stress her out with his brooding. He *was* doing his best to be involved, but many of the notions of modern manhood seemed to have passed him by. They didn't talk about anything. The thought of him being around more after the baby was born became somewhat less reassuring, but Celeste did her best to bat it away. She didn't want anything to take the edge off her bliss.

When he got up to give his speech, it took John less than two sentences to turn the focus towards his daughter. Beaming with pride at the idea of becoming a grandfather, John was keen to dispense advice. When Celeste was born it was more than enough to convince him that angels existed, which was more than enough to inspire the naming process. If she wanted to carry on the trend, transforming it into a full-blown family tradition, wouldn't Angelica be adorable? Yes, he meant for a boy. Character building.

It was the most natural thing in the world to laugh along with everyone else and give a mysterious smile whenever anyone asked what Celeste was considering, name-wise. The truth was, she wasn't sure. Like finding out the gender, it had felt like too much of an assumption to pick names out for someone she wasn't sure she'd get to meet.

But it was the most ordinary thing in the world for an expectant mother to look ahead. Feeling braver than she had at any point yet in this pregnancy, Celeste started making preparations as soon as she got home. It was time.

Tomorrow morning, she was going to investigate signing up for antenatal classes but in the meantime, Celeste pulled down her mother's battered copy of *What to Expect* – a less-than-subtle wedding present. This pregnancy had a future and then some. Celeste owed it to the baby to get ready for their arrival rather than continue to worry about it not coming.

PRESENT DAY

DECEMBER

Paige

ALL THIS TIME OFF was taking its toll. Before, Paige would never have suspected she'd start climbing the walls so soon. Almost a month of her sentence remained, stretching ahead towards eternity.

"Are you alright?"

Paige turned to Luke, knowing she must have looked at least halfway down the route towards all-out mania, hair sticking out at odd angles thanks to raking her fingers through it. The lie would be far too obvious if she tried to answer Luke's question in the affirmative. Two and a half weeks of sick leave had done things to her head.

"I need, God, I don't know." Paige noticed Luke's surprised expression and laughed. "Oh, not religion. Not like that. But I do need... *something*. It's all so, so, my life, I mean and I..."

How could she make him understand? Especially when she couldn't sort it out in her own head?

"Do you ever think in life that you're coasting?"

Luke being Luke, probably not. He was a man with a perpetual plan, but Paige had to start somewhere. Not that she wanted to blame everything on her mother, but Margaret's grand plans for her daughter's life had curbed ambitions for everything outside the prescribed course towards accountancy.

Paige groaned. "I used to go out and do stuff. While I was studying, doing the thing that she had set out for me, I was also the woman in the tie-dye T-shirt pestering people with a clipboard. I spent whole Saturdays banging on about saving the bees and whatnot."

"I remember." Luke had a soft, fond smile on his face. Did he think of those days with nostalgia, that time when he loved Paige, and she was oblivious to his affections? "Striding around the high street."

Paige sighed. "I miss being that person. When did I let that stuff go?" Probably around the same time she stopped having all that student-y free time.

To Luke, the solution was obvious. "Then we'll find you a cause to get excited about again. There's no shortage. Any one of them would be happy to have you back, I'm sure. World's as on fire as it ever was." He paused and considered. "More so."

"True."

Paige didn't want to have to admit that those fires had dulled inside her. Maybe it wasn't just a lack of time that had pushed all this stuff to the wayside. You needed fervour to get in people's faces. But there was no reason why she couldn't fake it for a little while, right? And Luke made a compelling point, if Paige could get invested in the hopelessness of the environment a few years ago, the worsening situation was bound to be a motivator.

Gratefully, she nodded at Luke. She ought to have known that moaning to him would end up in something solutions driven. You could put the clipboard down, but that didn't mean you'd stop hearing its call forever. If Paige knew her husband, and she did, he'd have a list of suggestions for her within the week.

EIGHT YEARS AGO

JANUARY

Paige

"T his was a mistake." Paige's voice was tentative. Even with Luke's arm draped over her, casually, as if it belonged there, she had felt her convictions firming up overnight. She knew it was treacherous to say the truth, that it betrayed all the glorious things he'd whispered in her ear last night, every searing kiss.

Couldn't Luke understand though? Anything between them, a relationship or whatever else he was looking for, wasn't going to work. Not with Paige's head still so full of Owen. If she couldn't banish her ex from her thoughts, then none of it would be fair to Luke. She'd bog them both down.

Or maybe Luke did understand that they'd made a blunder together between the sheets. To Paige's surprise, he nodded. Despite her resolution, she felt a tiny stab of disappointment. Even though she knew that he needed to agree to it all being a mistake, it would've been courteous of him to fight for her a little, wouldn't it?

"So… we're agreed?" Someone had to say it out loud.

"Yeah, course. We got carried away. Shouldn't have happened." His voice was too light, too casual, but he was saying the words Paige had asked for. She couldn't complain. "Don't think either of us should apologise but, you know, why don't we pretend we didn't do anything? I crashed here after I had one too many with the Dominos, right? Innocent platonic sleepover."

Was he that good an actor? Did he regret saying those things to her last night? Had he spent the wakeful hours of the night like Paige had, wishing he could take everything back? Paige's trembling ego was such that the last thing she wanted to hear was that Luke hadn't meant it when he told her how beautiful she was, how desirable, a goddess in his presence.

No matter how much Paige wanted to know what was going on in Luke's head, she couldn't bear to ask him why he wanted to unravel their night of passion as much as she did.

"I mean, I'm game if you are." She rested her hand on Luke's arm. "Couldn't bear the idea of losing you as a friend."

A glimmer of a wince flashed across his face and Paige's heart quailed. Had it already happened? What she'd said was the truth. She was already on the verge of tears at the idea of Luke slipping out of her life.

It didn't matter that everything yesterday had felt downright apocalyptic. In time, she'd survive Owen's desertion. Minutes and weeks and months were all the healers she needed. Already, his good opinion meant a lot less to her. But if Paige pushed Luke away, which she knew she'd do if they dove straight into a relationship, it might well be the end of her. Better to try and rewind.

PRESENT DAY

DECEMBER

Paige

PAIGE HAD SPENT THE best part of three decades taking the ability to sleep through the night for granted. Only when that ability abandoned her did she realise its value. At night, the walls, her bedding, even Luke started to feel like they were all pushing in on her, the glowing hands of her alarm clock regarding her with disappointment as she stared right back at them through the dark.

When she just couldn't drop off, it felt like less of a waste of time if Paige could do something productive with the gaping maw of all those night hours. Sure, it was the worst thing possible for so-called sleep hygiene, polluting her whirring mind with blue light, but was lying awake with that carousel of worries going to be any better for her sanity?

It was such a tiny thing, a grain of sand, a tiny little sweet pea – she seriously doubted that it had ever progressed to blueberry size – but Paige felt the baby dividing up her life. It should have been easy enough to get over. After all, the biological reset button had been slammed with such speed that Paige might never have realised she was pregnant in the first place. She hadn't even been sure she wanted it, not totally. Had her doubt triggered the miscarriage?

What she needed, in the absence of a developing pregnancy, was reassurance. On the forums, it was somehow harder to feel sympathy for women who had living children when they lost pregnancies, even if they didn't feel their families were complete. Couldn't they be grateful for what they already had?

If anyone heard her thoughts, Paige would have no choice but to admit that it was an illogical, unreasonable jealousy. Yet another thing to add to the pile of terrible impulses she could never express. Deep down, she knew you shouldn't have to Pollyanna the situation after a baby came away, be made to appreciate that you still had the use of your legs when your arm had come off.

Even so, Paige couldn't muster as much compassion in the face of problems such as having to break the news of a miscarriage to a no-longer older sibling or the struggle of having to keep it together for the sake of a living child. Such thoughts rendered her monstrous, so selfish and lacking in proper feeling. But what Paige needed were more stories with greater relevance to her own still-childless experience. That way she wouldn't get bogged down by these resentments.

Huddled under the covers or slipping off to the living room when the shared bed felt too suffocating, Paige dipped in and out of the message boards, bathing in the digital gleam of women who were all going through the same thing as her. The same questions were repeated over and over, highlighting the glaring gaps in public understanding of what it was like when you lost a child in pregnancy.

When will the next period be? When is it safe to start trying again? When will the horrible feelings ebb away just a little bit? Is there anything that could have been done? Is this much bleeding normal? How can I keep it together around friends and relatives who are pregnant? Is it a betrayal to be thinking about a next time already?

It seemed what they were all concerned about, fixated on, was moving on, getting to the finish line next time round rather than taking the time to feel what had happened. But Paige knew she wasn't being fair to all these strangers looking for answers rather than judgement. There had to be other sites where women talked about that sort of thing without the urgent pressure of needing a baby in your arms right there and then. But it was in the name: Mumsnet.

Even though she was only a handful of weeks from her own experience, Paige felt like some kind of elder states-woman compared to so many pushing their questions out into the void. It was a comfort, almost, to be someone with knowledge of her own to pass on. She had it in her to be constructive, to post comments of her own and share what had happened to her. This was making a virtue, the lemonade of miscarriage lemons, putting what she had learned out there as lessons for others.

Maybe it was the lingering fatigue that caused those scanty feelings of happiness to ebb away. Everything started seeming that much less helpful as the tiny spring of solace dried up. It was so relentless. There were so many women in pain with the same thoughts rattling around their skulls, left alone by tragedies that hadn't been prevented. To make it all worse, there were plenty who came to say that they'd had multiple losses, four or five over the course of time spans so short they felt unbearable, mere months or so many deaths crammed into a year. How could anyone bear it?

*

One of the perils of too much time on one's hands is the temptation to delve into the almost limitless depths of the internet. It was a little while before Paige could pluck up the courage to go searching for what she really needed, but before too long she broke. No matter how many accounts she dug up, Paige couldn't get enough stories of other people's miscarriages and pregnancy losses.

She knew it was beyond morbid, that it wasn't going to change anything that had happened to her. She wasn't sure if it was even helping to process her own experience. But Paige kept browsing for more content, hoping to find as much as possible that would chime with what she'd been through.

One problem poked out further than all the others. Every single time Paige heard or read about a woman's experience of losing a baby, she felt as if she couldn't breathe until she knew if the lady in question ended up with any living children afterwards. Without that closure-granting information, Paige was in free fall, hurtling over a missed step on the stairs towards oblivion. Her own story was still achingly unresolved. She couldn't accept the same thing in others.

Without Paige realising what she was doing, she got into the habit of trying to find out online before getting further into accounts. It wasn't always possible, but in cases where the woman in question was some variety of public figure, Wikipedia was often eager to divulge snippets like marital status and offspring. Paige just had to see what kind of fate had been granted – vital that she knew if the newsreader talking about her past traumas had managed to grow her family, or if the equal rights campaigner got to come home to any living children at the end of a busy, productive day.

It didn't matter how much it felt like cheating, this background research. What did the world care if Paige tried to read the last page first, devouring her pudding before she ate her greens? More than that, it wasn't fair on those poor lost children either, Paige knew that. Going on to have a healthy pregnancy didn't tie a bow on any parent's hurt or ever make that family whole. Babies didn't replace babies. But Paige couldn't stop her mind from revolting against reality in those in-between spaces. When was a story ever finished?

The thing about all her research was that Paige wanted to be in control of it. It wasn't fair when stuff leapt out at her. She flagged ad after ad as a sensitive subject, as Paige's digital cookie trail stalked her wherever she went on the internet – even with liberal use of incognito mode – haunting her with gurgling infants that could never be hers.

And other reading material in general was proving difficult. Too many books proved impossible to trust, taking jarring detours into back alleyways full of lost babies where the plot developments weren't handled in a sensitive way. And then forgotten whenever the script called for it, the losses erased from a character's back story as soon as they posed narrative complications.

The usual welcoming arms of historical fiction had started to cross too, barring Paige from their former sanctuary. No matter how hard she tried, she couldn't get into the old sweeping romantic sagas she used to love. Epic battles and political intrigue from long ago stopped appealing. Contemporary novels didn't provide much joy either. They were proving too distracting and so often Paige found herself losing patience with problems that didn't seem all that pressing. Who cared if Sally nailed the big presentation or Monique got together with the local cupcake shop owner?

Crime was the answer. Paige used to dismiss thrillers as being far outside her literary wheelhouse, but the jagged edges and death waiting around every corner suited her right down to the ground at this moment in time.

Until it didn't.

The book made a satisfying thud when it hit the bedroom wall, dropping to the floor in a crumpled mass of wayward pages. Paige was pleased with her overarm technique and couldn't bring herself to care all that much about making marks on the wall.

The noise was enough to summon Luke. He poked his head round the door with a question on his face.

"They skip this part," Paige said with acid in her tone, not bothering with context. Her husband could catch up with her line of thinking. "Every story about this sort of thing, they cut out chunks of the story. They skip over the weeks and months, or years even, until she's ready to live again. Or she's already got another baby, a replacement, and everything's happy again. Because that's the obvious, easy fix. No one wants to wallow in this bit or drag it out, but... what else can you do?"

As he tried to tease out meaning from her diatribe, Luke's eyebrows furled together. "Another bungled miscarriage storyline?"

Paige sighed and nodded, adding another no-go title to her mental list. With a disappointing lack of success, she'd already tried to scour the internet for some kind of warning database, resources to help steer the bereaved away from thoughtless content. Let alone something that could provide suggestions that might do something to help. Doesthedogdie. com didn't even scratch the surface, reporting the obvious stuff and leaving it there. Everyone knew about the Red Wedding scene in *Game of Thrones*.

"There are... some more specific books and stuff for this sort of thing, aren't there?"

Not enough. Paige sighed. "Course there are. Sensitively written, frank accounts of miscarriage experiences. People giving their advice on what worked for them, how best to heal. And some of it is saccharine enough to put my teeth on edge. Oh, and do you know what feels even more like an insult? Where does it make total sense for all the baby grief titles to appear in the bookshop? Next to all the smug smiles and cradled bumps. Where else could you possibly put stuff related to reproduction? Doesn't matter that the outcome isn't quite as joyous, all gets crammed into the same box."

Paige could hear the bile pouring out of her, flooding in the wrong direction, towards an inappropriate target. None of this was Luke's fault. He hadn't designed the shelving system. On the tip of his tongue, Paige was almost sure, was the suggestion that she looked online for that sort of thing, avoid the in-person potential pitfalls. She had to cut him off. "Excuse me for wanting a bit of escapism from all that."

"I know, love. Makes sense. I'm sorry."

"I didn't mean it like that. Not your fault." Paige smiled. "Or your problem to solve."

"We'll see about that."

The ghost of a wink let Paige know that her husband was joking. She went over to nestle against him. "Would be nice to get a heads-up for this kind of stuff when it comes up though. It'd make it easier when it feels like the moment to seek it out."

Trigger warnings made so much more sense to Paige now. They weren't a fad or some liberal affectation, not some label to show how switched on you were to experiences other than yours. If you didn't think they were necessary, then you were lucky. Not superior to or stronger than those around you.

"Let me know whenever you want something pre-reading, I can always screen things for you."

Paige kissed the sweetest man she knew on the cheek. If Luke ever stopped trying to come up with suggestions to make things better, he'd be quite the changed person.

FIFTEEN YEARS AGO

MAY

Celeste

WAS SHE MAKING SOMETHING out of nothing? Even now, so many months into a pregnancy that was clearing every milestone, well after her resolution to get ready for this baby, Celeste couldn't always shake the feeling of dread. The bout of cramping during week seventeen had scared her so much that she'd ended up in the midwifery unit to make sure it wasn't the beginning of the end. It had been fine, nothing to worry about, reassurance given, the giddy wow-wow-wow of the heartbeat coming through the machine was a starburst of joy.

There were times when it was so difficult to be sure that it was all alright. Celeste didn't want to make a fuss. The baby was still kicking, weren't they? At least, Celeste was almost sure the sensation was there. They'd said something at the last scan about the placenta being at the front and when she'd looked up what that meant, Celeste felt like cursing. Muffled movement.

Only two days until her next appointment. It was fine. Nothing to worry about. The doctor wouldn't find anything wrong, and she'd be wasting everyone's time if she jumped the gun now.

She kept telling herself that all the way to the car. Two days was an eternity. Better to get things checked now. Just in case. She didn't give Stephen a choice, merely informed him she was going, and he could either drive her or stay at home.

All the staff at the midwife unit agreed with Celeste's logic – to her relief and terror all at the same time – and with very little discussion, she was dispatched to the hospital for another ultrasound. Celeste couldn't bear to look at the screen this time. The truth was frightening – what she'd been fearing ever since she saw that second line on the pregnancy test, had almost been expecting all along and hoping with every fibre of her being wouldn't come to pass – and Celeste couldn't trust her eyes to interpret it.

There was a reason they didn't let you see the screen in the early set-up when they suspected things weren't going well. They didn't want you to jump to conclusions when you weren't trained what to look for. This late into the pregnancy, when the baby and its movements should be obvious, there should have been every reason for joy. Another show for the entertainment of everyone in the room.

Celeste clutched the midwife's hand, her thoughts in overdrive. Should she have waited for Stephen? They'd agreed it was better for her to head in while he tried to find parking – a challenge at the best of times – but now that meant she was in this moment without him. The doctor had offered to hold off until Stephen arrived, but the urgency was too much. She had to know. Now.

They were all holding their breath as the wand moved over Celeste's big belly. The entire process must have taken less than a minute, even though she couldn't tell whether it had been a second or an hour. It was impossible for Celeste to look at the doctor after the probe was removed from her skin.

"I'm so sorry. There's no heartbeat."

It was over.

A primal wail burst out of Celeste's chest, wordless and immense. Somewhere in the middle of the churning mass of thoughts, the fresh layers of grief wrapping themselves around her brain and her heart, was the leaden thump of realisation. They were going to have to try. Again. Finally, Celeste understood Stephen's immediate certainty after they knew they'd lost the first baby.

Back up the legs would go, carefully timed to her cycle. Old hat, really. Been there, done that. They could keep going until they ended up with that living child in their arms. It was almost a comfort to know they'd done the whole conception after loss thing before. Twice now, they'd kicked off the process of trying for a baby and they'd got results. And look how much further they'd come this time.

Celeste's shattered heart ached at the thought of what this new loss meant. Her second child was dead too. There were so many things that would have to be undone now: hopeful baby bits and pieces to return, connections to unravel to protect everyone involved. She thought dully about how she was going to have to call off the baby shower she wasn't supposed to know was happening. Her mother, surprisingly influenced by what Celeste was sure Gail would have otherwise written off as "an American affectation", had plunged into planning headfirst and failed to keep the secret.

Everyone would know. Maybe third time would be the charm and people could stop feeling sorry for her? It hurt to hope for the future. There was another labour to get through before there could be thoughts of any other babies.

The practice run of last year had turned out to be preparation for the big show. For the first time since that hellish missed miscarriage, Celeste was grateful for the way it had panned out. The decision to take the pills and give birth rather than have the doctors scrape them out hadn't felt like a choice at the time, but it turned out it was the right way to go.

If she'd had the surgery, Celeste wouldn't have any idea what to expect now. Here, she was an old hand. Just like she'd already managed to conceive again after loss, Celeste had birthed a dead baby before. Having a live one, now that would be uncharted territory. This one might be bigger, so much closer to life, heart-breaking in their proximity to the finish line, but there was some level of reassurance in the familiar.

There were stark contrasts though. Having sucked down the initial batch of tablets, Celeste was going to have to come back to the hospital to give birth. The two-day wait felt like forever, but there were things to be done, people to call, a bag to pack.

Celeste went through each task robotically, trying to keep her stomach as still as possible. They'd warned her the baby would still move around, a dead weight floating in liquid, drifting around for Celeste to feel. It made it all the harder to extinguish the little flame of hope that they were wrong, that this baby who'd made it so far, almost to eight months, would defy all expectations and emerge into the world alive.

With the miscarriage, the birth had been a full stop. It still gave her guilt to think that she'd flushed the toilet afterwards rather than scoop them out. Maybe they could have found a reason for why that baby had died. Even so, pulling the handle had marked a definitive end to the process.

Now, the closer Celeste came to meeting her second poor, dead child, the more fearful she became of what might happen, her response. Would she want to touch them? Could she bear to see their face?

She stayed quiet and did what she was told, swallowed her next round of medication, and waited for them to take effect. Celeste lost count of the hours in that darkened room, the number of doses.

It was difficult to concentrate on anything, flipping through TV channels at random, picking up and putting down the tattered paperback she'd stuffed into the hospital bag without thinking too much about her choice, the quiet, gentle conversations of the kind midwives who came in and out of the room to see if there was anything they could do for her. Celeste lost track of the personal details she'd divulged, trying to make connections, accepting several cups of tea for the sake of having something warm to hold onto.

Throughout the long day and night of that stage of the labour, Stephen sat in the corner. The only noise from him was the slight rustle as he turned the pages of his newspaper. He was careful to hide the trembling of his hands as much as possible. It was easier for Celeste when he tried to get some sleep on the low couch in the corner of the room.

By the small hours of the morning, the period-like cramps intensified to outright contractions. After a *rest* decreed by the doctors, Celeste was hooked up to the synthetic oxytocin drip to get active labour underway. A grimmer version of what this moment should have been, a quieter, sadder form of what might have happened if the baby wasn't already dead.

Time became patchy. Through a haze of pain, Celeste was dimly aware of someone plumbing a second drip into her. When they didn't have to worry about the baby, they were prepared to give you the good stuff. The opiates blooming through her system dulled the edge of the contractions and Celeste had something more concrete to focus on: the five-minute increments at which she could press the pain management button to get the next fix.

When Celeste began insisting that she needed to use the toilet, the midwives assured her that it was time, that the baby was coming. Embracing the familiarity of these sensations once again, Celeste bore down, feeling something sliding out of her. For a horrible, heart-rending moment, everything was quiet and still, even though Celeste wanted to scream. All along, she'd hoped against hope that the doctors were wrong, that her little miracle would come out swinging. As she crouched next to the bed, on her knees with a tiny body dangling between her legs, Celeste was certain her child was dead. Had they told her the baby was breech? She couldn't remember.

Celeste knew they'd never let this happen to a live baby. Rather than waiting for the next contraction to wash through Celeste to get the head out, they'd have been tearing her open to help her child breathe and both parents would have cheered them on. One last surge, a final push and the baby slid out into the midwife's waiting arms.

And it was then that the silence was truly deafening. As the midwives busied themselves with the bundle they'd taken from her, Celeste crawled up onto the bed. Her teeth chattered with what felt like cold, but the midwives told her it was the effects of the adrenaline.

They knew what this was, they knew what to say. How many women had been guided through the delivery of a dead baby before her? They'd already told her that this was the private delivery room they used for bereavements. Getting to it required you to pass the fewest other doors on the ward. Even so, there'd been one or two points throughout the period they'd been sealed inside when Celeste had heard a baby's first cries. Unlike now.

One of the midwives came to crouch down next to Celeste. "Do you want to know?"

Unable to speak, Celeste nodded.

"It's a little girl. We're just giving her a quick weigh. Then would you like to hold her?"

Again, Celeste nodded. Throughout labour, she'd wondered what she might want to do at this point, feared and longed for it in equal measure. Murmured conversations with the midwives had made it clear it was Celeste's choice and that whatever she wanted to do was right. Not wanting to know Stephen's opinion, fearing his dismissal, Celeste hadn't dared to ask him. Now that the moment had arrived, motherhood took over. She couldn't imagine not holding her child.

The white towelling bundle was eased into her arms and Celeste looked down at the face she'd been dreaming about for what felt like her whole life, certainly for the last eight months. In the dim light, it looked as if most of the baby's exposed skin was almost purple. With a lurch in her stomach, Celeste tried not to think too hard about the compression of the birth canal while her poor daughter's head was stuck inside. Around the mouth and nose though, was the pinkness Celeste had imagined.

The bruising didn't matter, neither did the peeling skin on her tiny hands – the deterioration Celeste had been prepared for. The baby was beautiful. Her daughter. Celeste could have stared at her forever. The delicate button nose, the curve of her cheek, the beautiful little mouth, the eyelids that Celeste couldn't quite convince herself wouldn't ever open. Until a few short days ago, this gorgeous baby had been tucked inside Celeste's womb, alive and kicking. And now she was here, but dead.

Celeste couldn't summon the courage to ask for a camera. When the suggestion had been brought up before, Stephen hadn't thought it was a good idea. Before he could say that it might be easier for them all if Celeste put the baby down, she took the opportunity to memorise every feature of her face.

It might have been kinder to give her husband the benefit of the doubt. But she didn't want Stephen to urge moving on from this baby the way he had the last. He was present, here for Celeste in this moment, and she didn't want to push for something he wasn't capable of. If he couldn't understand Celeste's need to preserve this time in resin, that was a shame for him, but it wasn't going to stop her from doing what she needed to do.

"Do you have a name for her?"

Celeste tried to think of the names they'd discussed for girls. Somehow, ones for boys had come so much easier. Classic, strong names that would fit the strapping young lad they pictured together. Maybe Stephen had been more partial regarding gender than he'd wanted to let on. This fairy child, their ethereal little girl, would she suit any of the old lady names that Stephen favoured? Somehow, she didn't seem to fit Dorothy or Eleanor or Ruth.

"Baby will do, won't it?" Stephen's voice was soft and gentle, but somehow firm enough to make it plain that no wasn't an acceptable answer in his book. "For the forms?"

The midwife who'd asked about names swivelled her eyes towards Celeste, deferring to her. Even though the baby was dead, Celeste was Mother. She was in charge. But she didn't know. She was afraid of making the wrong decision. Celeste parked her disappointment. Stephen *was* the baby's father, after all, he did get a say. And Celeste couldn't think what to name her anyway.

As if the midwife could read Celeste's thoughts, she gave a small, sad smile. "You can always change it down the line. We can put 'Baby' for now. Doesn't matter if it ends up being a placeholder."

Though Celeste was reluctant to put the baby down, she did have to submit to getting checked out by the medical staff. She lowered Baby into the cold cot – a fridge on wheels – that had been brought in. Then Celeste lay back on the bed, trying to fight the surprising giggles that came when it took three people to wrestle the stirrups into place.

"New equipment," they apologised multiple times. While all the focus was on her nether regions and the stitches she needed, Celeste turned her head to look at her husband. She couldn't quite dare to wonder how Stephen was feeling about the twisted realisation of his dream of fatherhood. Staying quiet, Celeste watched as Stephen reached down into the cot to rest a hand on his swaddled daughter, stroking the soft skin of her cheek.

It passed like a dream, the short window of time with their girl. Not just because Celeste sensed Stephen's keenness to get away. He didn't decline when the nurses offered them the chance to wash the little body or dress her in the tiny clothes they'd supplied, but it was clear that he didn't want to. He accepted the hand and footprints though, the tiny wisp of fair hair, the memory box.

When they were left alone with Baby, Stephen scooped something out of the box and handed it to Celeste. A storybook. Her voice shook as she read aloud, but with Stephen's arm around her and Baby bundled in her lap, Celeste knew that this was the closest they would ever get to an ordinary family moment.

As soon as Celeste was cleared for discharge, when the doctors were content that her uterus had shrunk back down and all the forms about the post-mortem were completed, Stephen began to gather their bags. No amount of time with Baby would have been enough, Celeste could see his thought as plain as day and she even agreed with the sentiment. So, there was little point in lingering. If Celeste didn't let Stephen lead her away from Baby, she would have spun the time out forever.

EIGHT YEARS AGO

JANUARY

Paige

AS MUCH AS PAIGE felt the unbearable need to talk it all over, she knew that confessing to Kelly about her night with Luke would make the situation — whatever was going on between them — far more real. If Paige could keep it to herself, maybe she could forget, undo, reset, make the shift in her friendship with Luke go away. Denial would make things go back to the way they were before if she could give it enough time.

It was lucky Kelly was wittering on about an interview she'd tanked – but somehow still managed to land the sales job – and how she was keeping her fingers crossed it would be enough to tide her over until the next batch of student finance came through. And then there was the essay she hoped Paige wouldn't mind looking over, just a sanity and grammar check. She wasn't expecting her to go above and beyond or anything.

Then, as Paige had been lulled into a false sense of security, Kelly took a breath and shot her friend an incisive look. "Okay, I've got to say this. I'm surprised Luke hasn't taken advantage of this window yet."

Paige jolted at the cattle prod of Kelly's words. It was clear that their library study session was destined for an extended bout of serious non-productivity. "What are you talking about?"

Eye roll, sigh, twitch of the eyebrow. Kelly's response felt somewhat rehearsed before she slipped into a studied air of mild innocence. "Oh, just that you and Owen never stay broken up for long. I know, I know, he's been all definitive this time, but you've been sure of that before. When the two of you were having a bit of a breather a few months ago, or whatever he convinced you to call it, Luke was swearing blind that this time he was going to tell you how he felt for sure. And then he bottled it. I don't want him to end up black and blue with self-flagellation if he leaves it too late this time."

The sheer confusion on Paige's face must have done the talking for her. There was another theatrical sigh from Kelly, followed by something of a smirk. "He's been in love with you since freshers'. Don't tell me you didn't know."

"Don't be ridiculous, Kell. That's... that's mad. He isn't... I mean, he doesn't feel that way."

"You can't be *this* dense, can you?"

"I don't know what you're talking about." Even though she wasn't going to be able to take in a word of it, Paige bent her head low over her textbook, wishing for once that she had long enough hair to swing down over her cheeks. Anything to hide the scarlet flush. Luke Tilney in love with her? That was, well, flattering to say the least. But he had more sense than that, didn't he?

"Oh, come on. He hasn't been too subtle about it. Respectful, sure. That's our boy to a T. But you can't not have known *anything*, surely?"

Kelly's incredulity was infuriating. For Paige, the anger blooming in her gut was easier to cope with than the idea of this secret pining. "Kell, don't do this. Men and women are perfectly capable of being friends without those sorts of feelings getting in the way. Stop being so heteronormative, you're better than that."

"Sure, guys and gals can be mates without the merest sniff of lurve whatsoever. For example, *me* and Luke, excellent friends. Not least because he's been mad about you from day one. I couldn't get a look in if I tried, makes it much easier to keep things nice and aromantic."

Now Kelly had come out and said it, Paige wasn't sure that her friend's revelation didn't make an uncomfortable amount of sense, even without the night of magnificent surprise passion. Luke was... Luke. One of Paige's dearest friends, a confidant, a shoulder to cry on as well as being a total laugh.

Had... had he been planning what happened between them? What had felt at the time like a spontaneous night of searching for comfort in the arms of a friend was beginning to feel that little bit seedier. What if Luke *had* been taking advantage of the "window", as Kelly had put it?

"But... but he never said anything." Did Kelly know Paige was lying? She and Luke had agreed to keep their little night of sexcapades between them, after all.

"With the amount of mooning you've been doing over Owen, how much of a chance would Luke have had with you if he did?"

Paige shifted in her chair, uncomfortable in a way that had nothing to do with the cheap plastic under her bottom. They needed to get better seating in here. How were people meant to concentrate, study for their degrees, if they were subjected to such conditions? What did all that tuition fee money go on?

She couldn't keep ignoring the truth bomb, Kelly's awful knack for hitting the nail on the head. It was a bit uncanny, really. Better for all concerned if you weren't exposed to Kelly's sharp scrutiny all that often. Not least because once she'd handed out one of her insightful observations, you couldn't unlearn what she'd said. Even though Paige hadn't let slip about sex with Luke, it was obvious she wouldn't be able to pretend anymore that it hadn't happened.

*

A shadow crept past the corner of Paige's field of vision. Heart hammering, she turned to look. It was just one of the neighbourhood cats. The hostile tortoiseshell with nothing but disdain for the world in her expression, Paige had seen that one before. Actually, the cat wasn't alone. Death was keeping her company, a broken little body hanging out of her mouth.

"Why the hell are you looking so pleased with yourself, you evil thing?" Paige spat. "Bloody murderer."

With a surge of tremble-inducing anger, Paige realised what must have happened. That cat had emerged from *their* garden. Paige's efforts to keep the garden stocked with an exciting range of bird seed, catering for as wide a range of wild birds as possible, to her housemates' amusement, was in fact cultivating an all-you-can-eat buffet for the local feline community.

She slammed into the house and groaned. Her frustration had nothing at all to do with the cat and Paige knew it. If he was in love with her, why had Luke gone along with her plea to forget about the night they'd spent together? There was no other choice. She had to get some answers.

"When you said it was a mistake…" She didn't want to finish the question, knowing how much it was going to change things between them if she kept chasing an explanation.

This time, she was the one to turn up at Luke's with a takeaway. A peace offering complete with naans and several bottles of Cobra. With intense relief she found Luke alone, his housemates magically somewhere else for the evening.

Curiosity was nipping at the base of Paige's skull, too insistent to ignore. She had to know how Luke felt, hear the truth from his lips. The door to the point of no return was already yawning wide. Even if Paige could somehow keep pretending it wasn't there, she had to find out which side of it they were on, and whether they were together.

Luke was inspecting his nails, avoiding Paige's gaze with an air of casualness. When he began to speak, his voice was once again measured, reasonable. "If memory serves, *you* were the one who declared it a mistake."

There could be no doubt in either of their minds what the *it* was that they were referring to. The last time they were alone together.

"But you agreed," Paige pressed.

"I did." There was nothing in Luke's expression to give him away. Everything was calm and assured. If Paige didn't know better, thanks to Kelly's intel, she could believe that Luke was relaxed, indifferent to everything she was saying. That there was no hidden torch for her.

But that was all down to his surprise acting prowess, surely? Unless Paige had managed to snuff out all those feelings Luke had kept secret from her for so long? Nothing like being begged to pretend that sex hadn't happened to convince you once and for all that a cause was lost.

"Well," Paige fiddled with her jacket cuff, "I know why I... I mean, it was all too soon after..." She didn't want to say Owen's name. "It's just... why did you think it was a bad idea?"

For far too long, Luke was silent. When he looked up to examine a spot on the wall, rather than look at Paige herself, the neutral expression he'd been wearing had vanished. Something genuine, something raw, was beginning to bleed through.

"That wasn't how I wanted our first time to be. Don't get me wrong, I'm not being all virginal about it, loading firsts with all this meaning or whatever. But I... I had to believe that afterwards, once we finally, when we'd had that break-through, that you wouldn't be able to push me away because I wasn't the person you wanted."

A strange, strangled note had crept into Luke's tone. It was devastating to Paige, laying her cruelty bare. His eyes flicked to meet hers at last. They were dark with intent, urgent and primal. It was clear to Paige that they weren't friends, not just friends anyway. Hadn't been for some time. Even if she wanted to try and cram them back into that place, it was obvious how impossible that effort would be. She'd lose him altogether if she kept trying.

"I should have held out. Made you wait for it. Rather than indulging you with some kind of pity shag. Or whatever it was you wanted from me that night."

"Oh." A blush rose from the liquid centre of Paige's belly. They were teetering on the edge of something significant, her and Luke. From the way he was looking at her, Paige was almost certain Luke wasn't going to let her mess everything up again, that he really did still want her. At that thought, a rush of gratitude mingled with every other feeling swirling around her abdomen. "You've got quite the high opinion of yourself then."

"Do I?" It was a growl of a challenge, scorching heat radi-ating from his eyes.

Pretending she wasn't trembling with desire, a languorous sensation unfurling through her veins, Paige nodded with a teasing smile. "If you think delayed gratification is the way to play this, you must believe the payoff will make the effort worth it. Ends justifying the means and whatnot."

"I think I'm equal to the task." There was more to it than swagger. He had plenty of substance with which to back up that playful confidence and Luke knew Paige was well aware of that too. Even wrapped up in so many layers of emotional complexity, their night together had been worthy of a glowing five-star review.

"Is that so?" A happy little bubble rising in Paige's throat was enough to convince her that maybe she could have some fun with this situation too. "Do you expect me to believe that if I were to beg you to, right now, you wouldn't have sex with me?"

"That depends."

"On?"

"How do you plan to beg?"

From the cocked eyebrow to the soft curve of Luke's lips, Paige couldn't imagine how she'd ever been able to think of him in platonic terms. Allure was coming off him in waves, helped along in Paige's head by vivid flashbacks to the sight of him without his clothes. If Luke wanted her to plead for him to touch her, Paige was a breath away from getting down onto her knees in supplication.

"I didn't say I was planning to."

"Well…" Luke moved until his face was much nearer to Paige's, close enough to kiss but only if she leaned forwards. They were dancing together towards the brink. "If we're dealing in hypotheticals, then I can say with confidence that I wouldn't so much as kiss you should you ask me to. Even if you said please."

"No?" Disappointment made Paige sound like a petulant child denied a lollipop. "Not even pretty please?"

"Absolutely not."

Paige moved forward by millimetres, breathing in Luke's intoxicating musk, still maintaining a hair's breadth of gap between their lips. "What if I fluttered my eyelashes?"

For a moment, she thought he was going to break, that she'd won. But as Luke's hands settled themselves on Paige's hips, neither pushing her away nor pulling her any closer, just resting there, her wavering sense of control over the situation evaporated. When she felt the tickle of Luke's breath on her ear, any illusions over who was in charge melted away.

"I'd be a terrible friend if I gave into such a move on your part, wouldn't I? You'd regret it in the morning, I'm sure. Experience has taught me that much, and I'd hate to take advantage of you. Can't let ourselves get into bad habits, you know. So, I wouldn't slide my fingers up the back of your neck as I tipped your face towards mine. And I'd never trace the line of your jaw as we began to kiss."

The pressure of his fingertips increased inexorably, a feather-light squeeze deepening to a firmer hold as Luke kept talking, detailing the litany of increasingly rude things he would never dream of doing to her. The way those same fingers holding Paige against him wouldn't scoop her up as she wrapped her legs around his waist, how he wouldn't press her up against a wall and that it was lucky that none of this would come to pass.

Why? Because there was no way he'd be able to make it to a bed this time around. It would be a miracle if they didn't end up breaking any furniture. Bang goes the security deposit. A terrible blow to a poor student's finances.

It was the most intimate moment of Paige's life and yet they somehow still had their clothes on. Her eyes flew open, seeking Luke's searing hot gaze. "How can I convince you?"

"Convince me of what?" The delighted smile was wolfish and dangerous.

"That I want you. Only you." Her words came out between ragged breaths. It wasn't a mere desire not to think about him anymore, she couldn't say Owen's name. The last thing Paige wanted was to give any more form to the spectre in the room with them. If she wished hard enough, it would go away, and she and Luke would be alone together.

Her cheeks were on fire. "And that I want you to do everything you just said."

Luke shrugged. "I don't know. Take me out to dinner, tell me I'm pretty. There's no telling what I might get talked into after a bottle of wine or three."

"Tomorrow night? Caravello's?" Could Paige wait that long? An entire day? It would be worthy penance though, and she'd do it. It was only fair, after how long Paige had made Luke hold out for, even if she hadn't realised.

But it seemed that she and Luke were of similar minds. "I don't know, that's such a long time away."

Frustrating man. Paige was on the point of pouting as she tried to tease out a solution. "But you said you weren't going to kiss me."

But before Luke could answer, Paige managed to solve the puzzle on her own. The sleeping princess didn't have to wait for a handsome stranger to come along and instigate her cure. Paige's fingers raked through Luke's hair as she pulled his mouth towards hers. Like magnets of opposing poles, once they'd snapped together, she knew there'd be no pulling the pair of them apart again without a whole lot of force. Damn right.

PRESENT DAY

DECEMBER

Paige

PAIGE DIDN'T SEE ANYTHING like enough of her parents. While Margaret had made it difficult to spend any time together, as a unit or even one-on-one, the same accusation couldn't be levelled at Russell. It was far too easy to let the weeks slip past without popping by to see him. And he was being respectful, courteous, giving Paige her space.

Not that Paige was avoiding Celeste or anything like that. The tentative warning that Russell had issued about keeping Celeste out of all the miscarriage chat had been weighing on Paige. She didn't know what to make of it.

So, when Russell suggested a visit, Paige couldn't think of a good reason to say no. As she crossed the threshold of her father's house and leaned into Russell's welcoming hug, Paige felt awful for having stayed away.

"Hi, Dad. Is Celeste upstairs?"

Russell shifted from foot to foot. "No. She, er, she went out."

"Oh." Paige was thrown. "But she knew I was coming round?"

"Ah… yes."

It was considerate of her, Paige supposed. A relief too, given that she didn't know how to handle the pregnancy loss chat around her stepmother now.

Russell looked lost for a moment and then smiled. "Fancy a good old-fashioned litter pick? We can have a wander and I'll show you the verges where the council's been going to town on wildflower planting. I think you'll like it."

Civic-minded Russell's take on environmentalism. It had always been his way. He knew his suggestion would go down well. It was something the two of them had filled otherwise idle Sunday afternoons with back in the day. Such outings happened to coincide with the times when Paige couldn't stand to be in the house with her mother for a moment longer. The air was too thick with the lingering results of Margaret's surprise announcement in that odd in between time when the divorce was yet to go through and the three of them were still living together.

When she thought about it, Paige had no idea how they'd managed to coexist in such stifling proximity. Maybe the father–daughter rubbish clear ups were as much for Russell as Paige, his way of looking out for her as well as seizing the opportunity for a little breathing space.

A stroll in the sunshine on the hunt for discarded crisp packets was an excellent suggestion. Rather than trapping each other in the front room they could be out together in the fresh air. A far better prospect than stilted small talk stretching into pained silences, Russell straining his mind for anything that might comfort his grieving daughter without upsetting her further until the blood vessels in his brain popped from the effort of it all. For one thing, it was so much easier to discuss uncomfortable topics if you didn't have to look the other person in the eye.

"Do you think you two will try again?"

Paige stopped in her tracks, wondering how frank to be about the subject. "If I'm being honest, we weren't trying as such this time around."

"Oh."

"Don't get me wrong. We wanted this baby. Very much." Paige didn't want Russell to get the wrong idea about Button. The loss wasn't a relief. It had been an adjustment made and undone in a very short period. "It wasn't something we were gunning for, if you want to put it that way."

A sympathetic smile played across Russell's lips. "You two have plenty of time if you wanted to leave it for a while. And it's not as if it's a requirement to have children."

"We do have time." Paige acknowledged. The other part of the equation was something she'd been grappling with. Did she *want* to go the whole hog and actually try? The accidental pregnancy had been so perfect, putting her in that position before she had to think about it. And even if Paige decided she wanted to be a mother in the first place, were children something she wanted right now?

Before the thoughts could climb on top of her, swamping her brain, Paige knew she had to move the conversation on. If there was one slim upside of loss, it was the breaking down of a few barriers, granting licence to ask more questions than she might have done otherwise. She wasn't going to admit to Russell what was behind the cracking of her reserve, didn't want to give him ideas about bright sides.

"What about you and Mum? How much planning went into me and Annie?"

If Margaret weren't a hundred miles away, she'd have been the obvious person to talk to about this. Or at least she should have been. But Paige's father was right there, in possession of the information she was interested in, when the question tripped off her tongue. Her cheeks were flaming at the thought of her own parents getting down and dirty. But Paige passed off the blush as exertion as she darted forwards to scoop up a discarded water bottle. It seemed that the discomfort was mutual as Russell gave a nervous cough. Too late for Paige to question whether she wanted the low-down on her own conception.

"Well, don't tell your sister this, but we were a bit surprised that she came along so soon. Thought it would take a few more, er, practice rounds. Some dear friends of ours had been having no joy for months and Mum was beginning to get concerned we might go through something similar. But then she was barely off the pill and, well, bam."

You had to give him points for trying. Paige and Russell looked away from each other. However, in the moment she averted her gaze, Paige was almost sure she could detect a hint of pride on Russell's face. The male dream. Potent enough to make an impact as soon as it was possible.

"It was enough to make us that bit more careful when we were thinking about having another one. We decided that spring was a lovely time of year for a baby."

With her birthday coming right at the end of May, Paige found herself appreciating the amount of consideration that had gone into the timing. With such irritating fertility in her family background, maybe there wasn't anything to worry about, no matter how often Paige was plagued with thoughts of difficulties in the future. They'd managed to get pregnant once without a whole lot of effort. Whenever she and Luke found the courage to try again, if they did, they'd be following a stellar track record. And this time, things would be alright.

Feeling generous enough to steer them away from any other embarrassing revelations, Paige asked about how the bathroom renovations were going. Russell's relief about the safer conversational ground was palpable. The thoroughly middle-class topic of home improvements was rich enough to carry them all the way back home.

THREE YEARS AGO

JUNE

Paige

PAIGE COULDN'T DENY THE obvious. She'd never seen a happier bride. Celeste was radiant. That being said, Paige's experience of weddings was limited – most of her friends were yet to tie the knot – and Celeste wasn't doing herself or her groom any favours by playing up the gaping age difference between them with her beachy curls and tea-length lacy frock.

There was such a carefree giddiness to Celeste that day. To both the bride and the groom if Paige was being honest. So much so that there was no denying the loved-up nature of this match. And it did mean a lot to Paige to see her father happy. Ever since Margaret dropped the bombshell of her dissatisfaction with the life she and Russell had built together before skipping off towards the bright stage lights of Devon, Russell had been consumed with competing concerns for the people in his life.

If he could miss something so fundamental about his own wife, in what ways was he failing the others around him? Far ahead of any of his own concerns, Russell had an overpowering need to make sure that everyone was alright, that he was doing everything he could for them. It killed Paige to see her father so convinced that it was his own inadequacies at fault rather than holding Margaret responsible for never speaking up about her unhappiness.

Those worries were a world away as Russell smiled dopily at his new wife. The sight was working something loose in Paige's heart, something she hadn't even noticed was there until that night, that moment on the edge of the dance floor under the shifting disco lights.

No matter how little Paige approved, irrespective of her opinion of Celeste, Paige didn't think it was doomed. Some marriages *could* be built to last. If you had the right person by your side.

"Well, if they can do it, I suppose anyone can."

"Come again?"

As soon as she realised that she'd said the words out loud, Paige blushed. Could she backtrack? But looking at Luke, the man who loved her more than anything, whose devotion had never been in doubt, she knew she couldn't keep her bubbling stew pot of thoughts to herself. Not when so many of them were about him.

"Maybe we should be the ones walking down the aisle together."

Before Paige knew what was happening, Luke had whisked her into his arms, dragging her with him into the middle of the throng of dancing guests. "I can't believe you just did that."

With Luke whispering into Paige's ear, his arms around her waist, pulling her close, it was impossible to know what his expression looked like. He couldn't be quite as scandalised as he sounded, could he?

But could Paige blame him for being angry with her? It wasn't as if she'd come out with the most romantic of proposals. She hadn't done it right at all. Maybe Luke would let her take it back, chalk it up to the heady fizz of champagne whisking Paige away from her senses.

She was shocked to hear that tone from him though. It was clear what his answer to the question she hadn't asked would be, which felt oddly disappointing. Maybe they could pretend she'd never said anything at all.

So long as they were together, Paige didn't need anything else. It was for Luke's sake, really, that she'd even thought of getting married. There'd always been something of a romance deficit on her side of the partnership, or so it felt. But maybe getting hitched wasn't something that would address that. The divorce had been enough to hold Paige back from that sort of thinking. Why didn't she know how Luke felt about marriage?

"Sorry, didn't mean to tread on Dad's coattails," Paige mumbled.

Before her worries could rattle on any further, Luke drew back and shook his head, the widest smile on his face, one with a wicked hint to it. "Oh, not because of that. Though it makes sense that you'd want to steal the bride's thunder, jealous pixie of a stepdaughter you are."

While Paige grimaced at the officialness of her new relationship with Celeste, Luke was getting ready to throw a fresh distraction her way. "It's more that you've *ruined* what I've got waiting for you at home."

Paige's eyes widened.

Later that night, back at their flat, in a cloud of candlelight and forget-me-nots, Paige had to admit that Luke's way of suggesting that they should get married was a little bit more fairy tale than hers. She'd leave romantic moments to the master in future.

FIFTEEN YEARS AGO

AUGUST

Celeste

"STEPHEN?" EVER SINCE THEY'D left the hospital, he'd been quiet. At the long-awaited follow-up appointment, he'd asked sensitive, thoughtful questions. About Celeste's test results. About Baby and her post-mortem. About the future.

All the while, tears had trickled down Celeste's face. It was easier to leave the questioning of the doctor to Stephen, especially as he was doing such an excellent job of covering everything she'd thought of. But when the kind consultant turned to Celeste and asked if there was anything else, all Celeste could think about was that period of uncertainty.

"Could I have done anything? I... I was concerned about movement, which was why we went in. If we'd come in earlier, if I h-hadn't hesitated. Could... would it have made a difference?"

Eyes full of shining compassion, the doctor reached over to hold Celeste's hand. "There was no sign of infection and your daughter's condition – the limited deterioration observed in the post-mortem – was such that whatever happened to her must have been quick. You did everything you could for her. It was the right thing to come in when you did. This wasn't your fault."

Celeste couldn't bring herself to look over at Stephen. She couldn't do anything but finally give in to the sobs that broke to the surface. By the time she was in control of herself again, it was much too late to catch Stephen's reaction, let alone try to gauge it.

"Should it be what the two of you choose to do, I would encourage you to try and have more children. The fact that we couldn't find any reason for your daughter's death is encouraging, from a future-focused view if nothing else. I'm so sorry that we couldn't give you anything definitive, but we were able to rule out lots of nasty causes that might stand in the way of other pregnancies. The biggest hurdle is getting pregnant again. We'll make sure to look after you when you get there."

It had seemed impossible to Celeste that she could have walked out of that appointment with hope in her heart. Poor Baby was another blip. A larger roadblock than the miscarriage. But not necessarily something that stood between Celeste and living children. They were going to get through this. Stephen's certainty had carried them through last time, maybe hers would do the job now.

But Stephen still hadn't said anything in the car. When he finally responded to her question, it was enough to make Celeste wish he'd stayed silent.

"There's something *wrong* with you."

Everything shifted. The bubble of hope in Celeste's chest popped, drowning out everything else the doctor had said. Even though she knew Stephen was right, that there was no other conclusion that could have been reached, she flinched. It was an impossible feat, but Celeste knew she had to try and stand up for herself.

"They didn't find anything," she whispered.

"Well, they didn't look hard enough, did they? *She* was normal, no obvious defects, that's what they said. She'd have been *fine* if *your* body hadn't murdered her. Clearly nothing the matter at my end." He continued to stare dead ahead at the road in front of the car. His words were a deadly hiss.

The timing couldn't have been better as Stephen pulled into the drive. "I'm not going to give you the chance to kill any more of my children. Got to make sure of that."

His door slammed and he was gone before Celeste had the chance to process anything he'd spat at her. She didn't know why she was surprised. Was Stephen so afraid of his own grief, of the reality of losing Baby that he had to find something, someone to pin the blame on? In the absence of anything concrete from the doctors' investigations, Celeste had to be it.

From Stephen's point of view, the logic was more than clear. He thought he'd been trading his old wife in for a shinier new model, one with the sorts of bells and whistles he was looking forward to using. And now it was clear he'd been sold defective goods, no matter what reassurances the doctors gave.

With a twinge of annoyance, not the emotion Celeste might have ever expected in this moment, she realised she was going to have to make friends. Hiding away from the world had only been possible this far with Stephen's protection and now that was gone. She hadn't even noticed when he'd withdrawn. No wonder she was in shock. Leaving the car felt like too much.

The world knew she was faulty. With an obvious bump, everyone wanted to know you, to have a claim on your stomach, to give advice and make a connection with you as an expectant mother. It had irritated her so much at the time that Celeste hadn't ever thought she'd miss the treatment once it had gone. But it was going to take so much more effort to find fellow parents of the dead.

In the absence of anyone else to talk to about what had happened, Celeste knew she needed to find community. Not least because this latest development would mean she was going to have to depend on the mercy of her disappointed parents.

PRESENT DAY

DECEMBER

Paige

PAIGE KNEW SHE WAS brooding even before Luke homed into view with a concerned expression on his face.

"Are you alright?"

What was the point in pretending? "No."

He offered Paige a steaming mug. "Do you want to talk about it?"

It felt like her head weighed a ton as she wearily rested it against Luke's shoulder. She cradled the tea's comforting warmth between her hands as she considered her options. It was obvious that Luke's offer to talk was more than genuine. He wanted Paige to let him care for her. But was it going to make a difference? "It's nothing I haven't told you before. I don't want to keep dumping everything on you."

"I don't mind."

Paige blessed him for saying that, whether or not it was ultimately true. He had to have plenty of his own problems churning around in his head, the loss of pending fatherhood and everything being so far out of his control. She knew she should ask Luke how he was, but she couldn't. "It wouldn't be fair."

"None of this is. For either of us."

"No, I know."

They both stared into empty space. "It feels like you need to talk to *someone,* love. If you don't want it to be me, then what about Annie? Or one of your friends?" For a moment, Luke paused, as if trying to come to a decision. Was he going to remind her about the counsellor's card he'd given her a few weeks ago? Paige had been ignoring it ever since she'd dropped it into her bag.

"What about Kelly?"

"Are you mad? Not interested."

"You two have been friends for the best part of ten years. Are you going to keep on punishing her for one lapse? You said she was excited about the card designs. She probably doesn't even know what she did, how much it upset you. Can't you give her the chance to apologise?"

Paige's gaze swivelled back to the floor, and she pushed an angry huff out of her chest, trying to keep her temper in check. "But that's at least half the point, Ook, she didn't realise. It means I can't trust her anymore. She might do it again."

"I don't think you're being fair."

His confusion was enough to make her mouth quiver. "You can't take her side in this."

Luke's eyes widened in alarm at her implication. "I wasn't... I mean, what she did was horrible. But if you explained, then... I mean, if you never give her an opportunity to apologise, how can it ever be right between you two?"

Before she snapped and said something she knew she'd regret, Paige took a breath. And another. It was enough to prod the rational side of her brain into wakefulness. "You have a point there."

"It was bound to happen one of these days."

"I know I need to forgive her. And, and I need to find someone to talk to. I'm not ready yet though." Her voice dropped to a whisper. "It all hurts so much."

It was the easiest thing in the world to allow herself to be folded into Luke's embrace. He kissed her hair. "I know, love, I know."

PRESENT DAY

JANUARY 2016

Paige

ONCE PAIGE HAD RETURNED to the office, fit and well enough to be working again, the clenching tension of her first week back relaxed inch by inch as her workmates behaved around her much as they ever had. Maybe there was a little more gentleness than usual, enhanced understanding when Paige made the odd mistake, but there weren't any overt references to the spectacle she'd made of herself. Or the reason behind it.

Still, she found herself struggling with small talk. It sent her heart racing to think that what had happened could come up at any turn of the conversation. Zack might mention that his date from the other night had gone so well that he was almost certain he'd met the mother of his future children. Or Jia and her boyfriend might have an announcement to make.

How far around the office had Paige's news gone? Did they all know about the miscarriage? Did she know if they knew? If they were aware of the broad brush strokes, would they want to know any of the grisly details? Would she have been curious about someone else's experience if the roles were reversed? She'd be lying if she tried to pretend there wouldn't be a little morbid fascination.

As chats stretched on, Paige began to wish for signs, some acknowledgement of her loss, or the public freak-out that had followed it. She felt like she was lugging a neon placard around with her and the longer everyone went without making any allusion to it, the more it weighed her down.

What if it was down to Paige to say something? Did they all think that *she* was the one acting strange for refusing to dispense the permission required for them all to talk about it? Once a day or two had crawled by, during which Paige had managed to excuse herself for a few brief cries in the toilets to get a handle on her broiling emotions, it was easier to go with the flow. They were all sticking with the established precedent of don't ask, don't tell.

But then something came along to break the spell of silence. Aisling crouched down beside Paige's desk, shooting a furtive glance over her shoulder to check no one was in earshot before she spoke. "We're finally doing it."

Paige's eyes flew wide open with panic at Aisling's conspiratorial whisper. Finally doing what? Where had this sudden plotting sprung from? "Huh?"

"We're crashing Kwame's poetry slam. Tonight. You *have* to join, no excuses."

"You're kidding me." For the first time in who knew how long Paige found herself grinning. Something foamy and distracting was bubbling around in her chest. "He wants people to come?"

Aisling's expression, her eyes glittering, her mouth quirking to one side, betrayed her. Clear admission of guilt, as well as an explanation for such secrecy. "Well, not as such. But he was talking to Layla, you know, the new lady in IT. Anyway, I heard him mention it right down to the when and where. That's basically the same as an official invite for someone quite so shy and retiring as our dear Kwame."

"Maybe he was trying to impress Layla? Can't imagine he wants a whole cadre of us to turn up and cramp his style."

Aisling's smile morphed into something a little wicked. "Oh, I'm sure that we'll be teaching him a lesson to remember the perils of trying to be interesting in sharing office goss. Don't you want to go along and cheer him on or whatever? You're always so supportive of all our outside stuff."

Why was it so important for Paige to go along with them? And then the penny dropped, skittering into place. Aisling was doing it for *Paige* as much as Kwame, trying to find something to cheer her up, give her a night out with a purpose so they didn't have to run the risk of talking about babies. Paige's heart brimmed with all the unspoken thoughtfulness shimmering in the air around her.

She grinned back at Aisling. "Go on then, you've talked me into it."

*

Not sure what to expect later that evening, Paige's smile was still on her face, widening with anticipation for what was coming. She had to hand it to the work gang, they'd been right to drag her out. This was going to be fun.

Sneaking into the pub without being spotted by Kwame was a downright thrill. With Jia smirking next to her, giving Paige permission to find it all exciting and so many kinds of ridiculous, she could relax into her glass of wine and not devote the smallest scrap of brain space to miscarriage. No one around her was thinking about it either. Paige was beyond grateful.

Until Kwame took the "stage". Under the spotlight pointed at the bare stretch of wall behind the microphone stand, he was soulful, earnest, and oblivious that he had a far more familiar audience than he'd been expecting. Less than a verse into his performance, and Paige felt her soul draining out of her mouth, which was hanging open in horror. She couldn't believe what she was hearing.

As she stumbled outside, sans handbag, not caring about the wine stain spreading across her favourite scarf, those searing words rang in her ears. *Formless one, yet to meet, gone forever, unknown by so many corners of the universe.* It *couldn't* have been how it sounded, right? Not from Kwame. Paige was being oversensitive, reading way too much into something innocent and unrelated to everything she'd been through.

If she could catch her breath, stop every fibre of her from hammering away, Paige knew she'd find a way to endure the rest of the evening. She scrambled to put an escape plan together. March back in, give her apologies, invent some emergency of Luke's that she had to go back home and deal with, no matter how implausible that would sound to anyone who actually knew Luke – a man more than capable of dealing with his own crises. Oxygen was all Paige needed to make it to the next moment.

The haunted, pleading look on Aisling's face as she crept out to join Paige put paid to her hopes of a dignified exit. Everyone knew. Aisling had already sussed out Paige's inter-pretation of Kwame's verse and how little she wanted to share her thoughts about it with the rest of the group. No one would be fooled if Paige tried to pretend.

But what if there was more to it? They hadn't wanted to discuss it at the office, but what if they were trying to force the topic now?

"Please tell me you didn't know he was going to do that." Paige's voice was faint.

It was almost impressive that Aisling's lily-white skin managed to pale even further. She looked like a ghost under the orange glow of the streetlights. "Of course, I didn't. I'd never…"

Nodding, Paige could already feel the tears welling in her eyes. With a lurch of embarrassment, she turned and scurried away. Realising that she was leaving her purse, her keys, everything apart from her phone – clutched tight between icy fingers – behind in the pub wasn't enough to make her go back.

Even with the cold night pressing around her, she needed time alone with her thoughts. There should have been fifty different credible explanations to justify what had happened under that spotlight. Maybe Kwame had a girlfriend who'd been through pregnancy loss. Or Paige's stolidly unpoetical brain had misinterpreted what was meant to be a clever metaphor. Or Kwame had a past life as a woman where he'd garnered first-hand experience that he'd been keeping very quiet about until then.

But none of those made as much sense to Paige as the anguish flaring in her gut that Kwame had taken something from her and her alone. He'd laid claim to an experience that wasn't his for the sake of *content*. Sure, he wasn't posting it on the socials, and he hadn't invited any of them along, but Paige felt so used. It was wrenching that she could believe something so insensitive of quiet, thoughtful Kwame. The tears coursed down her cheeks as she marched deeper into the night.

*

"Um, Paige?"

Kwame. Paige's heart took a nosedive, plummeting until it lodged somewhere next to her feet. When she looked at Kwame's face, it sank through the carpet. Maybe the loss adjusters on the next floor down would find some use for the broken thing.

In the small hours of the morning, what had happened at the poetry night had felt like the push Paige needed to hand in her notice, run away and never have to see any of her colleagues ever again, including Kwame. Especially Kwame.

Somehow though, in the cold light of day, Paige had managed to drag herself into the office. Sensible, practical grown-up that she was, she hadn't even called in sick. She'd come to face the music, in the full knowledge that no matter how much she longed for the chance to skip over this moment, it had come. A sheepish Aisling had deposited the errant handbag onto Paige's desk without comment, but Paige wasn't getting through this bit without having to talk about it.

Kwame wasn't a bad guy. There was no denying his essential niceness and Paige didn't want him to have to stew in the mess of what had happened for any longer than necessary. She couldn't get around what he'd said, in front of an audience, no less. But it wasn't like it was his fault that those words had come out of his mouth while Paige was in the room.

"I want to—"

"You don't have to explain."

After everything that had wormed through Paige's brain at 2 a.m., it was true. This was Kwame. He wouldn't have set out to hurt her. She didn't have to hear whatever he needed to say about the why of what had happened. About how his sister had a miscarriage at fourteen weeks a few years ago. About how hearing about Paige's loss had stirred up old memories. How this was his way of processing all those churning thoughts.

"Seriously, man. We shouldn't have been there in the first place. I'm the one who owes you an apology."

Kwame shook his head with fervour. "But I mean, I… I wanted you to know. Well… it's… None of this stuff gets talked about. And I wouldn't, I mean, I could *never*… I wouldn't talk about it lightly. But I didn't want to assume… er, it's not my place. Not with your loss, or even hers really. I mean, it's not as if… if I were the father or…" The tips of his ears flamed with the uncomfortable acuteness of his embarrassment.

With a trickle of compassion that soon yawned into a roaring flood, Paige couldn't deny that Kwame was more than justified. She didn't have squatter's rights to the moral high ground. More than that, if she wanted to change the conversation, to get more people talking about the losses, to erase the invisibility of the grief she felt, she couldn't go around dictating who got to discuss miscarriage and who wasn't allowed to mention the topic.

The idea of anyone jumping down Annie's throat if she dared to mention miscarriage was enraging. Would Paige feel any different about that scenario if she had a brother rather than a sister? Since it was clear that Kwame had the qualification based on proximity, it wouldn't be fair for his gender to exclude him from discussing pregnancy loss.

"I'm sorry, K. That we all pushed in, that is. And thank you. I know you were doing it for you, but it's good for people to talk about it." It was a smaller, more hesitant voice than the one Paige used around the office. "I, um… is there any chance you'd maybe be prepared to send me that poem? I feel like I didn't give it a proper listen the first time around."

"You don't have to."

"Oh." Paige's eyes widened. Had she crossed the line? "It's okay if you don't want to. If it's, um, private or… or whatever," she finished weakly. "But I'd love to read it properly if I could."

Bless him, Kwame nodded. Even if he didn't want to share his poetry, Paige was halfway sure that he understood where she was coming from. He fiddled with the button on his shirt sleeve and gave Paige a shy smile.

She was seized by another generous impulse. "And if you ever wanted to… to talk about it. Well, I'd suggest we go for a drink. I mean, like a coffee or something." The thought of having a man with some level of miscarriage experience for Luke to talk to was beyond appealing. "I bet… I bet you would have been a brilliant uncle."

Stopping, Paige laughed at herself, her utter presumption. "I'm jumping to conclusions here." He did say his sister's loss was years ago. "Did… did your sister go on to have any other children?"

Kwame's smile widened to the point of beaming. "Two boys. And I try my best on the uncle front. She… I mean, none of us ever forgot about that first child. Whenever JoJo reckons that she can get away with it without having to go into the details, she'll say she's got three kids. And her sons know about the miscarriage. She never wanted it to be a secret."

"She sounds brave."

"In that, totally. Bit cracked the rest of the time but that's got nothing to do with the children. Your big sister never stops being your big sis, even when she's supposed to be a grown-up, a mum and everything."

Paige could relate. Annie was still pretty much the exact same person she'd been as a teenager. Her personality had been set in gelatine well before then. Of course, Annie didn't have children and Paige couldn't see that changing any time soon, but motherhood didn't have the power to alter her sister's essential Annie-ness. Had the brief period of pregnancy done anything to change what Paige was like as a person?

A polite clearing of Kwame's throat brought Paige back to the moment at hand. "You... um, just because the two of you are in the same club, that doesn't mean you have anything else in common or anything. But, ah, would you maybe like to meet my sister?"

"I'd love to. Maybe she could join us for that coffee sometime? I could bring my husband too."

"JoJo might suggest we upgrade it to cocktails."

Paige laughed. "Well, if we *have* to, I guess that would be awesome. I think the chance of us getting on just went way up. There're at least two things we've got in common now."

Once a relieved Kwame had made his way back to his desk, Paige went to find Aisling. Before the other woman could make a break for it, as the panicked expression betrayed she was desperate to do, Paige gave her a hug. It wasn't Aisling's fault that the night had taken such a turn, and the last thing Paige wanted to do was punish her colleague for the impulse to take her out for a diverting evening. "Thank you."

"It was just a bag," came the mumble from Aisling.

"Let's do karaoke or something next time instead."

"Deal." Aisling gave Paige a reassuring squeeze.

FIFTEEN YEARS AGO

SEPTEMBER

Celeste

CELESTE COULDN'T SLEEP. OR that was what it felt like. Even though Stephen had left her with the impression that he was turning her out of the house, it turned out he was just planning to leave her. Better for his purposes – he knew where to find her, or at least where to send divorce missives, but she had no idea where he'd gone. Whenever Celeste sobbed, there was no one there to hold her anymore.

And what she gained in not having to answer to Gail and John, she lost in being stuck in a home that wasn't really hers anymore. The outside world was too full of prams and bumps, all serving as painful reminders, triggers for Celeste's grief as if such things were needed.

She didn't blame Stephen for not wanting to keep the house, with the nursery they were halfway through decorating. His empty side of the bed taunted her as she stared at it through all the dark hours of the night, shuffling out of the covers come morning feeling as if she'd been squeezed through several wringers and sicked out, to then be battered with hammers. It was a holding pattern that couldn't last.

Before too much longer, Celeste was going to have to figure out what to do next. Move out, get a job, find a way to support herself. The allowance Stephen had granted her for what he'd called this "transition period" — all communication coming through his solicitors and Gail since he was far too disgusted to talk to his own wife — would only last for so long. If she hadn't given up her job when she'd married Stephen, a regressive choice that Celeste regretted, a loss this late would have granted her maternity leave. Just as she'd been before her pregnancies, Celeste was dependent on her husband.

To change that, to sort her life out, she had to find a way to rest. If she mentioned her insomnia to the GP, they'd skip straight to bringing up antidepressants again, or maybe even tranquilisers if she let slip too much of the truth of what was happening. As if they could make up for not saving Baby by medicating her out of the aftermath, insulate her from the more shattering effects of grief.

Chamomile tea, that was supposed to help, wasn't it? Maybe there were some other natural remedies to try. Everything sleep-related reeked of lavender, there had to be a reason for that. Sucking down endless pills and tablets, more than she'd had to take so far, wasn't the way Celeste wanted to live the rest of her life. Having to live it at all, and alone to boot, was hard enough. She didn't want to be dependent on pharma forever.

A trip to her local health foods shop confirmed her instincts. And kind as all the medical staff had been, the patient practicality of the sales assistant had blown Celeste away. Or they were just excellent at their job, sending her off with a raft of goodies to help the situation. Chamomile tea for before bed, lavender oils for creating a calming atmosphere, valerian root and passionflower to help with her anxiety. Celeste hadn't had to go into chapter and verse on her situation at large, the divorce had been more than enough to elicit the sympathy of the kind sales lady who was more than prepared to give her a nudge in the right direction.

She wasn't completely naïve. It would take more than a good night's sleep to convince Celeste that putting her faith in alternative remedies would have saved her child, but it wasn't as if anyone at the hospital had been able to do anything for Baby. She never wanted to feel that helpless again.. No harm in putting in the work to see what else the world could offer her.

Before long, it was like an intricate puzzle. Maybe Celeste had missed her calling in life. It was too late to retrain as a nurse just to delve into the medicine cabinet so it wasn't as if she could compare this to conventional medicine. Anyway, this made much more sense, matching up a need or a symptom with something in the herbal world. If this was how Celeste managed to stitch herself back together, she couldn't care less how anyone else decided to judge her for it. She was going to rise, to carry Baby – and the other one – with her through life, not descend into further misery and sleeplessness.

PRESENT DAY

JANUARY

Paige

I N HER SISTER'S COMPANY, Paige could relax in a way that felt so rare these days. She could even make a confession or two to Annie, safe in the knowledge that judgement would be kept to a minimum.

"I want to talk about the miscarriage. All the time. It doesn't matter what the conversation is, before long I'll be trying to figure out how to turn the conversation round to..." she felt her voice wobbling, "to the baby."

Annie's expression was kind. "It's only natural to want to talk about it."

"Is it? No one else seems to think so." Hopelessness seeped out of Paige's pores. "It's just so... over. There's no tissue, my boobs are as flat as they ever were. If I can't even mention what happened, what does that mean for her?"

"Her?"

Paige shrugged, a little embarrassed that her flight of fancy had slipped out. Not even Luke knew how she'd started picturing the baby. "It's silly. Nothing really. A feeling. I think it might have been a girl."

"It." There was a half-smile on Annie's face as she shook her head. "She. She'll always be a part of you. It's not the way it should be, she should still be with you in body as well as spirit. Even if you never mentioned her again, never even thought about her, you'll always have been pregnant. You'll always have made a life."

Tears already swimming in her eyes, Paige nodded, gratitude surging in her heart. So few people got it, the impulse to linger over what might have been, rather than bowing to the urgent pressure to move on with her life.

"Have you considered giving her a name?" Annie was hesitant. "Maybe it wouldn't help, but you could, if you wanted to."

"I... I thought about it, yeah. But it seems so... extra. She never got to *be* anything. It's me being, I don't know, wistful to invent a gender for her in the first place. We called them Button, as a pregnancy nickname. Luke didn't think it was a good idea to give the baby a proper name."

"Did he say he didn't want to name them?"

"No." Paige frowned, trying to remember his precise words, what Luke's estimation of personhood had been. "I don't think so."

"You could try suggesting it to him again? Maybe he'd want to?"

"Maybe." She was far from convinced. But the idea stuck. Once Annie had gone, Paige kept turning the thought over in her mind. It seemed that visits from her sister often turned her towards wonderings over who her child might have been.

Something floated to the front, a feather drifting on the wind.

"Molly," Paige whispered to the mirror. She didn't know where the name had come from, but there was something to it. Molly wasn't anywhere on the list Paige and Luke had cobbled together through those short weeks of delight, galloping ahead to a time they were barred from now. When all hope was gone, the list had been stuffed at the back of a drawer, languishing until they might need it again. It was a secret Paige could hug to herself, no need to share it with anyone else.

And then she smiled at her own sense of hubris. Button would only ever be Button, no need to project something onto them that wasn't going to be. From that point on, Paige knew that Button would always be a them to her. She was glad to have tried a name out, if only to help her realise that they'd never needed another one.

PRESENT DAY

FEBRUARY

Paige

S INCE IT WAS SO difficult to hunt out a window in Margaret's frantic schedule and Celeste seemed to have disappeared off the face of the earth, Paige wondered about going to seek wisdom from an even more senior generation. Wasn't that what you were meant to do with your elders, go and ask them about their stories, see what there was to learn from what had gone before?

But these weren't the sorts of stories you could depend on people wanting to share, even if asked. Heartache warped minds. Sure, people from Granny Ruth and Nana Dot's vantage points would have seen it all over the years, baby losses and all. But that didn't mean they were good at dealing with any of it. The twelve-week taboo was something handed down from their cohort, along with that famous stiff upper lip. The one that stopped you in your tracks when it came to expressing anything the least bit distressing. Not in company.

It might well have been the sort of attitude that women from that time hadn't initiated, but they were so steeped in it that the will to push back was long gone, even after permission to talk about it all was given. Paige didn't need to go and visit her nan. She was fairly sure she could predict Dot's response. Never one to suffer fools, to put up with what she referred to as festering or wallowing in any of the stages of grief, Dot would come out with something bracing about not grumbling or keeping your pecker up. She wouldn't want to dwell.

Granny Ruth was a harder one to anticipate. There could be no doubt that she'd had a hand in Margaret's general repression. The pursing of her lips whenever anyone referred to her daughter's late-in-life antics was a dead giveaway that Ruth didn't approve of Margaret's dream chasing in the slightest. But was that a reason to deny Ruth the chance to comfort her granddaughter? Paige owed her a visit. While Ruth was lucky enough to still be as sharp as ever, there was no mistaking the frailty slowly overtaking her.

The morbid notion that there was no knowing which social call would be the last she paid to her grandmother made Paige even more reluctant to drop by. She didn't want to run the risk that her lingering memory of Ruth would be her own granny dismissing the loss of Paige's baby as not worth the tears.

A phone call out of the blue put paid to her cowardice. Even before she heard the news, Paige felt like it was her fault. She'd conjured this development out of the tangled fog of her depressive brain.

"Granny Ruth's gone."

"Oh, Mum." The swell of sympathy, of outright guilt, swamped everything else in her head. "Are you alright? Do you want me to come down?"

As her senses caught up with her, Paige crossed her fingers behind her back —in case Margaret could somehow pick up on the gesture down the phone line. Death was already firmly stamped across her mind. This was such a shock that she knew she'd need time to separate her grandmother's demise from the loss of Button. It wasn't as if Paige would be able to provide much support for her mother if she went down to Dorset anyway.

"No, that's alright thank you, love. Derek's been terribly helpful."

No surprises there. Paige limited her disapproval to another unseen gesture: pursing her lips – an unconscious tribute to her dear departed granny. It would have been so much easier if Paige could find it in her to like either of her parents' new partners. She didn't want to come off as a petulant child of divorce, forever hoping that her mum and dad might decide to give things another go. That was the last thing Paige wanted for Russell, so it was just as well that Margaret had such a distraction to keep her away from potential regrets.

Not that Margaret was ever prepared to admit that she and Derek were having anything so pedestrian as a romantic relationship. Theirs was an artistic meeting of minds or something like that. Creator and muse, perhaps. Whatever else was going on though, Margaret sang exclusively from Derek's hymn sheet.

Right on cue, Margaret started up. "We've agreed that it makes the most sense to do the service somewhere around here. It would be far easier to arrange locally. Then I wouldn't have to…"

Rolling her eyes, Paige soon lost the thread of whatever else Margaret was prattling on about. Yes, it was perfect logic to hold a memorial service over a hundred miles away from where the woman had lived her whole life, where her friends were. Maybe Paige could get Annie to sway Margaret away from Derek's no doubt well-meant meddling. She couldn't summon the energy for such a tiresome conversation with her mother.

By all rights, *this* moment should have been Paige's first adult encounter with grief. It was the way things were supposed to go, grandparents shuffling off in a pale imitation of what it would be like when her own parents went in their turn. Children weren't meant to go first.

And so, the blow of Ruth's death didn't land in the way Paige had once imagined she'd feel when the day came. She'd miss her granny, of course. But Ruth was in her eighties. She'd left plenty of memories behind her and other people who loved her. Many would grieve the lack of her presence in their lives. That was the whole point. Granny Ruth had been granted decades in which to make an impact, leave the world a different place than the one she'd been born into. She'd had a life. Unlike some.

*

It wasn't that Paige resented the gathering held for Granny Ruth. Far from it. Paige loved the old woman dearly and wanted her grandmother to have the best send-off possible. Despite Margaret's initial Derek-influenced planning impulses, it all seemed to be coming off alright. There'd been hearty sighs of relief all round when it was accepted that maybe Dorset wasn't the best location for the funeral.

But with that wrinkle smoothed out, there was nothing to stop the event itself from digging fingers into the tenderest spots of Paige's heart. The tears prickling at her eyes were for Button, not Granny Ruth. It wasn't fair that she couldn't mourn her granny the way the woman deserved.

For a life well lived, a funeral was as much a celebration as it was a sadness. You could pore over old photographs, hunt out family resemblances and chuckle your way through layers of nostalgia, steeped in disbelief that you never knew this fascinating detail or that of an existence that stretched off into decades well before you were ever around. For example, why hadn't Paige the slightest clue that Granny Ruth had been a champion track and field athlete in her youth?

The infinite potential of a life unlived from beginning to end weighed heavily on Paige's shoulders, rendering her mute when it came to the point when she was supposed to contribute to the collected stories of her granny. In the end, she stole away to sit in the car, staring hard at the texture of the steering wheel until she'd gathered a firmer grip on her churning emotions. She wanted to do better for Granny Ruth, but Paige's bandwidth for grief was tapped out.

*

Paige and Annie were overdue for a catchup. Trying to spend a bit less time hiding away from the big bad world, Paige suggested a shopping trip. Good chance to nail a gathering flock of birds with a single pebble. The problem of what to get Russell for his birthday had been weighing on her mind, after all. A second opinion on woollens wouldn't go amiss.

"Hey, Peep."

Paige bowed. "Oakley."

They laughed and wandered off towards M&S. "How are you doing?"

"Oh, you know. Fine."

"Mmhmm. And how are you really doing?"

"Wouldn't it be the polite thing to let me get away with the bullshit answer just the once?" Especially in public. Honest truths could be tiring, and Paige wasn't in the mood.

"Nope, can't let you off the hook. That's what everyone else does, surely?"

Rather than admit how right Annie was about that, Paige twitched her mouth and stared at mannequins as she considered the original question. She appreciated that someone wanted to hear the truth, not the breezy brush off. "I don't know how I am. I can't help but think, well, I wondered about maybe talking to Granny Ruth about the, about it, before, well, it was too late."

"Oh. Before she died?"

"Kind of hard to have much of a conversation afterwards."

"I don't know. You could have hit Celeste up, seen if she had any ideas on that front." Annie gave Paige a sympathetic look. It was just about possible to predict what was going to come out of her mouth next. "Maybe it was for the best? You know what her generation can be like. If you dwell too long on all the people who went missing, you'll never look forward, never serve those who are still here. I think that's the homespun wisdom."

Yet again, Paige knew her older sister had a point. "How did you get to be so wise?"

"A heroic quantity of hard drugs."

Paige stuck her tongue out. Something Annie had said had lodged in her head like a burr. All the people who went missing. "Do you think Granny Ruth ever had a miscarriage then?"

"I have no idea. But I can't see her wanting to talk about it if she had. I remember when one of my exes found out that her gran had lost a child at three weeks old. Some gastric defect they hadn't caught. When Nisha tried to discuss it, the old woman shut the conversation down like nobody's business. Couldn't handle it. Culture's the same all over, you bury that stuff deep and never let it out."

The conversation no longer fit the knitwear mission they were on. How inappropriate would it be for Paige to drag Annie into a bar? Would the time of day alone make her look like a total alcoholic? Then again, Paige was more than capable of going cashmere-blend spotting with a Cosmo or three swilling around inside her. She had more licence these days for less socially acceptable behaviour.

And so, the barriers started coming down. "Do you think that other children are something you want?"

Paige swirled her straw. "Haven't made up my mind yet. I think so, it's… well, scary." Not something she wanted to get into there and then. "What about you? Any little bundles of joy in your future?" She'd always wanted to know where Annie stood on having children and it hadn't ever seemed like the time to ask.

"Bit more difficult at my end. I don't have all the ingredients to hand like you do."

Charming way to refer to Paige's husband. "Stop evading."

"Wouldn't it be the polite thing to let me get away with the bullshit answer just the once, little sis?"

They smiled at each other. "Seriously though, if you were with someone, even if it meant adopting, or you had to do the whole single parent thing, to spawn or not to spawn?"

"You're worse than Celeste. Feels like she does a lot of digging on Dad's behalf."

"She's been avoiding me. Since the loss."

"Celeste? I'm sure that's not true."

Paige let it go. It wasn't as if she really wanted attention from Celeste, more that the oddness of her stepmother's behaviour was rubbing her up the wrong way. With the turn in conversation, it was only after Paige had made it home, armed with purchases she already regretted, that she realised Annie still hadn't answered the question about if she wanted to have children someday.

With a guilty lurch, Paige realised how little she knew about the current state of Annie's love life. When was the last time she'd mentioned seeing anyone? Paige couldn't remember the last time her sister had introduced her to a girlfriend. Were children a sore topic for Annie? Did she feel like her chances were slipping away? A better sister would have the emotional capacity to find out, Paige knew.

FIFTEEN YEARS AGO

NOVEMBER

Celeste

IT WAS LIKE DATING again. Maybe the divorce that Stephen was shoving through the courts at full speed was steering Celeste's thoughts in that direction. But in a lot of respects, the mechanics of the process she found herself in the middle of were the same. You made a connection one way or another, arranged to meet, and when you did, started to test the waters to see if having something in common, this specific something, was enough for you to want to keep this person in your life.

Celeste was more comfortable with trying to make loss parent friends than trying to fill Stephen's vacant spot in her life, but it was a marginal thing. The idea of confessing what had happened to someone in the know was easier than hopeful small talk about the future with a potential boyfriend – how often would she have to crush someone else's dreams with her story and its repercussions? Even so, any kind of one-on-one interaction felt like far too much for Celeste for the time being.

And yet the inevitable fix ups kept coming. In a way it hadn't after the miscarriage, it now felt like everyone and their dog knew someone who knew someone who'd lost a child. News like this was public domain. You didn't have a choice about hiding it. A neighbour's daughter had a stillbirth half a decade ago or their colleague had heard of someone in their cousin's family who'd had a twin loss. Did Celeste want their number? She didn't know whether to be relieved or annoyed that these connections were piling up, silent tragedies coming out of the woodwork.

Gail was especially insistent. As if she could make up for her failures in offering comfort after the miscarriage by forcing someone on her daughter who had a better chance of understanding. But Celeste's paper-thin defences didn't take much of an assault from her mother and before she knew it, she was sitting down for coffee with the daughter of a friend of her mother's friend through church.

It didn't go well. After Celeste had cried all over the understanding woman before being able to get any words of her own experience out, the sympathetic lady – full-term stillbirth with two subsequent living children – suggested a group session might be an easier way to start. When there were more stories in the room, it was less awkward that you weren't the one doing the talking. Seemed like it was worth a try.

Though she'd never been to anything like it, Celeste imagined the support group session was a lot like an AA meeting. Community centre, small circle of chairs, packets of expectant biscuits waiting for the break. Bubbling over with nerves, Celeste sat and stared at her hands during the introductions, dreading the moment when her turn came. She was too overwhelmed to absorb even the most basic details of anyone else's potted history.

"I… um. I lost my daughter back in May. I was… I mean, she, it was… I was thirty-one weeks along. We… the doctors, no one knows what happened. And then my, my husband left me." Celeste's gaze was rooted to the carpet. She dragged a shoe across the floor.

One of the other women sitting in the circle — Zara maybe? — gave a small snort, sharing a meaningful look with her neighbour. "Looks like we've got another one."

There were a handful of knowing smirks firing off around the room. Celeste was almost sure she heard someone mutter the name Emma.

Her brow furrowed. "I don't understand."

Possible-Zara grinned. "You've walked into a room of folk with dead children brandishing a failed marriage to give yourself an edge in the sympathy stakes. Next time you'll have a limp."

"And an eye patch." The next woman's tone suggested they'd all seen this sort of thing before. Celeste wondered what form Emma's attention-seeking crimes had taken.

The group leader seemed to have reached the point where she felt the need to interject. "Maggie, Hannah, that's unkind." Was she about to hiss how vulnerable Celeste was?

But Celeste could already feel the laughter rising in her chest, cleansing and surprising. It was like being back at school. For what felt like the first time in months, years even, she was giggling. The sheer relief in not being the most tragic person in the room by as gaping a degree as usual was enough to bring her out of herself, just a little. And she hadn't taken any offence. Suddenly, it was Celeste's goal to be in a position where she could be that tiny bit salty to someone in circumstances like her current ones. Not in a cruel way, but a little something to break the veneer of overwhelming tragedy.

"Maybe I'll have had an unfortunate accident in the kitchen before the next meeting and force you to look at my full-thickness burns."

That earned her a snort from the first woman who'd spoken. "Good one."

The group leader seized on the opportunity to smoothly guide the session towards a more conventionally healing place, asking Celeste gentle questions about the loss of Baby and the fight with Stephen.

There were more tears, how could there not be? But the fellowship, the freedom to admit actions and thoughts that would shock or baffle most, was what Celeste needed to lighten the load, no matter how fleeting the relief might be.

After they'd wrapped up the support meeting, Celeste found her exit barred by a united front of Hannah and Maggie. "Sorry. Didn't mean to call you out like that. It's just been so refreshing not to have to deal with our resident story topper for a little while. Would have been very difficult to have to welcome another one into the group, sometimes you have to draw a line."

"Although," Hannah chimed in, "might have been interesting to see you and Emma compete. We could take bets on how many meetings it'd take before one of you ended up in a full-body cast."

They all cracked up. Maggie slipped an arm through Celeste's. "So, we were wondering if you fancied coming for a coffee – or something stronger – show there's no hard feelings?"

With that, a two-on-one social situation didn't seem so daunting. Celeste had assumed that Maggie and Hannah were old friends, but in fact they'd met about six months ago at the support group and bonded over how many times they got reprimanded for cracking out the dark humour.

"But it helps, right, to share? You wouldn't keep coming back if it didn't?"

Maggie set three lurid cocktails on the table and slid into her seat. "It does. Nice to be in a room of people who get it. But I'd be lying if I didn't say that part of the appeal wasn't our after-hours session. So, you'd better earn your place, or we'll have to kick you out."

Rather than rise to the threat, Celeste nodded meekly and sipped her drink. The other women seemed to sense that she was a little too wrung out to be able to join into the conversation much and were content to leave her to chip in – or not – as she wanted. Letting the chat wash over her was more than enough.

"Someone tried to pull an 'everything happens for a reason' on me the other day."

Hannah rolled her eyes and swirled her straw. "Ugh. What did you do?"

"Waited her out. After a while, she muttered something about God's plan, but she had the grace to look embarrassed about it."

Stretching out a hand to rest on Maggie's shoulder, Hannah added, "I can't understand why people don't *think* about what they're saying. Like they're trying to tell me that I'll end up with a *better* baby because of losing Nora, or agree and say how she's in a better place. As if there's anywhere better than with her *mother*."

"As if what happened to my Johnny was…" Maggie stared off into the middle distance before blinking hard and exhaling. "Found an excuse to leave after that."

"Good for you. It's like anyone who chooses to start a sentence with an 'at least'. Any shred of logic along those lines can get in the bin."

"Yeah. It's the utter earnestness that gets me." Maggie stabbed at the ice in her glass. "Like they think it's actually going to help. If they can't give me the reason why I had to have my baby die inside me, they can keep their clichés to themselves. Someone was wittering on at me that my time would come, and I'd know the joy or something like that. I want to be brave enough to brandish photos at them, make them get that he was a *baby*. Not just a loss. I gave birth. My time came. It went in a hurry too.

"People just do not want to talk about any of this stuff, they'll grab at any excuse to sweep it all under the rug. We're crap with grief in this country. There are plenty of times when I don't want to get into it but knowing when I *could* if I wanted would make all the difference. That I won't get dismissed if I want to talk about my kid."

In time, Celeste hoped she'd feel able to share too. Maybe if she kept failing to pipe up, Hannah and Maggie wouldn't invite her along again. Even here, there were things they had that Celeste didn't. There were no photos of Baby for her to show the world what, who, she'd lost. Her child didn't even have a proper *name*. Everything about Celeste's time with Baby had been so fleeting. It was this part of Celeste's life, the after, that was forever.

"The first words out of my husband's mouth after we knew we'd lost our first baby – missed miscarriage – was that we could just try again."

"Oof. And you want us to feel sorry for you that he peaced out? No, girl. Lucky escape." The gentleness of Maggie's words and the way she covered Celeste's hand with her own made Celeste feel safe. Someday, she'd be able to open up about Baby too.

PRESENT DAY

MARCH

Paige

DURING A LULL IN Celeste's interminable gathering to celebrate Russell's birthday, Annie flopped into a chair opposite her sister. Paige had her feet tucked up under her, curled like a cat, enjoying her solitude while everyone else was busy in the kitchen. The glass of wine in her hand was doing its best to smooth off the rough edges.

She'd been flirting with the comforting thought of religion. Why couldn't Paige pull a Celeste and surrender everything to some anonymous higher power? Not God, but Demeter or whoever Celeste preferred. Slightly more palatable. Paige knew she had it in her to get over the strain of the constant eye rolling at some point and get on board with all that nonsense if she was prepared to put the effort in.

But with faith came scratchy notions. If there *was* some greater purpose, some grand design, that meant there was a God out there in charge who was cool with the idea of smiting innocent clusters of cells. A deity who punished without discrimination. For Paige, rejecting her natural secularity wasn't worth it. Overall, she decided it was easier to deal with the random cruelty of nature than the whims of divinity.

Annie interrupted Paige's musings. "Well, I'm not going to bother asking how you are. You'll tell me off." She sniffed. "Your only sister, not allowed to care about you."

Paige pouted. It looked like Annie had been at the bottle too. "Most considerate of you, sister dear. I'm... up and down."

With a sympathetic smile, Annie's eyes flicked over towards the glowing threshold of the kitchen. Luke seemed to be taking charge. It was for the best. Celeste didn't cook meat often and clearly appreciated the assistance in basting. Somehow though, Paige's offer of help had been rebuffed. She was to sit down, relax. Keep her distance, it seemed, from Celeste.

"How's Luke?"

"Why?" The sharpness, alarm, in Paige's voice was a bit too obvious for her liking. Why didn't Annie ask *Luke* how he was?

"Why do I want to know how my brother-in-law is? Because I'm in love with him and I'm trying to gauge when's the best time to let him know."

The giggle eased some of the tension building up in Paige. She liked tipsy Annie. The veneer of goofiness was quite the novelty. "Oh, if that's the case, he's... he's fine. I think." Her laugh now, tinged with bitterness, made her sound heartless. "No, I know. That man is A-okay."

"What is it?"

"It's like..." Paige trailed off. She didn't want to keep digging this up, over and over. But it was pressing on her mind, insistent and unrelenting. And Annie was safe to talk to. "I've tried to talk to him about it, the miscarriage, and he swears it's not the case, but it's as if he isn't affected by it at all. I don't want him drenched in mourning, weeping at the skies or anything, but..."

"You want to see a bit more emotion from him?" Annie's eyes were kind and gentle, a sure sign that she had something to say that Paige wasn't going to enjoy hearing.

"It would be nice to feel a bit less alone in this."

"He… you've met your husband before, haven't you?"

Paige's eyebrows banged together in a frown. "What are you talking about?"

"Well, one of the many reasons why he's the one for me is the way his actions always speak louder than his words. He does stuff in his own way. Luke copes with all of this by looking after *you,* hadn't you noticed?"

"I…" Paige's eyes sank to the ground. "Maybe."

"Talk to him. Even if it's not what comes naturally, he'd try anything for you."

"You're a soppy drunk."

With a wolfish grin, Annie drained her glass. "It's important to notice these things, keep tabs, when you're trying to get between married folks. Right, into the breach, let's see if they've salvaged the chicken."

*

Paige knew it wasn't healthy to spend so much time rattling around on her own in the house. She'd declined the offer to join Luke on his trip to gather materials for whatever DIY project he was working on. Getting some fresh air for its own sake seemed like enough of a reason to pop out, maybe she'd get some milk they didn't need to justify the stroll.

As she stepped out of the house, Paige turned her head and almost turned tail. Slamming into her with the power of a runaway freight train was the realisation that Mrs Next Door – they were on nodding terms if nothing else, and Paige couldn't quite remember the name on the parcels she accepted every now and then – might not just be getting a bit tubby. Paige nodded at her neighbour, smiled, and accelerated down the pavement, keen to get away.

What if Mrs Next Door was pregnant? That gentle smile, a little disbelieving that this was happening at all at her age, the carefree laugh. It all served to rub in Paige's face that she'd failed to foster life. Rightmove wasn't the answer, but that didn't stop Paige from firing up an idle search on her phone as she wandered along the footpaths. She didn't even know if it was true, but she couldn't breathe with the idea of a pregnancy that close to her, an eventual baby that wasn't hers on her doorstep.

It seemed there wasn't anything inspiring to be found on the market, lots of characterless new build white boxes but no converted windmills or charming cottages anything like in budget. Giving up on that plan, Paige grabbed the milk and headed home. Mrs Next Door must have gone by now. As Paige was counting the change in her pocket, she jumped as a black-and-white shape darted across the path ahead.

A long time ago, Paige's dislike of cats had shifted to a low-level phobia. It was impossible to trust the coin flip snap in temperament that would cause a docile kitty to lash out and leave a person with gouges through their skin. But there was something about this cat. Maybe it was the complete lack of sympathy in its eyes that made everything seem so much more bearable in the moment.

Not caring how it might appear to anyone passing by, Paige plopped herself onto the pavement a couple of feet away from the formal moggy, the patterns of its fur making it look like a distinguished tuxedoed gentleman on his way out to a film premiere or cocktail party.

"I lost my baby."

It could have wandered off. The cat could have interested itself in the rustling bush that ran alongside the pavement, trying to scare up an elevenses snack. But it stared at Paige instead, yellow eyes full of contempt and mystery. The barest sliver of encouragement was all she needed to keep talking.

"I'd be showing by now." Paige held out a hand in front of her stomach. "I keep picturing the bump. It's hard not to think about it, how far along I ought to be by now. This week would bring me to nearly six months, I think."

She didn't think. She knew. It was somewhere in the region between hard and impossible not to plug in the dates, do all sorts of pregnancy maths to figure out what could and should be happening. The thought of June rolling round without Button making their debut into the world was corrosive.

"Every month now, I swear that maybe I'm pregnant again. Even when I know it's not possible. But it turns out that pre-period boobs feel the same as early pregnancy boobs. You know, well, you don't. But sore when I'm going downstairs, tender enough to get my attention. I never knew before. Or maybe I've forgotten the finer details of what it was like and I'm conflating things. Either way, whenever I'm thinking I might have pulled an immaculate, Mother Nature kicks me in the unmentionables to make sure I know my place in the scheme of things."

She told the cat everything there was to say about her lost little Button. Even though that didn't amount to much. The cat couldn't brush Paige away with breezy assurances of next time or debates about personhood, when the soul arrived or departed, or blithe nothings about God wanting another angel. Those were the worst, making her want to tear her eyelashes out by the root.

If the cat were given half the chance, it would have devoured what had been left of Button without a second thought for the ladles of sentimental detail Paige was offering up. Still, it was something for her to say the words out loud and have them heard, witnessed, by something with a beating heart.

A week or so later, Paige saw the cat kissing up to a smiling couple brandishing something for it to eat. "Flirt," she said with a smile, not loud enough for either of the enthusiasts to hear her.

Though she had the odd temptation to do so, Paige never repeated the feline heart-to-heart. But it'd been enough to teach her that maybe there wasn't so much to be afraid of lurking behind those slitted pupils. Even their cold calculation was something you could put your faith in. If you could count on a cat for anything, it was a dash of self-preservation.

FOURTEEN YEARS AGO

JANUARY

Celeste

AFTER MAGGIE GOT PREGNANT again, it wasn't a huge surprise when she withdrew a little from the support group. Pleased as everyone was for her, there was a certain level of tension that no amount of assurance from everyone could dispel. Hannah had been distraught.

Celeste understood. In some ways, she had it easier. Her future didn't hold that kind of pressure. Stephen had removed himself from the equation, so there would be no baby. The question of when to try again was moot. As for Hannah, she'd lost her buddy in the trenches. Everyone wanted, needed, for Maggie's pregnancy to go well, but it was difficult to remain close to the situation if you were the one staring at negative tests every month.

Knowing how difficult pregnancy after loss was when you'd "only" experienced miscarriage as opposed to a stillbirth, Celeste felt a little guilty for not being able to support Maggie. Maybe one day she'd be able to pay things forward, but as it was, she was still too close to Baby's pregnancy. It was also a source of guilt for her how much she enjoyed becoming Hannah's new Maggie.

They started meeting more often, for lunch and for coffee. After one of their catchups, Hannah checked her watch. "Bugger, I'm running late."

"Sorry, didn't mean to keep you."

"Oh, didn't mean it like that. I've just got an appointment. Actually, I've been meaning to mention it, you should come with me sometime, to reiki."

Celeste's eyebrows furled together. "Don't you do that for fertility?"

In their conversations, Hannah trod lightly when it came to her conception efforts. She knew it was something of a sore point for Celeste, who was doing her best to make peace with the certainty that she wasn't ever going to have a living child. Better to squash the hopes of the future than to ever put someone else through this hell with her. It hurt, to ignore that impulse she'd felt in the immediate aftermath of Baby's death, but Stephen had decided how it was going to go the first time around, so why was it such a surprise that he did the same after the second loss?

Hannah, at the other end of the scale, was going full tilt towards trying to make a sibling for her lost daughter Nora. Whether it was competitiveness or jealousy, Maggie's pregnancy was acting as a spur, or possibly a thorn in Hannah's side. The GP couldn't help yet with fertility assistance, but there was always acupuncture. And now reiki, it would seem.

"No, not necessarily. I never talked to Mags about it because she looks down her nose at all that stuff. Her loss. There's a bit of a faith-y element to reiki, but it's like yoga or meditation. No more out there than either of those. Really though, I find it this brilliant way to relax. Like a deluxe massage. Not just someone paid to rub you down. Little bit of love, little bit of care. Maggie was never open to it – guess she didn't need to be – but given how you go on about herbal remedies, I think you'll like it."

Celeste hesitated. On one level, she felt seen by Hannah, validated. But on another, she found herself crawling with apprehension over what this observation might lead to. It was all well and good debating the relative merits of infusions and supplements, but Celeste dreaded the personal attention. She felt rancid.

Something had to be wrong with her, something deep inside that the doctors had missed. Her soul? Something that couldn't be measured with conventional methods but still had a tangible effect on the inner workings. This healer would take one look at her and her aura or her chakras or whatever was wonky would give her away as someone beyond saving.

Proving Celeste's sheer transparency, Hannah's eyes widened with understanding. "Don't want to make you do anything you don't want, but I remember feeling like that." She reached out a hand so she could squeeze Celeste's. "Sage doesn't judge, I promise."

Celeste tried to hide her smile. There were advantages and drawbacks to hanging out so much with someone who'd been through the same experience. They hadn't been able to find a reason for Hannah's loss of Nora either. "I'll come."

Hannah beamed. "Trust me, it's so you."

After that, it wasn't long before Celeste was ensconced in a candlelit room, breathing deep to inhale the incense rather than remember the delivery room with its similar low lighting. She knew what Stephen might have to say about what was going on. He'd scoff at the sheer nonsense of it all. Maybe that was even more reason to lean in. Wasn't this experience offering her everything she was so desperate for: a safe space in which to release her worries, her fear, her pain?

Once Sage got to work, Celeste thought she could sense some level of connection through the healer's touch, affection even. Maybe it was only happening because Celeste was paying her. However, for the weight of the world to be lying in someone else's hands, even for a little while, was a wonderful sensation. As a long heavy breath streamed out of her mouth, she felt a knot in the pit of her stomach unravelling. Or at least loosening, ever so slightly. It was enough to feel like a transformative easing of an awful burden.

A thought floated up to the surface of her mind. There was no going back. She couldn't return to her old self, the naïve, trusting version of Celeste who existed before loss. The one who trusted Stephen's judgements implicitly because he knew so much more than she did. That woman was as good as dead.

Celeste wasn't her anymore. She wasn't the mother to a living child. She wasn't a wife. There was no way for her to move on from what had happened. She never would. But all she could do was to move forward with her life. She felt such a surge of gratitude towards the healer's gentle patience, the care radiating off her for Celeste and her children, the way Sage had acknowledged those little souls without question during the intake discussion.

Leaning into the alternative methods meant accepting so much outside the bounds of what you could see and feel. This was Celeste's way forward. Nothing else had helped so far and contorting yourself to remain within the lines of "normal" was absurd when all it did was hurt.

PRESENT DAY

APRIL

Paige

MARGARET'S PUPPETEERING OF HER daughter and her life choices hadn't ended when she went through with the degree course her mother wanted. In the vain hope of getting some variety of support in kind, Paige had gone without complaint to the excruciating spring production of Margaret's theatre troupe. This was, after all, what she'd run off to Devon for, a realisation of frustrated dreams she'd carried with her all her life.

In previous years, it had been so much easier for Paige to find ways to avoid her mother's am-dram productions. But she'd made her promises before disappearing after Granny Ruth's funeral and that was that.

Without Luke there to support her, it was as if she was missing an arm. It hadn't seemed important enough to ask him to rearrange his work trip. Somehow, Annie had also contrived her absence, leaving Paige alone to face the music.

If for Paige, the spectre of Granny Ruth was still hovering somewhere in the ether with Paige's lost child, close enough to start twining together, then Margaret might well have needed more support than she was prepared to let on. Being there was something constructive Paige could do.

Just a shame that an evening with the Durdle Door Players was the sort of experience rendered even more unbearable because Paige knew full well there were plenty of amateur dramatics troupes out there who were perfectly capable of putting on a decent show. Margaret's wasn't one of them, increasing Paige's general frustration that this was what her mother had dropped everything else in her life for.

The obvious person to blame for the assorted debacles was Derek, their director who clearly fancied himself quite the auteur. When you thought about it, their performances *were* something close to masterful. In every production they staged, something was off. Never the same thing twice, but always a single jarring element that sullied all other efforts. Not in such a way as to be disastrous, but enough to make Paige's evening agonising as she searched for plausible compliments.

It was often stuff they'd got right in previous years. Strange accent choices, questionable casting when there were far better choices to be found even within the troupe, Derek was an expert in the unexpected disaster. That evening, the audience was treated to the incomprehensible choice to bathe the stage in a sickly green glow. Not the most obvious lighting arrangement for Cinderella.

But Paige knew what these performances meant to her mother. For all the distance between them these days, it was satisfying to be able to play the supportive daughter. It wasn't as if she had a potential grandchild to show off. She had to do her bit. Which meant it was more than acceptable to down another glass of the slightly sour wine and contemplate how long she had to hang around before it was acceptable to push off.

Afterwards, she went to congratulate her mother. Before Paige could say anything, Margaret swooped forwards to fold her daughter into her arms. "Wonderful to have you here, darling."

Inhaling the familiar faint citrus scent of Margaret's neck, Paige felt herself relaxing. Hugs from her mother were so rare they had to be savoured and she'd been needing this one for a while. It was a relief that she hadn't had to ask for it. When they drew apart, Margaret's expectant face demanded Paige's review of the theatrics.

"It was a really…" she struggled to summon any acceptable word out of her brain, "memorable performance."

"Thank you, dear. *So* glad that I could get some family representation. Such a shame no one else could make it."

"I'm sure they all regret it."

Margaret beamed. "So, how are you?"

There was that question again. Paige paused, trying to decide how honest to be. "I've been better."

The dismissive sigh wasn't an encouraging sign. "You can't dwell forever, dear. Got to pick yourself up eventually. Do you never think that it might have been for the best?"

Even Paige's internal brain-Margaret was a little stunned by the question. They were steaming towards dangerous waters, but Paige had to ask. "What might?"

"Well, are you *sure* you want to have children in the first place? Right now, or, or possibly ever. You shouldn't feel any, well, obligation. Not for my sake. Or your father's, of course. We're all perfectly capable of getting on with our own lives. I know plenty of mothers would try to tell their children otherwise, but you don't have to provide any grandchildren for the sake of our fulfilment. I've said the same to your sister."

Good to know Annie had been included in this largesse too. Paige was all for equality for siblings, but this was too much. Why was Margaret picking at this? "What are you saying, Mum?"

"Everything changes once you have children. Your time isn't your own anymore. It's not something to be taken on lightly. Your father told me that your, well, that it hadn't been planned."

It felt like three or four sucker punches had landed all at once. At the top of the heap of surprises was the fact that Margaret and Russell still had any kind of meaningful interaction. Maybe they'd run out of other conversation topics at Granny Ruth's funeral.

"So, what? You resent us? We stopped you from swanning off and realising your dreams? Without us to hold you back, you'd have skipped off a long time ago?"

"I didn't say that." Margaret sounded as if offence had been taken, but Paige noticed that her mother stopped short of saying anything to rebut her argument.

It wasn't difficult to read between the lines. "I'm not you, Mum. I, we... I mean, sure, it might not have been something we'd planned on doing when it happened, but Luke and I do still want to have other children."

"There's no need to go rushing into it, that's all I want you to understand. You don't have to do anything you don't want to."

It was enough to make Paige want to snarl. "Maybe I should be referring to the Margaret Davis grand plan for my life. It would be good of you to let me know what timelines I ought to be sticking to. Of course, the last time I left you in charge of one of my life decisions, I ended up stuck in a career track that bores me senseless."

"That's not like you."

"Yeah, not generally one to answer back, am I? Almost as if I'm going through something significant and a bit of support from my own mother wouldn't go amiss." The giddy thrill making her heart hammer suggested Paige might have gone a bit too far.

"Not that. It's not like you to stick with something you're not happy with."

Was Margaret mixing up her daughters? Annie was the one with a spine when it came to their mother's opinions. "It is exactly like me! It's what *you* wanted. I'm the sensible one. The one who'll put up a token show of resistance but eventually fall in line with enough prodding. I do what's expected, don't I? The practical decision maker."

The frown was baked into Margaret's voice when she next spoke. "Oh, I don't remember it that way at all. You mean your university course?"

"What else could I be talking about?" There was acid in Paige's clipped words. "How do you recall those events then, mother dear?"

"My daughter was struggling with the decisions that would govern her future, and the endless dither and delay wasn't going to help the situation. I don't know about you, but I sometimes find it easier to process my feelings about something after a choice has already been made. Then you understand if anything needs changing. I cracked down, helped push things to the surface. Then you could sort things out for yourself."

Convenient for Margaret to cast herself as the hero. Of course, her version of how things had shaken out ignored all those promises she'd extracted from Paige and her insistence that her daughter stuck to them.

"You could have made that a whole lot clearer at the time."

Margaret blew out a short, huffy breath. "If you say so."

Giving up the fight was almost more galling than carrying it on, but Paige's head was filling up with woolly, baffling thoughts. Before she could figure out where she wanted the rest of their delightful little chat to go, Margaret picked up another tack, doling out manipulation by other means. "Well, if it's something you're set on, you should be able to answer the question: why do you want to have children? Why now?"

"I didn't say now." Anger knocked the rest of Paige's breath out of her. She shouldn't have been so stumped by what Margaret was asking. But her mind was blank, and her insufferable mother must have assumed she'd won the argument. Paige could almost see the smugness Margaret hadn't earned spreading across her face.

"I…"

Paige wanted to do a better job of mothering than Margaret had. It was what you did, a way to leave your mark on the world beyond your career. Given how things were already going, bringing work back into the discussion wasn't going to help. Even though she tried to resist the social media pressures, she couldn't help noticing that so many people her age seemed to be moving forward with their families and she was beginning to feel left out.

There was a hole in her life. Paige wasn't sure if it had been dug by the miscarriage, or if it was getting pregnant in the first place that made her notice it was there. Her arms were empty. They ached. And it didn't matter in the slightest if her mother ever understood.

PRESENT DAY

APRIL

Paige

NEXT TO WHAT HER mother classed as support, Paige knew she'd been taking Luke for granted. There weren't any rules, no edicts that stated he needed to grieve the loss the same way she did. There were times when she resented that he wasn't as outwardly broken by the experience of the miscarriage as she was, but would it be so easy to bear if he was the one breaking down in tears every five minutes because of it?

It was understandable for them to have had different reactions. At the end of the day, it was something that had happened in *her* body, not his. But watching someone you loved go through that much pain wasn't exactly a barrel of laughs.

Luke was her life raft. He was the man who'd wanted her at a time when someone else had discarded... no. These weren't romantic or flattering feelings, were they? Paige brought her desperate freight train of thought to a juddering halt, its brakes squealing and sparking in its wake.

It was time and past that Paige made sure her husband knew he was far more than a man-shaped crutch to her – the stabiliser to her rickety pub table. He wasn't the rebound who'd healed the hurts left behind by someone so careless with her affections. Luke deserved to feel like more to his wife than a carer, or a well-meaning nurse. Not to slam nurses, of course. But a romantic partner should feel loved as much as they loved in return.

Did that mean it was grand gesture time? A mad dash through the airport or spelling his name out with flowers on a panoramic hillside? Paige rolled her eyes. She was her own corny script-writer, churning out hackneyed ideas at the third act climax.

Before she could track down patisseries willing to bake her into a cake to jump out of, Luke brought her tumbling back to earth by coming into the room. The words were out of her mouth before Paige could devote any thought to what she was saying.

"We need to talk. I," she swallowed, "I wanted to say I'm sorry."

"What for?"

She raised her eyebrows at him. Was he going to make her list transgressions?

He shrugged, relenting. "You've been having a tough time. Lots to cope with."

"Doesn't mean I can get away with murder."

"Oh, have I been in danger?"

"I don't think I'd have killed *you*."

"I'm sure between us we could have stashed Kelly's corpse somewhere."

Paige laughed and poked her tongue out. "I wanted to… you've been…" trailing off, she tried not to look too pathetic

"I miss them too." His words were soft, sad. "Well, maybe not miss them, but it does make me sad, to think what we lost. I'm saying it so you know, not to… go further than that or anything. I was really looking forward to being a dad, even though it was so short."

Eyes shining, Paige nodded. There was more to say, but she wasn't sure she was capable. Luke seemed ready to save it for another time. Maybe they ought to have an early night or something.

FOURTEEN YEARS AGO

MARCH

Celeste

ANOTHER NIGHTMARE. THERE, IN the middle of her subconscious, Celeste saw her again. *My baby, my baby, my… Baby.* The words were an endless drumbeat in her head, no let up between thumps, no spaces in which to rest. This was wrong. In so many ways. Something that valerian or chamomile or lavender or any amount of Sage's time could never touch.

They needed a name. No, she wasn't a they. Before Celeste knew Baby was a girl – over too many months of grieving for one while looking forward to the other – thinking in gender neutral terms had become automatic. Stephen had said it was too sentimental to call them anything other than "the baby" while they were inside. Well, Celeste *wanted* to be sentimental, and it wasn't as if he was around to stop her anymore.

She'd never know whether the first loss would have turned out to be a boy or a girl, but Celeste could say for certain she had at least one daughter. Who deserved a proper name. This wasn't *Dirty Dancing*. Everyone needed their own name that wasn't just Baby. What better way to illustrate that she'd been a person?

At the support group, Celeste knew she was an object of gentle pity because of the blank space where her daughter's name ought to be. Everyone was too nice and too diplomatic to say so, but she could tell. And Hannah might have said something.

The only thing holding Celeste back was that it felt like it was too late. It wouldn't be official. They were gone, both of them. Even if she came up with the perfect name, would that make it true? Would it be enough to make it real? Maybe there was a way to amend a birth certificate? Well, that was deed poll, wasn't it? But you couldn't do it on someone else's behalf. And it wasn't as if that mattered anyway. Certificate of stillbirth, that was all Baby got, having not been born alive. And even that was far more than the loss before her had been granted. The first Baby Hartman.

Celeste wanted so much more for her children. As much as she'd been cheated out of a lifetime with them, the two of them had been denied lives, personhood, altogether. There had to be something she could do to mark them, to honour them.

As tears slid down her face, hidden in the weak moonlight, Celeste knew it was important to focus. If she didn't, she would lose the few memories she had. It was already harder and harder to think of her stillborn daughter as ever being real. As if Baby had been a fairy changeling all along, snatched away by the fates for some indiscernible reason, justice for some slight or transgression Celeste hadn't realised she was making. Maybe that was why Stephen hadn't wanted photos, anything tangible. That way, it was easier to let Baby melt away into dreams, where she kept finding Celeste anyway.

There had to be something. A tiny seedling of an idea began to sprout at the back of Celeste's mind. Without thinking too much about what she was doing, she snapped the light on, grabbed the first bit of paper she could find, and went in search of a pen.

*

It was time. Celeste had been left with so few mementoes. The tiny hand and footprints. The bundle of hair so small and wispy, Celeste was afraid to breathe on it. She was too concerned about causing it all to blow away. No photos. No body.

She'd had plenty of time to be heartbroken over so many additional losses. No chance to breastfeed. No first smile, first words, steps, school days. They hadn't even had a proper funeral for Baby. Stephen had signed away that right to the hospital and while Celeste was sure it had been a sensitive affair, there was no getting away from the fact that Baby had been laid to rest without her parents there and alongside other babies who hadn't made it to life either. She hadn't got her own ceremony.

Today, Celeste was making the most out of what she had. Creating something meaningful from what Baby had left behind. She lived in her mother's memory, and Stephen's — even if he didn't want to admit it. A handful of people in the world had ever seen Baby's face and it would take very little indeed for everyone to forget that she'd ever existed at all.

So, pulling from a dozen different sources, Celeste had put something of her own together. She'd lifted elements from a Japanese Buddhist ritual, but Celeste didn't think anyone would mind. Ever since she'd heard it, she'd been captivated by the term *Mizuko*. Baby wasn't a water child, as such, but it was refreshing to feel her experience represented by someone else's culture, even if the attitudes towards grief in the society Celeste lived in couldn't cope with this depth of love and loss.

But she had put more work in, to make this something of her own, something that felt right for Baby. Even though she was a terrible artist, she'd wanted to do her best to draw Baby's face. It had been painstaking work to try and get the picture right and after all that effort, Celeste was determined to set fire to it. She told herself that every year her artistic skills would improve, and she'd come back with a better drawing to transform into ashes in the woods.

In the middle of nature, her makeshift altar of candles arrayed in front of her, Celeste spotted a flash of colour out of the corner of her eye. Something was watching her. With curiosity rather than self-consciousness reigning, Celeste turned her head and looked into a curious set of eyes. The magpie tilted its – her – head. One for sorrow.

"Rebecca," Celeste whispered. Her daughter deserved to have her real name said out loud at long last.

By the time she was scooping the cinders of the portrait into a bag, ready for scattering somewhere with wildflowers, she was aware of another presence. It was almost like a cartoon, one of those anime things that Celeste couldn't make head or tail of. Through the trees, she saw an unmistakeable shape, far too big to be a rabbit.

The logic of it all was so obvious that she was almost surprised someone hadn't shouted it in her ear. Of course. Stephen might have cast her off to the point that she was no longer obliged to use his name, but he was still as big a part of the children as Celeste. He had held her hand, and Baby's, and waited until it was all over to run away. Even though Celeste wasn't a Hartman anymore, the first little soul who had shared her body always would be.

"Hart," Celeste said.

Only a bit over a year late, but her firstborn had a name at last too. If they'd lived, the council might have had a thing or two to say about her negligent parenting. No one else in the world had to be on her side, let alone her own ex-husband, but nature was her ally. Maybe if she squinted hard enough, she'd be able to make out the siblings out there somewhere, hand in hand. Magpie and deer. Rebecca and Hart.

PRESENT DAY

APRIL

Paige

As Paige had been dreading, and picturing in half a dozen different ways, she'd been summoned to see Celeste. None of the scenarios that shoved their way through Paige's head made any sense. She couldn't understand why Celeste had created this distance between them *now*. It left Paige bewildered as to what to expect from the social call. There was more to it than the studied innocence of Russell's suggestion that she pop by for a cup of tea.

Mercifully, Celeste skipped any pretence and got right to it. "I owe you an explanation."

Paige shook her head. This was what she kept coming back to. Even if Paige wasn't in command of all the relevant facts, Celeste wasn't Margaret. There didn't have to be any expectation on Celeste to see her, no burden of parenthood. After all, in years gone by, Paige would have been grateful that Celeste had made it so easy for them to pass each other like ships in the night.

As she opened her mouth, Paige wasn't sure how to put it. They didn't have to try and force anything that wasn't meant to be. Just because Celeste was married to Russell, it didn't mean she was obligated to join Paige's support network.

But Celeste held up a commanding hand to stop Paige before she got there. "I wouldn't expect you to understand yet. I haven't done my best by you, and I really should have. Me of all people. Well, you'll see in the future. You've inherited something. A... a duty, or an obligation. Maybe it's a calling to some. You do it almost without thinking about it, for others who end up walking the same path you have."

She swallowed and fixed Paige with an intense expression. It was several leagues more forceful than anything Paige had seen on her stepmother's face before.

"Russie... how much did he... has he told you anything about...?"

Even in that conversational pocket of gravitas, with the looming sensation that a steamroller of a revelation was incoming, Paige had to fight the urge to gag. What else was she supposed to do upon hearing her father referred to as Russie? Sickening.

"Tell me about what?"

"That I've lost two."

The shadow in her eyes let Paige know without a glimmer of doubt that she meant babies. There was nothing else she could be talking about. Paige shuddered at the thought of going through one loss, to come out the other side and into another pregnancy, only to be clobbered by yet more death. Then her heart quivered with panic. Celeste didn't have any children of her own. Now Paige knew that wasn't true. Celeste just didn't have any she'd been able to bring home.

"Miscarriages?"

Celeste's mouth twisted. "One of them was, yes. I should have been ten weeks, but we found out that they'd died a little while before that. And then it all came away."

"And the other?"

The lopsided smile became smaller, and far sadder. "We made it to thirty-one weeks that time. Everything was going swimmingly, sailing through every test. And then they couldn't find the heartbeat. I didn't know any better, I'd managed to convince myself I was still feeling *some* movement, even though it was somewhat less than usual."

Paige's eyes widened in horror. She could never have predicted that *this* was the reason Celeste had felt the need to keep her distance. "You had a stillbirth?"

The nod from Celeste was enough to flip Paige upside down and shake a cascade of uncomfortable feelings loose. Celeste was right, she *did* owe Paige an explanation. No, that would be wrong, heaping more unfairness on Celeste's head. She didn't owe anyone a damn thing. Paige wished she'd known, that was all.

"What is it?"

She grimaced, not wanting to admit her thoughts to Celeste. They'd sound awful. But she hadn't thought she'd ever be able to get the answers and here was the opportunity right in front of her. The sheer tender kindness in Celeste's expression was difficult to resist.

"I... I couldn't help wondering. Before today, I mean. You know, which was worse, a miscarriage or a stillbirth. And..." Trailing off, Paige knew she didn't have it in her to finish. Celeste wasn't a thought experiment.

Celeste's smile was still kind, but wan. It was clear that she understood what Paige hadn't managed to say. "Since you don't hear about miscarriages all that often, and stillbirths even less than that, stands to reason that you wouldn't come across too many people who've gone through both. It's natural to speculate. To be honest, I'm not sure I'm any authority. I can tell you for one thing that there's more support out there after you've lost a baby so late in pregnancy. From some people, anyway."

They both shuddered. Back in her day, Celeste must have had a Margaret or two of her own to deal with. Rather than getting into those specifics, she continued. "There has to be, you see, officially. Because it's all so much more public. Once the bump's been spotted out and about, well, it's the sort of thing that people notice. It's common knowledge that a pregnant woman's stomach develops a magnetic quality. It's everyone's property. If anyone knows there's even a possibility of a baby…" She spread her hands.

"They do their best to sand away layers of potential awful. Remembrance boxes, casts of the hands and feet, as many pictures of their babies as anyone can bear to take. Fundamentally, they're much better these days at guiding people through the process, letting them know what to expect from labour." Celeste's eyes were shining with tears. "I see her face all the time in my dreams, even after so many years. I never had an actual photograph of her though."

"They – she," Paige corrected herself, "she was a girl?"

Celeste nodded. "Rebecca. Stephen, my husband at the time, he didn't want to name her. She's down in all the paperwork as Baby Hartman. But as time went on, I couldn't help it. Makes her more real, you see. Because she *was* a person. What?"

The frown hadn't been voluntary. Her stepmother must have caught the fleeting wistfulness on her face. Though guilt was stabbing at the base of her chest, Paige wanted to give Celeste the space to talk about *her* losses first. Celeste seemed to still feel she had further explanations to give, but Paige knew she would have to make another confession of her own first. Now she knew the full truth, it was easier to admit this kind of thing to Celeste than she could have ever imagined.

"Of course she was," Paige whispered. The last thing she wanted was for Celeste to think that Paige wanted to reduce little Rebecca in any way. In these sorts of cases, at the very least, personhood could begin whenever the mother determined. "It's… well, I know it's mad, that we can never know for sure…"

"Know what?" Celeste was gentle with her prompt, but Paige knew she wasn't going to be allowed to get away with not finishing her thought. There was an edge to Celeste, in her voice, her words, that Paige had never noticed. Celeste had unsheathed something else, alongside her explanations.

"We can't know whether who I lost would have been a boy or a girl one day."

"But did you have an inkling, maybe?"

"Not really." Paige considered. "Maybe more of a wish, or, or a flash or something. Not at the time, it was such a short pregnancy, but afterwards. I think she *might* have been a girl one day. That's how I thought for a while, but now I'm not so sure."

"You're allowed to. You can even name them down the line. Or change it if it doesn't sit right. I did that. You can do anything you want."

How had Paige never given Celeste the least bit of credit for her grace, her generosity? In the face of a vanished thirty-one weeker, Paige's own loss felt insubstantial. There was no comparison when it came to poor Celeste's tragedy. But here she was, giving Paige permission to share with her, making room for her stepdaughter.

Clearing her throat, Celeste carried on. "After poor Rebecca, well, it didn't feel right to me that her sibling soul didn't get any sort of name when she got one. Everyone gets to decide for themselves what a miscarriage means. To me, it's a life. I lost one baby but two lives. So, a real name didn't feel quite right. After I got rid of Stephen's surname, it seemed fitting to think of my first child as Hart." She smiled encouragingly.

"Button," Paige replied.

"That's lovely."

After a pause, Paige looked back up at Celeste. "You said that it was two lives, but one baby?" She wasn't even sure how to phrase the question, hoping that the rising inflection would do it for her.

"Yes, love?"

"I just… how do you know? How do you make that distinction?"

Celeste looked thoughtful for a moment. "If you sit with these things for long enough, I don't know how to explain it, you find answers on your own. Whatever makes sense to you. And really, we all choose where to draw our own lines. It's a privilege of the situation, but also a curse. We don't have enough words for these sorts of losses, that's what leaves the wiggle room." She sighed. "What works for one person won't quite fit the bill for someone else. Miscarriage has the awful effect of making it sound like you did something wrong, that it's some sort of personal failing."

Paige nodded with fervour.

"So, how I see it is that a miscarriage is a loss of something on the spectrum running between a life and a baby. It always seemed rather important to me to draw some sort of distinction between dear little Rebecca and Hart, whether it was fair to them or not. Hart does tend to get a bum deal there, somewhat overlooked. I decided in the end to think of him as a him, to give him a little something else of his own. You miss them both, but… Rebecca was so much closer to life. We don't have anything like enough words to describe babies who are lost. Not in any way that doesn't sound hopelessly clinical."

She smoothed an imaginary crumb off her skirt. "And it's easy to end up resenting the way that miscarriages and stillbirths are so often lumped together, even when you've gone through both. It happens with all types of baby loss. We get crammed into boxes because it's more important to make everyone else comfortable."

"I'm sorry."

Celeste waved Paige's sympathy away. "That's what I've found, anyway. It makes a grim kind of sense. Folk are desperate to relate to your experience, to make it halfway understandable from their perspective. And, well, miscarriages are so much more common than stillbirths. It's hard enough to wrap your mind around a lost life, let alone one that was almost fully formed, a breath away from being ready to be born."

There was a pause and Paige's heart quailed to see Celeste's lip trembling. After all this time, it still affected her. But how would it not? Would it upset her further if Paige asked her how long ago it was that she'd lost Rebecca? And Hart.

Celeste shuddered. "Perfectly healthy. That's what they said about her."

"So, you never found out why?" That thought made it all seem so much crueller. It made sense that answers were out of reach for early losses, when a glob of tissue was all too easy to miss. But further down the line, when they could run all their fancy tests? How did that happen?

"Why she died?" Celeste shook her head. "Even these days, with whatever technological wizardry they've invented for fact finding, there's no guarantee of an answer. The closer you get to term, the less likely you are to find anything definitive, counterintuitive as that might sound. But you see, all the obvious reasons would have probably brought things to a stop before then. You know, issues with the placenta, physical defects, that sort of thing. At thirty-one weeks, your odds are somewhere in the region of fifty-fifty for getting a reason why it happened." Her face fell. "I lost the coin flip."

"I'm so sorry." The words were rote, automatic, repetitive, and yet Paige meant them far more than anything else she'd ever said to her stepmother.

With a sad smile, Celeste shook her head once more, taking command of the situation again. "No, dear girl. I won't take apologies from you. You've had your own hell to go through. We don't have to keep score. I've had more than long enough to glue myself back together. You shouldn't have to be the one to comfort me. I'm the one who's been failing in my responsibilities. I haven't been able to be here for you, or offer to be, at least. Not that I'd have wanted to push in, you might not have wanted that sort of support from me."

They both stayed quiet as that jagged little truth hovered in the air between them. Paige wanted to protest. She really did. But it would have been disingenuous for her to say that she'd have welcomed Celeste's intervention before she knew about her unique insights into her situation.

She'd pegged Celeste as a conduit to the sorts of stories she wanted, nothing more. At least Paige could relax that Celeste wasn't going to feel used now. This conversation was happening on the older woman's terms.

"When it happened to… it all felt so… so close to home. It brought everything back and while I wanted to… Russie tried… well, he helped me until I was ready to face you. Even though it makes me a total coward. But I want you to know how desperately sorry I was about your loss."

"Thank you." Lip trembling, Paige knew that if she said anything else, she'd dissolve into tears. Which would set Celeste off in proper fashion too. They wouldn't manage to continue their discussion for ages. Cathartic sobs could wait.

"I wanted you to hear… it won't be helpful to you when you're stuck in these after-months. Right now, it's all standing still, and it doesn't feel like there's a way out. But, I promise, time's the only way through. It's selfish, I know, to want to say all of this to you. I imagine you've heard that or something like it plenty of times. But it was the one thing that made the... the later loss more bearable. I'd been through something like it already and I knew that someday down the line I'd... that I'd never forget either of my children, but that I'd be able to cope with living again. You never move on, just forward."

Shuddering as if a great weight had eased its way off her shoulders, Celeste rolled her neck. Then she raised her eyes to meet Paige's gaze. There was more to say, but it seemed to be getting easier for her to get through it all. And Paige knew she needed to hear it. The way Celeste was describing what she was going through, the time-stuck nature of the weeks making their treacly trickling progress, was a clearer sign than anything else that Celeste had been through the same experience. And worse.

"It's too easy to torture yourself with what you might have done. Whether it's nine weeks or thirty-nine, I think we women have our ways of convincing ourselves we could have found a way to save them."

All ease had been temporary, banished now. Celeste's chest was heaving. Paige was desperate to stop her stepmother in her tracks, to assure her there was no need to keep going. But Paige couldn't make herself get the words out. If she were being forced to be honest, she'd admit there *was* a need. She had to hear what Celeste needed to say.

"Especially when you're holding this perfect little baby, this person who was growing so well up until... until the last moment. Even though you don't know for sure when that was. In utero SIDS. That's how I began to think of it. Even though SIDS is far less common than it used to be, and still-births are still..." She shook her head. "Early on, if you lose them, the odds are high that they were never meant to stick, painful as that is to know. Chromosomal abnormalities and such, I'm sure you're aware. Of course, you are. You'll have done your research. I know you, spreadsheets and data." She gave a watery smile. "But once you've made it past all those dangerous moments, beyond those first few months… you convince yourself you're safe, you know?"

Celeste sighed. "I'm so sorry. I'm doing a terrible job of comforting you, my dear. I don't mean to torture you with trimesters. I thought better late than never and now, well, I'm—"

But Paige was shaking her head with vigour, stopping Celeste in her tracks. "You're being real. It's what I need."

Paige couldn't make herself say it, her mouth plugged up with impossibilities, but she was hoping that this exchange might be liberating for Celeste too. Strange how much could bubble up once you unbottled it. And these feelings must have been with Celeste for a very long time, no matter how hard she normally worked to keep them inside.

"I used to get so angry," Celeste whispered. "Born sleeping was such a poisonous nonsense to me, a little dash of euphemism to make it easier for the rest of the world to deal with. My daughter *died*. She was ripped away from me before I had the chance to meet her on the outside. Anyone who ever dared to talk to me about living with the angels or being called up to heaven, they'd get a cold stare from me if they were lucky." After a beat, her eyes flashed with something a little wicked. "Physical violence if they weren't."

This was a side to Celeste that Paige had never seen before. Maybe Russell didn't have such odd taste after all. If this Celeste stuck around, maybe there was a chance for a better relationship between her and Paige in the future.

"You must have lost quite a few friends that way."

"Well, if you want to call them that. Some people do start to distance themselves from you. But if that's their reaction, you're better off without them." She cocked an eyebrow.

"Preach. Everyone wants to move on." Her stepmother's comment about moving forward, rather than on, had struck a chord with Paige.

"And you can't do anything, take the next steps — whatever they might be — in a hurry. You'll hurt yourself more in the long run if you try. Remember them with love. Even when it breaks your heart to do that. Even when it doesn't hurt but feels like it should. Move forwards, with them in your heart. Not on without them."

Paige nodded, grateful to hear her own thoughts coming back at her. If she'd ever considered herself to be an elder stateswoman, her credentials were nothing compared to Celeste's.

Everything she'd ever known about Celeste felt like it was coming apart at the seams. Maybe she'd imagined Celeste's deeply dippy nature, needing to find something objectionable about New Mummy, inventing a reliance on wishing on stars and the bogus properties of crystals. Childish, childless Celeste. None of Paige's impression of her had been real.

Already kicking herself for it, Paige knew she wouldn't be able to shut her wonderings off if she didn't ask the question cluttering up the front of her skull. "It's what everyone says. That you can try again. Like you can replace the one you lost…"

She tried to find the words to prove that she was different to anyone who spouted those empty platitudes, who wanted to skate over the pain and skip to the happy ending. Another baby wasn't an easy solution, a plaster that healed everything under it without question and in a trice. More than anything else, Paige hoped that Celeste understood that she didn't have to answer if she didn't want to.

Biting her lip, she had to come out with it. "It took a while, but I think I still want to have a baby, even though I can't have Button. But you, I mean, did you not want to? After…" she had to say the name, "after Rebecca?"

"I…" Celeste brushed a fingertip across her lips, musing. "You have something, someone, that I didn't have back then. Luke's one of the good ones. Someone who'll hold you in the darkest moments. Like your father."

It was good to know that Russell was in that category, but Paige found herself hoping that Celeste wasn't about to go into more detail. There were some things you didn't want to know about your dad.

Feeling merciful, it seemed, Celeste sighed and smiled. "It's a moment that will test a relationship like no other. There will be times when you'll just need him to be there. He's the other half of your whole, the fellow parent, the one person in the world who stands any chance of understanding the uniqueness of the life you lost together."

There was no arguing with her assessment of Luke. He was the best. Paige's safe harbour. She didn't know the first thing about Celeste's ex. It wasn't hard to make the leap from what she'd already said, and the fact that the marriage hadn't survived. Paige ached for the Celeste of yesteryear. A woman who deserved someone kind and giving.

"Maybe I should have realised that my Stephen wasn't up to the job of making a family with me after the first time we went through pregnancy loss. We were both so lost… we convinced ourselves that a child, any child, would fix the situation. Plenty of people go through miscarriages, after all.

"But following that second failure, after Rebecca's death, Stephen was… incapable of forgiving me. One loss, he could just about get his head around. After I'd had two though…

careless. To say that I was damaged goods in his eyes would be to put it mildly."

Rage coursed through Paige's veins. "It wasn't your fault! She was healthy, they told you that. And even if she hadn't been, you'd have done everything you could for her. I know you would."

"Thank you." Celeste reached out to place a gentle hand on Paige's knee. "It takes time to come to that sort of thinking though, on one's own behalf. Too long for us. In some ways though, I wonder if I'm grateful to Stephen. I was ready to keep dipping my heart into hell to try and get what I wanted. Before he left, I was preparing myself to try again, to spread my legs and hold onto hope for a living child. But," she looked wistful, "he put an end to things and that was that."

"What about with someone else?"

"I could never quite bring myself to inflict that on anyone after Stephen. I'd already lost two. For all that the doctors assured me it wasn't anything I'd done, or hadn't, that there wasn't anything we could have tried to prevent the losses, we never knew what it was that put an end to either of them."

She heaved out another breath. "I'd have done it all again to get back to her, gone through that hopeless labour as many times as I had to so I could have the chance to hold her again. But life doesn't work that way, no way to return to moments already gone. For all of Stephen's total inadequacies, *he* was my partner for those pregnancies. Going into the future, well, the idea that I might take those failures into a new relationship, curse another man, a better one, with having his hopes dashed over and over. It was too much for me."

"It could have been a problem with him though." Paige had to defend Celeste. For all that it didn't make any difference to what had happened. "And it's not like you need a huge amount of input from a guy to get the, er, process started. Nothing at all after that."

The kind, patient expression on Celeste's face spoke volumes. Paige wasn't saying anything that hadn't been said or thought before. "I considered that. Doing it on my own or finding a different route to it. But things were in such a terrible place after Stephen left, even though it was the best thing for us. Not completely his fault, the separation. It never felt like the right time for me to try again. I couldn't bear for the third time not to be the charm."

"You're still young," Paige whispered, not even sure she meant what she was saying. Her voice caught. Was she really suggesting she wanted another sibling? People in their forties had babies all the time. It wasn't impossible at Celeste's age. Maybe Russell's ready fertility was one of the things that had attracted him to her in the first place. If she got the right nudge, could this still happen for her? Paige started crossing every mental finger that she wouldn't have to hear too much about it.

But Celeste interrupted Paige's train of thought with a sunny peal of laughter. "Liar. But I think that's the sweetest thing you've ever said to me. I can't go back there though. Sure, women my age have done it, but... it's not on the cards for me. I know I'll never be your mum, not that I'm trying to be. I'll never have a child I get to take home. I will always be Rebecca's mother, and Hart's. I've... I've made peace with my situation as much as I can."

She was tugging at her sleeves, in what seemed like a subconscious effort to hug herself. There was a gentle rocking back and forth motion that Paige longed to interrupt, but she was rooted to her own chair.

"I know it's the modern thing to take the plunge on your own. I suppose I could have tried that. In the end, it was easier to let Stephen take the choice away from me. I never had to put myself to the test again. The longer I left it, the less I felt I could trust myself with carrying another baby. I couldn't get away from the dark thoughts about what sort of disaster might befall a third. I haven't been pregnant for fifteen years. I don't think I could bear to put myself back there."

Paige wanted to keep arguing, keep fighting for Celeste's children, re-litigate what had already happened, but she could see the resignation on Celeste's face as plain as day. What good would it do to convince her that a different route could have been taken? Paige didn't want to add to Celeste's guilt. Maybe it wasn't just Celeste's guilt at play.

There was a puff of an exhale from Celeste. "And if we couldn't have saved either of them, there was nothing to do to guarantee a future pregnancy. I wasn't brave enough. Better to wait until I met your father, someone happy with the children he's already got. And if I can do a little bit to light the way for you, that would mean the world."

Paige returned Celeste's smile with gratitude. "My experience doesn't hold a candle to what happened to you though."

"Darling, don't be ridiculous." For once, Paige didn't mind Celeste calling her that. They'd reached a deeper level of intimacy than ever before. All their normal rules of conversation were off. "If losing what I lost means that I can only sympathise with people who've had it worse than me, then I wouldn't be able to talk about death with almost anyone else. I'll admit, sometimes when people are going on and on about their grandparent or their dog, I can get a bit short with them. But you don't want to play Top Trumps with grief. It's a hollow victory. Besides, I'd like to think that sometimes I can help people find some kind of perspective, especially when it's babies. I'm always going to be the woman whose children died before she could know them. No one wants to be that sad sack."

"I... I had no idea."

Celeste smiled. "There was a certain amount of design in that. It felt important to tell Russell about it in our first few months together, introduce him to some of my remembrance traditions. But I asked him to keep it from you girls. It's not the sort of thing I like to broadcast after all this time. Sometimes it's nice to be just me, keep the baggage out of sight."

"So, you don't like talking about it?" It was part of the problem, not that Paige blamed Celeste. But out of sight, out of mind was the way of it too often.

"Oh, I didn't mean it like that. Just... after a while, it can be too much to be the one responsible for introducing my dead babies into the conversation. Even for those who know, well, people don't want to bring up particular topics without permission. But it can be hard to grant it sometimes."

Turning Celeste's words over in her mind, Paige frowned. She looked up at her stepmother. "If I asked though, you'd want to talk about Rebecca?"

"Oh yes." It was like a shaft of sunlight had spilled onto Celeste's face. Enthusiasm lit her up. Relief was doing something similar to Paige. Everyone else got to bang on about their children in endless detail, why did loss parents have to be left out in the cold?

"What would you like to tell me about her?"

"Rebecca was beautiful. I know everyone says that about their children, even when they're more like misshapen lumps with serious side-eye. But she was perfect, button nose, delicate tiny mouth. A baby. I was so grateful for that. Throughout that awful labour, I thought that maybe I wouldn't even want to hold her afterwards. I was afraid of what my own child would look like."

"But it was fine? I mean, you wanted to. And you said she was alright?" Paige winced. "You know what I mean."

"I do. Well, she was dead, of course. Poor mite. And, given that she'd been gone for a day or two before she came out, there was some…" Celeste swallowed, "some deterioration. The skin on her… on her hands, and across her stomach, it was peeling. But after she was wrapped up, Rebecca could have been sleeping. I thought I might be able to look at her eyes, but the lids were still fused shut. Takes a while for them to open in the womb, you see. And we never got that far." She gave a shuddering sigh.

After what felt like an eternity, Paige could move again. She got up, crossed the room, and flung her arms around Celeste. Two grieving mothers, united in something at last, they hugged each other close.

*

A little while later, once the tears had subsided, and a concerned Russell had fetched hot drinks before retreating again, the sheer relief of everything being out in the open almost splitting him in two, Paige was trying to sift the surging sea of questions crashing around her head. There was still so much to talk about.

It was as if Celeste could see right into her brain. "You can ask me anything." From the look in Celeste's eyes, Paige believed that she really meant it.

"Am I…" Paige swallowed. "Am I being ridiculous? Sometimes I wonder if I'm blowing this out of all proportion. As if I haven't really earned the right to… It was only seven-ish weeks." It wasn't fun to confess that out loud. She didn't want to have to ask if she had a right to be as upset as she was, but she couldn't help hoping that Celeste's powers of telepathy would hold up, that she'd read the need for permission to feel in her expression.

Celeste, kind, generous Celeste – how could Paige have ever thought badly of her before? – reached over and patted Paige's hand. "I don't think we can ever predict how these things are going to affect us. No one gets to be a yardstick. It's not like there's an allotted amount of grief you get for a loss, codified by how far along you were when it happened. Some people can brush themselves off after a later loss and worry they're not human for not feeling as cut up as someone who had an early miscarriage. I've seen it all." She winked. "Years of support groups. None of us know what's going through anyone else's head."

"I guess." Paige wasn't convinced.

"Don't fall into the trap of trying to compare yourself to anyone else, that's my advice. That's the sort of thing social media does to you. Everyone shows off the light moments and hides the dark. We might have all gone through similar experiences, in essence, but we're all different people. Makes sense that we'd have different reactions to what happened. Of course," Her mouth settled into a tight line, making Paige fear what was coming next, "I'd suggest that you don't make the mistake of trying to belittle someone's stillbirth by trying to draw comparisons between that and something that happened rather earlier in a pregnancy. Where they didn't have to rip themselves apart to birth a child everyone knew would be dead before they came out."

Paige's stomach lurched. "Someone did that to you?"

"I don't know if you've noticed, but there are some folks out there who are desperate to make any conversation about them, regardless of a total lack of relevant experience to bring to the table. They can aways be depended on to make do with what they've got. Et voila, a six-week miscarriage becomes totally relatable to a third-trimester loss. Better than having to listen to someone else."

It was all too plausible. Paige nodded with a sardonic grin. "I don't know anyone like that."

They shared wicked smiles.

Paige knew she was going to have to ruin the moment of solidarity. "What... was it like? Being pregnant again, I mean?" There was a flush of selfishness in her, but she couldn't help wondering about the time between losses, the trying again, the second pregnancy – before it all went wrong. What if Paige was heading down the same path? She had to prepare.

"You, well, when you lose a pregnancy, it's more than that. More than a baby. It's a whole life. All that potential gone away to nothing. For no reason at all, most of them. Or it's before anyone might be able to find out why."

Celeste was wrapped up in her thoughts, lost in the realities of what she'd said. But then she looked over at Paige, guilt spilling across her face, making her eyes shimmer. "Sorry, that's not what you asked. I wasn't trying to make anything worse for you. Even when you've been through it yourself, you don't necessarily know any of the right things to say. Thoughts float to the top and..."

"But at least you have less fear of saying things anyway," Paige chipped in, hoping she could nudge the conversation back on track.

Celeste shook herself and they reflected smiles at each other.

"That joy of an uncomplicated first pregnancy. That vanishes too, I'm afraid. I know," she cleared her throat, her lip quivering for a moment before she carried on, "I know that I never got to have a successful one, but the second pregnancy, for all its moments of joy – and there were plenty of those – carried a lot more stress with it than the first. Even before I got to the end of it. Even when I got past so many milestones with no cause for concern, I could never quite relax. Maybe my body was preparing me for another loss."

"I'm so sorry." For a fleeting instant, Paige wondered if she was making things worse for Celeste. Was this conversation too much for her? She'd been keeping away for a reason, after all.

And Celeste seemed to confirm those worries with what she had to say next. "You don't have to keep saying that. But I... I don't like digging it up over and over. The pain of... it's all too much. Perhaps it makes me a coward, but it's easier to keep it all inside. Means I stay functional."

She had an apology of her own clear in her eyes, for staying away after Paige's miscarriage. Was Celeste trapped between generations, torn between the reserve of the Granny Ruths of the world and the trendy frankness of Paige's cohort? Paige hated the idea of burying what had happened to her, locking it away in a dusty corner of her mind and only bringing it out for these sorts of conversations, with fellow members of the club. But she had to respect Celeste's choices. By now, she knew better than anyone what kept her sane.

On the other hand, Celeste's preoccupation with alternative higher powers, ceding her autonomy to random ephemera and superstition, was making more sense than ever. They were something to put your faith in that didn't rely on your own judgement. You could surrender some of your own decision making to the universe in exchange for a little peace of mind. Better by far than submitting to the cold randomness of bad luck unlinked to any greater plan. Saying nothing about the remote cruelty of a God in charge of everything who smote people on a whim.

With a start, Celeste's eyes bulged. Her own words must have come back to her, responding to Paige's query about being pregnant again by describing how she'd been bracing for another loss all along. "I shouldn't bring things down with my maudlin nonsense. It doesn't mean anything like what I went through will happen to you! It's only for me that Hart and Rebecca go hand in hand. You're not going to have to go through all that."

"It's not nonsense." Paige was firm. "I'm so grateful, honestly. Good to talk with someone who gets it." *And then some*, but she didn't want to pile it on too thick.

There was still more for her to say, more to get through before this lengthy and unexpected conversation could be allowed to end. "I just… I didn't think it was going to affect me this much. It was a few weeks. If that. My pregnancy, I mean. But it feels like I've cracked into pieces, that I can't find my way out."

She was whispering, but Paige knew it would soon be time to stop, that she was skirting ever closer to proper danger, to thoughts that were too difficult to bear, let alone express. The more she confessed to Celeste, the less Paige knew what she was going to come out with next.

Celeste's mouth pulled to one side, and she spread her hands. "It was a life. Doesn't matter how far along it was before they came away. But while that's how *I* think of miscarriages, yours means as much as *you* want it to. There are yards of difference between a wanted life that didn't happen and one that you choose to put an end to, for whatever reason. It's easy to be fabulously angry at the universe for taking away your choices. None of it makes sense afterwards.

"This may help, but then again it may not. I am one of very few people I know of who's had a stillbirth and still wanted to have children who didn't go on to have them. And some of the blame for that lies at Stephen's feet rather than biology, or, or luck or whatever you want to choose as a culprit. I know miscarriages are far more common, but if babies are something you want, you can find a way to make that happen. You do have Luke – not that a man is ever the be-all and end-all, but he's one of the good ones.

"Whatever you decide to do next, or maybe you've already decided what that is — you don't have to tell me either way. If you'd like to, of course, please do. What I'm trying to say is that I'm here for you no matter what. Very much in the pro-Paige lobby." Celeste gave a short laugh and shook her head.

"Sorry, my dear, I know I'm rambling. What I'm trying and rather failing to tell you is that there's no wrong way forwards in your situation. If you never want to have to contemplate another pregnancy ever again, that's more than understandable. If you want to find another way to have a family, I will do everything I can to help you, that you're prepared to allow anyway. I don't want to tread on any toes. And if you find yourself wanting to try again, that's a wonderful thing, but not without its own struggles. Then again, you already knew that."

What on earth could Paige say to that flood of utter earnestness? Things didn't end quite there, but before either of them suffered emotional burnout, they needed to default to something repressed and British. The weather *had* been unusually warm of late.

On her way back from her father's house, for the first time that Paige could remember, she was glad Russell had married Celeste. And not just for his own sake, so that he wouldn't be alone. It was good to see Russell happy, regardless of how Paige felt, or had felt, about the partner who made him so. But now she could recognise that Celeste deserved the same thing. His goodness, Russell's kind patience and general contrast to what it seemed Stephen had been like, Celeste had earned them all.

While Margaret's surprise bid for freedom had hurt her husband, Celeste had been through far greater devastation in her life than Russell. It shouldn't have been remarkable for her to have found a partner who was nice to her. For so many reasons, that ought to have been a given. But since it was sadly the case that Celeste hadn't had the best treatment, Paige knew her father would be doing his utmost to make up for everything that the universe had inflicted on his second wife before he met her.

Paige didn't know how long this détente would last between her and her stepmother. One revelatory conversation with Celeste, something in common with her, wasn't going to change everything. Knowing her difficult past didn't do away with all of Celeste's eccentricities. Even if it did make it easier to cope with them. Celeste had a lot more currency with Paige now, the benefit of the doubt was hers for life. Even so, it would be somewhat disingenuous of Paige to treat Celeste in a *completely* different way because of what she knew now.

PRESENT DAY

MAY

Paige

IN THE END, HEALING crept up on Paige by surprise. It wasn't just the conversation with Celeste that helped her turn the corner. Being less afraid to say what she was really thinking didn't hurt either. Annie would have been beyond proud of Paige's honest responses to queries about how she was doing. Letting herself use Button's name in conversation helped to make them feel more real too.

She'd been expecting Luke's birthday to be difficult, after Christmas had plunged her into such turmoil, with a vice-like longing for the way things ought to have been, picturing herself pregnant in the middle of events. But the celebrations came and went with one small pang of heartache. She even managed to enjoy herself throughout, something that might have felt like a betrayal to her poor vanished Button even a few short weeks ago

It's only been a few months, Paige reminded herself with a shaky sigh. Sometimes it was hard to remember that such a short period of time had elapsed, especially when it felt like several lifetimes had slipped by her.

She was furious with herself really, but the edge of that anger had already dulled once she noticed it was there at all. Why couldn't this zen have parcelled itself out a bit? If there was any justice in the world, a point already proven invalid, the tranquillity would have been fed into her veins as a steady drip ever since the hammer blow had landed that Button was gone. That way, it might have made her feel a bit less like carving out her own heart not so long ago.

How annoyingly predictable. All it took to cope was time. Probing her feelings like a tongue pushing against a wobbly tooth, Paige tried her best to take stock of what was happening within her heart. She was still sad about it, sure, but the miscarriage didn't dominate every thought and sensation in the way it had done. It was difficult for her to know if it was just where she was in her cycle, hormones having their sway as much as anything else, but there was a sense of... of peace that had been absent before now.

Serenity was a relief, but it didn't feel satisfying, not overall. She was still in free fall. Well, not quite, but what she was experiencing was something akin to it. Like all those women who'd been through baby loss before her, Paige was almost sure she wouldn't feel truly settled until she knew what was going to happen next. Closure? Whatever it was, something was missing.

And yet there was nothing for it, no imaginings, no suppositions that could close the loop of Paige's life without her living it first. No one would make the decisions or dice rolls on her behalf. She knew the experience of losing her pregnancy wasn't going to destroy her. In a thin, uninspiring way, that was enough.

The hurt was still there, lingering underneath the new layer of scar tissue. But now it was as if the tide had gone out and washed the shore clean. The knowledge that she was supposed to be pregnant, that the undeniable slight bulge in her stomach was down to overindulgence rather than anything else, was hard to bear, but the gulf of sorrow didn't feel as yawning and insurmountable as it used to. Paige had survived, even if Button, or whoever they would have been, hadn't.

*

That night, as Paige slept, somewhere between a wish and a dream, gentle, unobtrusive sunlight dipped everything it touched in gold. It was a lazy summer's afternoon, a perpetual Sunday that somehow didn't have the prospect of work tomorrow hanging over it.

Paige was sat in a knot of grass, watching bubbles slip and swirl their way along the course of the river. The baby, her baby, was in her arms. That alone was more than enough to grant Paige a sense of peace. But the tranquil surroundings couldn't hurt either. It was Button, grown into a little girl. Tempted as Paige was to imagine a new name for them, she knew Button would be Button forever.

Button's eyelids fluttered. Even though there was no limit to the surging curiosity Paige felt with regards to every detail about her child, she didn't feel the need to check what colour her daughter's eyes were. It was enough for her to be able to look down and see she had Luke's snub nose and a few wispy curls of Paige's dark hair. When Button was a bit older, Paige would have plenty of hairstyle advice to impart. Though she might want to see if Button had inherited Paige's head shape first.

After an age during which no time had passed at all, Paige laid the baby down. Nothing would hurt Button here. She glanced down to see Button's eyes open, watching her mother and the world around them. She could see the butterflies and bees flapping around lazily. They were more interested in the wildflower blooms than the little girl, flying far too fast to be clutched in a chubby fist.

It was time for Paige to go back to the real world. The one where she was supposed to live through every day, rather than run her scenarios about what might happen and when.

Maybe she would be back someday. She could try to bring Luke. Perhaps there would be a dark-haired child running around to greet them, wrapping her arms tight around Mummy's waist, when Paige returned. There could even be siblings to tell her first child all about. Or maybe Button would find somewhere else she preferred to be, her own little bubble. Still, Paige knew this peaceful spot would be there, waiting for either of them that needed it. That was the main thing.

A thought crept into her head. Was this a preview of what would happen when she died? One day, she would leave her life and go on to whatever came next. When that happened, would Button be waiting for her, her own little psycho-pomp ready to escort her off the mortal coil? It did make the thought of death that tiny bit more welcome. She'd be with her baby again.

*

After all that relentless heartache, Paige was finally out the other side. She wasn't fixed, she wasn't who she was before, there was no denying that she'd been changed by what had happened, but she could breathe again at last.

How on earth had she managed it? It seemed important to at least attempt to retrace her steps in case she ever needed to recreate the process of putting herself back together. If she wanted to try for another baby, there was every chance she would end up right back at square one again.

But that wasn't as terrifying as it might once have been. The experience of the last few months kept slipping through her mental fingers. It was a struggle to recapture all those soul-crushing thoughts and feelings. The harder Paige tried to remember the sharpness of the pain, the way it had stabbed her all the way through her chest and out the back, the more remote it became.

The sense of loss was still there, never to be erased altogether. But the howling void had quietened. If anything, it was sheepishness that reigned supreme in her heart. Had she been making an almighty fuss over nothing? A few months on and the thicket of tragedy was a whole lot thinner than the towering thorny wall of relentless anguish she'd been convinced it was at the time.

"Don't be silly." Luke's eyes were soft when Paige confessed her worries to him. "You've every right to your feelings. Whatever they are and whenever they're happening, you should feel them. And you've had to work your way through a shedload of stuff." He took her hand and squeezed it. "I am glad you're alright though."

She smiled gratefully. "Me too."

It was time to start moving forwards again in their lives. Together. And she knew the step it was that she wanted to take. In bed, with Luke cuddled up behind her, Paige whispered into the darkness. "I want to try for another one."

"Are you sure?"

"No." Paige leaned her head backwards, curling herself closer against the man she loved more than anything. "But I keep coming back to the fact that I still want to have a baby."

She couldn't see it, but she could feel Luke's smile, warm as a radiator, even before she heard it in his voice. "I didn't want to push you, but I hoped that you might come around to that sort of thinking."

"You did?"

"Yeah."

"So, do you want to try too?"

Along with the nod, Paige was almost sure she felt a trickle of moisture. Luke was probably glad the lights were off. If he wanted to, he could pretend that he wasn't crying, rare event that it was for him. It was good to talk, to know that they were together again, back on the same page.

Paige didn't want to test that theory, but she needed a little bit more from this conversation before she could feel secure. "They, they wouldn't be a replacement, would they? For Button?"

She could hear the slight rustle of the sheets as Luke shook his head. "Not even if we wanted them to be. I mean, ages ago, before all this happened... when we both said that we wanted to have children someday, well, I know *I* wasn't picturing just the one."

"I wasn't either."

"There you go. So, we don't have to keep quiet about the miscarriage or anything, act like it never happened. Because it did, it's part of our story. We can always tell the kids, someday, that there should be another one at the table."

Paige's heart swelled with love for her husband. Together, they were moving again. They weren't pretending, trying to make the best out of a bad situation. It was more of an acknowledgement of what had happened, seeing what it meant for their future. There were still all sorts of possibilities.

"When you said you wanted to try..." Under the duvet, Luke's fingers were grazing the curve of Paige's hip, sweeping below the cotton fabric of her pyjama shorts.

"Mr Tilney, on a school night? You dirty thing!"

"Good to get the practice in," Luke murmured in between the kisses he trailed along her neck.

Afterwards, when it sounded like Luke was asleep, Paige could feel contentment coiling around her waist. All her fears, about never getting pregnant again, about… it happening again, about losing Luke… any of them could happen. But were they likely? She wasn't so sure anymore. Anything was possible.

PART TWO
THREE YEARS LATER

2019

DECEMBER

Annie

ANNIE SWIRLED HER PAPER straw around her glass, wishing hard that she hadn't decided to drive home later. Going for something harder than lemonade might have helped ease her into the festive spirit. One of the problems with starting a new job at the arse end of the year is that come the Christmas party, you're very much still supposed to be on your best behaviour.

It wasn't that she'd have preferred a sit-down meal to the buffet and drinks option – though it would have been harder to sneak quite so many of the pork and cranberry mini quiches with the more formal dining option – but it would have made it a bit easier to socialise. Bit sad that she needed people trapped in their seats to get a conversation started, but it was proving difficult to choose which knot of chat to break into.

Someone, it seemed, had noticed her social difficulties and was prepared to take pity on her. A woman with gorgeous curling black hair and a mischievous smile draped herself over the chair next to Annie. With a lurch somewhere south of her slightly-too-full stomach, she had to work hard to stop her mouth falling open.

If she hadn't been quite so instantly attracted, Annie might have been jealous of everything from the woman's easy grace to her daring fashion sense. Not that Annie was the least bit into victim blaming, but the cut of the midnight-blue dress drew her gaze like a magnet to the woman's cleavage, the curve of which was only emphasised by the silver pendant nestled against her luscious dark tawny skin.

The glint in her eyes, the suggestion of lip biting, made Annie more than a little worried that this glamorous stranger could read her thoughts. It was almost as if she was daring Annie to give in to every dirty impulse running through her head. She felt compelled to run her hands through this stranger's hair and mount her right there in front of her still-pretty-new colleagues. Worst possible time to get the horn.

It'd been far too long since Annie's last relationship, and she and Freya had been little more than sexless roommates by the end of that road. Even so, Annie had clung on tight when the inevitable break-up came. Pathetic as it was to admit, chaste hand holding was a hell of a lot more enticing than the thought of being alone. Paige's Luke was the exception that ground your nose deep into the mediocrity on offer elsewhere, rather than the rule everyone could follow. Having given up on her search for Ms Right a long time ago, Annie would settle for anyone.

Unless… could all that be about to change? Maybe Annie could justify her wild desire to slide her tongue into this woman's mouth if it was a prelude to true love. Not that Annie was sprinting ahead of herself. Not at all. But maybe this was what the fizzing sensation in her veins was trying to tell her.

"Wallflower."

Consumed by her inappropriate thoughts, she'd almost missed the fact that the goddess had spoken. "Huh?" She could have kicked herself for such a witless opener.

But Annie's saviour merely cocked an eyebrow before continuing with her gentle banter. "What are you doing here wilting on the edges? You don't look like a plus-one who's been ditched."

"Oh, no. I'm new, that's all. Joined Oscar's team three weeks ago."

The other woman's eyes flashed with victorious insight. "Ah, can't quite bring yourself to cut loose yet? Scared of cementing an early reputation as some kind of deviant party animal?"

Annie laughed. "Need to work my way up to that. What about you?" The plus-one comment made her heart sink. She'd have noticed this woman around the office, so that meant she was someone's guest. Therefore, odds were high that she was unavailable. Which got all kinds of in the way of Annie's brand-new ambitions for what to do with her tongue.

"Oh, I'm infamous for my legendary partying talents already. You meant if I'm here as a hanger on? Got me down as un-architectural?" The shrug was reassuring, as if Annie's new friend was as psychic as she seemed. "Said I'd keep Kitty company."

Kitty. The social pressure mounted as Annie racked her brains. The welcome tour felt like it had been such a long time ago. "Kitty, um, in legal?"

"Top marks for the new girl."

Scared of skipping over introductions and missing the woman's name, Annie stuck her hand out. "I'm Annie."

For a moment, she thought she'd judged things horribly. But after a beat, the woman slipped her hand into Annie's, sending tingles up her arm to the point that she wanted to check for goosebumps. "Juliet."

"So," Annie scrambled to find a question that was at least one iota less intense than what Juliet was doing for the rest of her life, "what do you do?"

"Oh dear. I thought we were flirting. That's a terrible pick-up line."

As her heart flipped over in triumph, Annie resolved to up her game. Batting her eyelids in as obvious a way she could manage, she lowered her voice to a husky whisper. "Something about you expecting a shedload of coal this year on account of your obvious status on Santa's list."

That provoked a dirty cackle from Juliet. "*Much* better." Her fingers were tracing their way up Annie's thigh.

If she didn't ask now, she'd never pluck up the courage. Right then, it didn't matter if it was just for a night or for the rest of their lives – though Annie was certain which of those options she'd prefer – but she was already burning up for the chance to get Juliet into her bed. The possibility she would say something to ruin the moment loomed large. She'd spent too much of her evening already worrying that she was showing herself up in front of her new colleagues as an unsociable grinch. Better to make the most of this golden opportunity.

"We could do the whole small talk thing, Christmas plans, the weather, how long you feel you need to stay to fulfil your obligation to Kitty. But… do you want to get out of here? We could go back to mine for," Annie licked her lips, more out of nervousness than an attempt to be seductive, "coffee?"

"Thought you'd never ask."

As soon as they'd turned the corner out of sight of the restaurant, she threw caution to the wind and pulled Juliet close against her. If she thought she'd been on fire with lust before, it was nothing compared to the inferno that ignited in her loins the moment their tongues touched. Maybe Juliet did this sort of thing all the time, but this was the fastest Annie had moved in a relationship since university. Well, ever really. She was already half in love with the daring stranger Juliet was turning her into, the sort of person who could ask for what she wanted. And right now, what Annie wanted was Juliet.

*

Once she'd sailed through to the wrong side of her mid-thirties, Annie had thought she was well past the days of the delicate dance of second-guessing herself about when to get in touch after a first date. If that was even how she could describe the night she'd shared with Juliet.

Sated by a string of exceptional orgasms – as if Juliet was capable of inspiring anything less dizzying – they'd fallen asleep together in a tangle. But by the time Annie woke in the morning, Juliet had disappeared like some kind of ghost of relationships future.

Before she could put too much effort into her plans to stalk Kitty to find her way back to Juliet, she found the scrawled note with a lewd compliment regarding Annie's prowess and a phone number in case she wanted to "do it again sometime". As if it was even a question.

But it did leave the ball squarely in Annie's court and she was caught between wanting to appear a little bit cool, or at least less likely to chase Juliet away, and the part of her that had been quivering with dismay since she woke to find Juliet gone.

The fear of coming on too strong be damned, Annie sent what she hoped was a breezy text. Her heart leapt into her mouth when she saw that Juliet had replied and once again Annie wondered if she should play the waiting game.

Keep it light, she told herself, *let Juliet take the lead*. But it wasn't long before they were discussing plans for New Year's, and it felt like the most natural thing in the world for them to make plans to meet up again for the big night – Christmases with families needed to be endured first. Annie ran to her wardrobe and started picking out her outfit like it was prom all over again.

If she could look half as sexy as Juliet managed without even trying, Annie would regard it a success. She'd been promising herself for the past year she would wear the burgundy jumpsuit she still wasn't quite convinced she could pull off, but to hell with it. Anyway, the hope was that Juliet would help rip it off her later – it was a tricky angle with the zip, after all – so it wasn't that important what she was wearing in the first place.

Until the moment Annie saw her again, she wasn't quite prepared to believe that she hadn't dreamed Juliet up. After a brief kiss hello, demure enough to be decent in public but bubbling over with the promise of what might happen later, they grabbed drinks and slid into a booth together, touching thighs and trading accounts of the holidays.

"We're a combo family, I guess. Mix and match of customs but all of the above, rather than an either or."

Annie tried to remember what Juliet had already revealed about her background, as if anything about Juliet wasn't memorable. Her nod and indistinct mumble felt like the worst kind of non-response.

Maybe Juliet didn't hear, or she was prepared to take pity on Annie. "Lots of people are convinced I'm Indian." She shrugged. "It's the colouring. But my dad's Nigerian and my mum's Finnish. So obviously I have to trawl all the way to the backwaters of Sussex any time we have a get-together, most natural of spots for the family pile. They've dug the roots in way too deep for even Brexit to winkle them out."

Wide-eyed, Annie scrambled for anything interesting to say in response. With the most diverse blood in her family hailing all the way from Donegal, she was so white she could almost illuminate the shady nightclub. If the disco lights were any brighter, she'd need sun cream. "I guess we're both a kind of bi then. Biracial, bi…sexual." Her clumsy tongue stumbled over the final word. Foot. Mouth. *Stop talking, stop talking now. You are* not *funny.*

Juliet's expression was one of exaggerated sympathy. "Oh, honey, who are you trying to impress? We wouldn't be ringing in the New Year together if I didn't think you were interesting."

"If I was going to lie to make myself sound more interesting, why would I choose being bi? It's just who I am."

But all that did was make Juliet laugh, in a way that might have been cruel if she weren't playing footsie with Annie under the table. "No, you're not."

Who was Juliet to tell Annie anything about her own sexuality? She knew plenty of people who'd grown up knowing exactly who they were in that sense. Before they even had the words for it, there were those who emerged from the womb with their identities intact. There were others though, folk who'd spent agonising prepubescent years grappling with all sorts of unexpected yearnings.

For Annie, the discovery of her bisexuality had been more like a light switch pinging on. A switch called Jasmine who sadly didn't bend that way, not that Annie had ever propositioned her or anything like that. But once she'd acknowledged to herself that it was more than a girl crush on an unattainable friend, that her feelings could be focused on more than one woman, there was no going back.

If anything, it made her dip back into her past and re-evaluate one or two things. Maybe her obsession with Kate Winslet had been a bit more than simple admiration of her turn as Rose Dawson. However, Annie's appreciation of women didn't wipe out the way she felt about men. Not everything had to be one thing or the other. Why was it so preposterous for her to be bi?

"How would you know?"

"Come on, it's obvious. And not just in the way you behave in bed." When Annie failed to return her smouldering look in kind, Juliet rolled her eyes, just a little. "Put it this way, have you ever had a serious relationship with a boy? I'm not talking school shit, walking around the playground hand in hand with everyone giggling and looking on because it's what's expected. We've all done that. I don't know about you, but Kareem and I never even kissed. Has a boy ever rung your bell *and* stuck around to buy you breakfast the next day?"

With supreme reluctance, Annie admitted, "no."

"My point exactly, sweetheart. You don't have to try and make yourself more palatable, you know, dangle the idea of grandchildren just to keep your parents happy or whatever. I see this all the time in children of divorce. So eager to please."

"I thought I was trying to be interesting?"

Before Juliet could fire off another comeback, Annie sighed and shook her head. She wanted to find a way to get off the subject. Juliet's psychoanalysis was pinching.

Not that she was half as accurate as she thought she was. Margaret had been clear that she didn't expect anything in that department from either of her daughters. Probably priming the pump in case anyone ever tried to wrangle her for childcare.

Annie couldn't think of anything less likely to happen, and not just because of Paige's reproductive challenges. Neither of them could run the risk of any babies becoming props in any of Derek's ridiculous productions. He and Margaret might be co-directors these days, but his bizarre final flourishes were still going strong.

Neither Annie nor Paige had the heart to show their mother the scathing online review of the most recent production which had dubbed it the height of car-crash theatre, dragging people through the doors with its power to provoke morbid curiosity, everyone wondering whether the dangling bits of set were intentional, or an actor was about to come to a grisly end courtesy of a snapped wire.

Without thinking too much about it – it was much too soon in the relationship to get into the thorny topic of her mother – the first thing that sprang to Annie's mind popped out of her mouth. "My sister's been having some trouble there."

"What?" Juliet cocked an eyebrow. "Finding her way out of the closet? Afraid that people might accuse her of trying to copy big sis?"

"Oh, no." Annie almost giggled at the idea. "No, she's hetero through and through. And she has the loveliest husband ever. I mean she's been having trouble with the whole producing-grandchildren thing. Doesn't seem to be able to conceive anymore. One loss and then years of nothing. I'm not sure I see kids in either of our futures at this point."

When she said it, Annie felt a pang. It was sad for Paige, sure. But the idea of neither of them having a baby, ever, was surprisingly sad. Part of Annie's problem was a lack of a Luke of her own. Someone to settle down with so that they could start tackling the fertility road together. Somehow, she and Freya had always found excuses to put it off. But the old biological clock wasn't getting any less deafening and she couldn't work out how she felt about it. The uncomfortable feelings were enough to distract Annie from the prickling guilt of spilling her sister's secrets.

"That's... wow. Sucks." Clearly keen to dispel the heavy mood that had settled over their table, Juliet pulled Annie up to dance with her. A daring gleam played across her face under the disco lights. What if she *had* found her Luke at last?

Few words passed between them from that point until midnight, but as their tongues melted together as one year ticked over into the next, Annie couldn't stop the butterflies pinwheeling around in her belly. 2020 became a far more exciting prospect than she would have ever thought a couple of weeks ago.

2020

JANUARY

Paige

SHE'D KNOWN THE TEST would be negative before she dipped it in the urine pot. Over the years, Paige had become a pro at this. One of those transferrable skills everyone kept banging on about: weeing on things with pinpoint accuracy. Maybe she should ask Pippa for a salary increase.

Just relax. Just try Chinese herbs, acupuncture, reflexology. "Just" was to infertility as "at least" was to baby loss, the prelude to ill-informed advice that solved a lot less than the dispenser imagined. Paige had never wanted to find that out. No one wanted to be a member of either camp, let alone both.

Just "do" IVF. She'd lost count of the number of times she'd been told that. Like it was a pill you popped or an order form that slung you a baby so long as you filled out every last box. Well, Paige had done it and still didn't have a baby to show for it. She couldn't shake the feeling that she was as done with the process as it was with her.

Those were quitting words and if there was one thing the infertility world hated, it was someone who gave up. If you couldn't lay your newborn living child in the middle of a maelstrom of used needles, how could anyone tell that you'd really tried? Everyone knew the bleak statistics about success rates and yet the narratives never seemed to end without a baby. She was being denied her little rainbow because she wanted to give up.

But Paige knew she was the reason for the failures. She hadn't gone into this last round with enough positivity coursing through her veins. They'd used up their last embryo, the sole hope for this frozen transfer, and it hadn't worked.

There hadn't been any more proper losses. Just a great big void filled with hundreds of negative test strips cluttering up landfill sites, not to mention pumping her with a pharmacy's worth of drugs in single-use packets. Well, plenty of people considered embryos that didn't implant to be somewhere on the spectrum of baby loss. Paige just wasn't one of them. She couldn't explain why not. The distinction eluded her.

Maybe it was her way of making Button matter that little bit more, to hold them closer to her heart, elevate her baby above everything that had happened since. Clearly, they were a miracle that she hadn't had enough of a chance to appreciate. The one time she'd ever been pregnant, and she hadn't even been trying.

Sometimes, Paige wondered if she'd imagined those few short weeks. Maybe there'd never been anything at all. Fresh griefs kept popping up, even such a long time afterwards. Of all the tests that she'd stuck in the bin, she regretted disposing of that singular positive one. Hubris had told her there would be plenty of evidence in the future of that second line. Positive pregnancy test meant baby. That was the deal. Where were any of Paige's?

It felt odd, sometimes, to reach back into the past when what she had come to think of as her bog-standard miscarriage had been the biggest grief in her life. It still was, really, but now it had competitors: endless disappointing appointments and furrowed brows that couldn't work out what was wrong, unwelcome news coming in dribs and drabs and massive bills. In all this time, she still missed Button. She'd learned to live with that loss. Infertility though was as roaring as the pain of miscarriage, just as all-consuming and endless.

The difference with infertility was its ongoing nature. It managed to edge everything else in Paige's head out into the void. There were no "at leasts" to be found within its gaping maw. She resented the universe for heaping more onto her plate. Sometimes, she wondered if she was leaning so hard into all her environmental measures for the sake of distraction rather than anything resembling altruism. She was saving her sense of self, not the world.

This wasn't the life Paige had pictured. The electric car, the composting, the wildflower meadows and all the reduce, reuse, recycle campaigns she was managing to push through were all things that brought her immense pride, but what was the point in it all? She had the time to pour her heart into renewable energy plans for local businesses and eco waste removal options because of that cavernous hole in her life where parenthood ought to be. She wanted to share it all with a little person she could call her own.

The familiar tug of guilt in the pit of her stomach distracted her from the other feelings. She wanted to tell Luke that he was enough, the way he did for her, but she wouldn't mean it and the last thing Paige wanted to do was lie. Sometimes, she wondered if that was what he was doing – reaching for the comforting untruth in the face of his wife's anguish. They were well past the morose days of her encouraging Luke to leave her for someone more fertile. He wouldn't put up with that talk anymore and she was grateful to know that even after everything, their marriage was for keeps.

It was a nagging ache in Paige, this overwhelming need for a baby. There weren't many more ways left for them to try to get back to potential parenthood. After two funded IVF cycles, the last transfer was a total gamble and an expensive one at that. But with that last embryo from the pathetic crop they'd managed to get with her scanty eggs, it had felt like a bet worth making. And they'd lost.

The time Margaret had asked her why she wanted a baby came back to her over and over. At the time, the question had stumped her. She wanted a baby because she wanted a baby. How could Paige put it into words beyond that?

She wanted something to show for the motherhood that next to no one acknowledged since Button had vanished. She wanted someone to pass her ideals on to, to carry them forward into the future. She wanted a baby because she wanted to create a universe to wrap someone in, a good, far more innocent one than Paige saw around her, for them to open their eyes and see the magic of the little things she was trying to do to make the world better, because she wanted to believe in the power of silly stories again, because she couldn't think of another way to rediscover her hope. She still wanted to do a better job of parenting than her own mother. Paige wanted a baby because she wanted to give Luke a child. She wanted a baby because there was nothing else in her heart or her head sometimes other than the endless longing for one.

This was something else infertility was doing to her. People who could get pregnant and stay that way didn't have to justify their desires for parenthood unless they did something terrible, something disqualifying. When it came easily, you didn't have to keep making the choice that this was what you wanted. Yep, her period was coming. Confirmation if it were needed that the pregnancy test wasn't a false negative.

It wasn't as if she didn't have anyone to lean on, but it did feel like she was running out of people who understood. The fact that Kelly had chosen not to have children was something very much in her favour, yet another reason why Paige was glad they'd made up. But it didn't mean Kelly was the same person Paige could turn to in times of strife. She'd chosen this, Paige hadn't.

The longer she went without a living baby, the more Paige clung to the likes of Celeste. She'd never seen that coming, that her stepmother would become a far closer confidante than her own mother.

There was more to it than the baby loss connection. JoJo's boys were huge fun but watching them grow up was no compensation for what Paige had been and continued to be denied. More and more, even when she met up with JoJo on her own, she'd come away from the interaction aching even more than when it started.

Celeste, for all that she'd warned early on that she didn't like talking about her own experiences, had never shut Paige down when she brought the topic up. Whenever she felt guilty for returning to the miscarriage, over and over, she told herself that it was good for Celeste to talk about her children in a way that was so rare in her life otherwise. There was nothing else for it, Paige needed to see Celeste.

Russell answered the door. "Pidge! Is there any chance you're here to see me?"

"I could pretend I am if that would make you feel any better?"

"Maybe next time, salve an old man's pride." Russell winked. "Does she know you're here or is this an impromptu visit?"

Paige couldn't remember the last time she'd made an appointment to see Celeste. Then again Celeste probably wasn't going to be the least bit surprised. She knew it was coming up to test time and that Paige would need support whatever the result.

"Seeing if I can catch her with her trousers down. And if you're worried about being old, you shouldn't have gone for such a younger woman." Now that Celeste and Paige got on, there was licence to make jokes about the age gap.

"But if I hadn't married my wife, I'd never have brought such true soulmates together."

With a laugh, Paige hugged her father. "How about dinner next week, just you and me? I need to tell you about the new recycling scheme for local businesses I'm working on, pick your brains if you've got any ideas."

It was still easier for her to talk to Russell about her passion projects than her… other variety of passion project. Celeste could be relied on to give him a digestible version of Paige's attempts at baby making as they progressed. Or didn't.

"You always want something from me." Russell sniffed theatrically and then grinned. "It's a date."

"Paige! I thought I heard your voice." Celeste surged forward and swept Paige into her arms. "How are you?"

The immediate wave of tears was probably all the answer she needed. It had become something of a routine: whenever Paige turned up with too many feelings to process, Celeste would wrap her up and stick her on the sofa with something noxious and herbal. She said it would do her good, but Paige was convinced it was a subtle form of revenge. Or that Celeste was throwing stuff in at random to see if she would notice.

Before Paige was ready to talk about the latest IVF cycle, she needed to satisfy her curiosity about something else.

"Is there ever anything you do just for Hart?" She understood why, but she and Celeste spent a lot more time discussing Celeste's second pregnancy, even though it was the experience of the first that bound them together. Button and Hart were the early losses. They had a lot more in common with each other than with Rebecca.

"Poor Hart. They get so overlooked. The thing is, though, Rebecca is the one I know how to miss. I held her, I saw her face. Hart was always so much further away – I suppose I'm somewhat to blame for allowing such a disparity between their signs. How often does one see deer unless they live some kind of forest-bound hermit experience? And when I do go to the woods, it's so much more often for her." She sighed. "But that's by the by. Rebecca comes first and there's so little I can do about it. Hart went on alone, maybe he's the herald of all those hypotheticals, the children we might have had, or lost, if Stephen and I had started to try again."

Paige wasn't all that sure she knew what Celeste meant, but she was well beyond disparaging her stepmother's fanciful notions. "I think I get that. I mean, we had embryos, but they're gone too. Nothing like as many as it feels like we should have… but that's beside the point. I don't feel the same about them as I do about Button."

There was a sympathetic nod from Celeste. "It's so individual. Some women grieve a failed IVF cycle as a miscarriage and who's to say they're wrong? For the two-week wait, they're pregnant until there's any evidence otherwise. An embryo can well be regarded as another little soul who didn't get to stay at the party."

That thought sent a shiver down the back of Paige's neck. Was she diminishing the cell clusters she'd been host to because they didn't stick? Should she be mourning four little lost ones rather than just the one?

"I think it's my way of drawing a line between them. Button made it further than any of the frosties."

When she'd first heard it, Paige had hated the term. But it was surprising how firmly it had lodged in her brain ever after. It was better than embabies, as far as she was concerned. Was she going to have to start carrying around more names on her heart? The prospect of more cycles, more failures to drag around with her, became even more daunting.

"You're in charge of however you want to think of them, my dear. They mean as much as *you* want them to. If to you, as the person it happened to, they were 'just a bunch of cells,' then that's what they were. But if they were a baby to you then they were a baby. No one else gets to make that distinction for you. For me, Hart has their place in my, well, heart. But they have to be content with playing second fiddle."

Paige stared into the depths of her mug of herbal concoction. It was clear Celeste already knew the results of this frozen transfer, but she still had to say it out loud. "The last embryo is gone."

"I'm so sorry, dearest."

They didn't talk about what might happen next, even if they were both thinking about it loudly. It meant a lot to Paige, just to sit in the wake of this latest failed dream and know there was someone else in the room who understood what she was going through.

FEBRUARY

Annie

WHIRLWIND ROMANCES, THAT'S WHAT they call it when things move fast. But that term was so limiting. It didn't matter how quickly their relationship progressed: any time spent in Juliet's company was like standing in the middle of a gale. This romance was already hurricane force. No one could blame Annie for holding onto what was happening with both hands.

Juliet opened the world up for Annie. It was beyond uncomfortable for her to realise how things had narrowed their way down in recent years, as if the whole family was holding its breath, waiting for Paige to have a baby. The palpable relief in being made to recognise there was more to her life than her sister's reproductive fate made Annie even more determined to get a life of her own.

But even in the middle of all the unbridled joy of a new relationship, it didn't take the old stirrings of anxiety long to resurface. Next to dynamic, firecracker Juliet, Annie felt so humdrum. What was the alternative? Surging further out of her comfort zones to go toe-to-toe with Juliet in an arena where she could only fall short? Going with the flow was about all she could offer, so she did her level best to be accommodating.

It was easier, and a lot more fun, to let Juliet choose where they went. Annie was way too beige to know that electro swing was a genre, let alone where to go to hear it on a night out. At least she was willing to go and try it.

Terrible habit to be getting into, comparing her current girlfriend to her ex. However, she was certain under the bright lights that Freya would be having a miserable time in the club even if Annie had had the slightest scrap of where-withal to drag her out. Freya would have been far too busy tutting at the sheer volume of the music to even notice the pink glittery drum kit that was making Annie smile. Still, even though Freya couldn't be a contender in the race to deserve Juliet's affections, there were plenty of other rivals.

Which made quiet mornings in bed together even more glorious. No one else for Annie to worry about there. She was scrolling through the news on her phone, Juliet curled at her side flipping through Instagram, enjoying the calm of the moment. A nice contrast to last night. Their lives together had peaks and troughs, rather than bumbling on at a comfortable, level, dull pace.

The contentment of such a point in time didn't stop troubling news from intruding on the bubble. Her fingers paused in their gentle stroking of Juliet's hair. "What do you think of this whole coronavirus thing?"

"Hmm?"

"That virus over in China, well, a bit more all over now. Italy. More places might end up like Wuhan, locked down."

Juliet shuddered. "Can't stand the thought of something like that. Shut inside for days, weeks on end. It's what they do to torture people. Solitary confinement. I'd rather be dead."

It had taken two, maybe three, dates for Annie to realise that Juliet's assorted opinions were varied, powerful, and ever so slightly overemphasised at times. Her emotions ran deep and sometimes she could wander too far into a hypothetical scenario of her own making, declaring that hundreds of hells would be worse things to experience than a world without chai. Or mojitos. They'd discussed more than just drinks, of course.

Bold declarations were where Juliet started off in arguments and if she were to be challenged on said declarations, she often opted to dig her heels in. Any hill was worth dying on. That had to be why her automatic response was to challenge almost anything Annie came out with. There were no quiet compromises in Juliet's world, only impulses taken as far to their extremes as possible.

Pleased to see a way out of the corner, Annie resumed smoothing Juliet's hair. "If that happened – I know, you don't think it could here and I hope you're right – but if, you could always come and stay here. I've got plenty of room since Krishna left."

Somehow, she hadn't got round to advertising for a new lodger. She'd found the whole thing too weird to cope with long term, no matter how welcome the rent money had been. The rush of relief when Krishna found a contract in Glasgow that was too good to pass up was enough to tell Annie that, fundamentally, she wanted to live with a partner rather than a paying guest.

Juliet twisted round to fix Annie with a provocative eye. "You'd get bored of me if I were around all the time."

All Annie could do was snort. As if that were the way round it would be. She wanted, desperately, to serve as a safe harbour for Juliet. They could hunker down and weather this pandemic thing together. If it came to it. Odd thing to find yourself hoping for.

"If you wanted to maintain an air of mystery or whatever, you could always take Krishna's old room. Plenty of space for either of us not to be underfoot all the time. Just promise me you'll think about it. If and when."

Juliet closed her eyes and pushed her head against Annie's duvet-clad thigh, cat-like. "If and when. The rent *is* nearly up on my shoebox of a flat." She sighed. "I'd go mad on my own."

As if she realised how close she'd come to making an actual commitment, Juliet shook herself out of the languid pose. Propping herself up on one elbow, she fixed Annie with a pointed stare. "Was that why you wanted a female lodger? Easy sex on tap if the mood took you?"

"What, no! That would be…." Annie struggled to find the right word.

"Oh, calm down. I'm not accusing you of being a predatory lezzer."

"I'm bi. Remember?"

"Sure, sure."

Every time she reminded Juliet about her sexuality, there was a flash of something. Sometimes, she felt the need to prod to make sure it was still there. She was still trying to work out what it was for sure. Jealousy? Competitiveness?

There was one small part of Annie that Juliet didn't have complete mastery over. Annie was long done trying to resist her magnetic attraction to her girlfriend. So, while 90 or so per cent of her was wrapped up with Juliet to the point of obsession, there was something within Annie that Juliet couldn't touch, couldn't quite understand even. Her attraction to men.

But then she caught sight of Juliet's disbelieving expression. She was humouring Annie, not prepared to give her the respect of simple validation.

"Oh, come on. I'm not a freaking novelty," she snapped. The idyllic morning mood had evaporated. "I'm simply not repelled by penises. It is possible to be into both men *and* women."

It was always prickly when someone tried to cram her into a box that didn't fit. She was more than a set of genitals, after all, why was it such a big deal that her sexuality was about more than that too?

An evil smile glinted across Juliet's face. "I know that bisexuality is a genuine thing, sweetheart. Don't you try and pigeonhole me as a bi denier. But, while we're on the topic, it's beyond obvious that you're a full-blown lesbian who can't quite bring herself to admit it. If I can ever get you to concede, I'll die a happy woman."

The satisfied smirk on Juliet's face made Annie want to groan. She was enjoying Annie's discomfort a little too much. It was her goal then, to unsettle, to make Annie doubt. Like a game. If she hadn't risen to the bisexuality jibes, Juliet would have found something else to tease her about.

There was a choice to make. She could either allow the tension to build, make more of a thing of this moment, or she could choose to let it go. "Shan't."

"Calm down, Virginia Woolf. Got to keep you on your toes."

"Are my toes all you're interested in?"

"That's more like it." Juliet leaned over to place a confident kiss on Annie's lips. There was a sly smile on her face as she reached across to cup Annie's bottom. "You know you love me really."

There was no denying it. Annie did love Juliet. Already. Madly. Deeply. Wanted to shout it from the rooftops. Would have done so already if she weren't so worried about scaring Juliet away and concerned about annoying the neighbours at such a delicate time. Before Annie could try and summon up the courage to say it to her face, Juliet had slipped away to the bathroom. The sound of the shower turning on was just about audible over the thudding of Annie's heart.

"You coming?"

FEBRUARY

Paige

WHAT WITH ONE THING and another, Paige's dinner with her father had been subject to a handful of delays. Somehow, when they finally came to sit down, she hadn't expected him to launch into a lecture about the emotional effects of miscarriage. Felt like a very strange role reversal.

Russell broke off and looked almost sheepish, as if realising who he was talking to. "I, ah, I wanted to try and understand things a bit more. I know I've got limited hope thanks to my, er, anatomical drawbacks."

Bless him for his earnest endeavours to be woke. Paige tried not to let her smile show her amusement as she listened to her father. Whatever he was about to come out with, she knew his take on baby loss was going to be fascinating. He'd come such a long way. Not super surprising given who he was married to, but still.

"Anyway, I was reading this book and it's amazing how much times have changed when it comes to miscarriage. For the better, of course. Back in the day, and I'm talking about the 1890s or so, women were constantly pregnant. They'd almost hope for a miscarriage, so they didn't have to cross the finish line again quite so soon, a reprieve from yet another mouth to feed, delaying what was going to come in the future."

Paige could see the trajectory of Russell's line of thinking. "You don't have to go back too many generations to get back to that mindset."

"And some of them are still so very keen to hand it down. It's probably where so many delightful people get the abortion as birth control argument from." He clapped his hands together. "So, we know what we're up against. Changing the conversation happens a little bit at a time. With more advanced testing, we catch more miscarriages, but fewer families think of them as blessings anymore. It's... I still wouldn't like to presume, but there are plenty of people who can't wrap their heads around the kind of grief they cause. Takes time to shift the attitude."

"Very true."

"It's coming at the problem from another angle. Understanding the evolution of the mindset. Back in the day... well, generations could be more fatalistic about miscarriage. If women, couples, weren't quite sure they wanted it, were even hoping it might go away on its own, a loss could be less of a tragedy. Now, people who want to keep their pregnancies have them slip away anyway."

"Yes." Paige tried to wrestle her own feelings back into their box. There was no way in hell her father was trying to upset her. Just in the same way he had in the immediate aftermath of losing Button, Russell was doing his best to help. She knew that.

Still, this wasn't what she'd expected from this dinner. There was a glimmer of disappointment that she wasn't getting a chance to discuss her latest efforts on the town council. That was the sort of thing they talked about normally and while she didn't want to shut him down, she was scrambling to try and figure out how to get things back on track.

"I'm banging on about it, aren't I? Sorry, Pidge. I got lost in the weeds of research and now I'm treating you like any of this is news to you. It's my roundabout way of explaining why I'm going to propose introducing miscarriage leave as company policy at my office. Wanted to get in there before I'm blown away by your next environment-rescuing measure."

"Oh, Dad." Paige reached out to take his hand. There were no words to explain how much this meant to her.

"I'm so sorry that the last cycle didn't take. This whole business passed unfair a long time ago."

"Thanks."

"Are you thinking about doing another round?"

"I... don't know." She and Luke had talked about it, a lot. But they couldn't land on any decision that felt satisfying. All conversations went in circles that left them both exhausted.

Calling time on trying felt so final, even if it had never been more tempting. To call or not to call, that was the question of mounting pressure. Plunging back into IVF would mean going back to square one, egg collection, again, but with full knowledge of what the experience would be like – more than just Paige's stomach had become bruised.

Russell cleared his throat, uncomfortable once more. "I might be stepping out of line, but if it's a problem that only takes money to fix, then it's something I can take care of. Something I'd be delighted to do."

If only the same thing was true of Paige's enduring streak of horrible luck. She swallowed. "Thank you, genuinely, Dad. I'll think about it, talk to Luke."

"Alright then, I've said my pieces. Nothing more to spring on you. Promise to leave more of the mushy stuff to Celeste in future. Now, there's one more very important question." He shot a meaningful look towards the specials board. "Should we get puddings?"

Paige felt a breath puffing out of her, relief rolling across her shoulders. She smiled. "I think we've earned them, don't you?"

"What do you fancy?"

"Anything that comes with custard."

"That's my girl."

MAY

Annie

J ULIET WASN'T SUITED TO life as an indoor cat. The pandemic had hit her hard in more ways than one. It had closed hospitality across the board, including the hotel she worked at as a manager. Furlough had helped to salve the wound, but it was obvious she was struggling with losing the steady stream of guests she could engage with on a regular basis. Annie didn't like wondering whether her company alone was enough for her girlfriend.

Several weeks ago, Juliet had been savvy. Her read on the situation had been clear-eyed enough to turn up on Annie's doorstep with a bag just before lockdown came in, filling Annie's heart with joy that she was prepared to take her up on her offer of moving in. A little less bliss-inducing were the times when the resentment came off Juliet in waves, so much having been taken from her.

Annie sympathised but knew she was in too different a place to be able to offer the proper commiseration. It didn't help that her life hadn't been half as derailed. She could work from home and her intense pleasure at having a live-in girlfriend again was lending the worldwide crisis an unearned rosy glow.

Poor Juliet. What rational person wouldn't be frustrated by the lockdown? Getting told you could leave the house no more than once a day was rough. At least things had eased off there of late. Juliet darted out of the flat at any opportunity and Annie did her absolute best not to resent that she seemed to need so much time away from her.

Juliet was a lot of things: generous, spontaneous, a pin-wheel of explosive oomph to the point that Annie knew she had to forgive her for such frustration in being cooped up. It was always a relief when Juliet found other ways to channel all that pent up energy. The kitchen had been a spattered mess by the time she was done with her most recent impulse.

The delicious curry that Annie had got out of the deal hadn't been a bad compensation for the sheer amount of scrubbing she'd had to do afterwards. Besides, you couldn't see the stains on the cabinets by candlelight. They'd had such a romantic evening. When Annie gave Juliet her space, good things happened. She had to keep bearing that in mind.

So, whenever Juliet came back in from her wanderings, Annie exercised supreme self-control in not hovering by the front door. She didn't want it to seem like she'd been waiting around for her. There was a level of plausible deniability in coincidentally happening to head to the kitchen for a mid-afternoon coffee at the same time Juliet arrived home.

"Hey! Who'd you see?"

Juliet jumped. "What?"

"Didn't you say you were meeting someone?"

"Um… no. Well, I was going to, but I ended up just getting a coffee and having a bit of a mooch about. Bit of a bust of an outing."

"Oh. You poor thing." It sounded beyond bleak. "You should have said, I'd have kept you company."

A fleeting expression clouded Juliet's face. Annie didn't want to try and interpret it, knowing the most obvious answer was that her efforts to get out of the flat had been in aid of having some time away from Annie, as opposed to communing with nature or anything else of that description.

Juliet shrugged. "It was nice to get some fresh air. Time to… think. You could probably do with getting out a bit more too, you know. What if you met up with your sister?"

"Um, yeah. I mean, you've got a point. It's just, I… I haven't talked to Paige much lately."

"Oh, I thought you two were close?"

It was difficult to explain why Annie had stopped checking in so often with Paige. Because she couldn't cope with hearing any more of her bad news? She knew Paige was thinking about another IVF cycle, even though the last one had been such a nightmare, leaving her bloated to the point of levitation and miserable even before it didn't work. And if Annie talked to Paige about major stuff going on in her life, she'd have to trade something in kind.

She wasn't hiding her relationship from her family as such. They'd be happy for her. She knew they would. But even though they lived together, Annie couldn't fight the fact that things with Juliet still felt precarious. As much as anything else, she didn't want her sister or her father to get invested on her behalf. Maybe all she needed was to keep Juliet to herself for the time being. Once they were ready to celebrate their third or fourth wedding anniversary, the time might be ripe to let her family know about her.

The truth was, Annie was avoiding Paige. She couldn't do anything for her sister, couldn't offer help at all until Paige wanted to accept it. It wasn't quite like admitting you were an addict before treatment could begin. Nothing quite so dramatic. But she couldn't talk Paige into something she wasn't ready for.

It wasn't as if the resistance wasn't understandable. Whenever anyone heard about fertility problems, even by proxy, they started brimming over with all sorts of useless advice. Relax. Go on holiday. You know what, stop trying altogether. Then it'll totally happen.

The one thing, people stressed, that you must never do, is give up hope altogether and try to move on, do anything else with your life. That would be admitting that there's something else out there other than what you've been promised by the universe and a hundred and one cruel pop-up adverts: a baby.

While she was still using excuses to avoid rebooking her fertility treatments – it was hard to tell if Paige thought the pandemic had done her a favour by derailing the next scheduled round, the disappointment seemed a lot thinner than it might have done a couple of years ago – she wasn't ready to consider anything else. There was nothing Annie could do to help apart from quietly doing her own research into what adoption might entail. Whenever Paige got there, Annie would be a well of useful information to get her sister started.

Of course, being childless not by choice was a thing. People who decided to move on from their home-grown efforts and put that dream behind them. But Annie knew in her bones that wasn't going to be the way Paige was going to go. That girl needed to become a mother again, to get to parent a living child this time around. It was so many kinds of unfair that she was going to have to make these kinds of choices to get there.

And who knew? Maybe someday Annie would be glad of the leaflets she'd been collecting on her own account. But all that was too much to explain to an irritable Juliet. She'd already been forced to move in, how would she feel about Annie suggesting they add a kid to the mix?

"I told you about all Paige's problems getting pregnant again?"

"Yeah?"

"Oh, there's no news or anything. I keep seeing all these stories about people who've had their fertility treatments cancelled and have no idea about when any of it's going to start up again. It's such a nightmare. And I know she's caught up in all of that and I'm kind of afraid to ask how it's all going." Annie sighed. "I'm such a bad sister."

"Maybe that's why you're convinced you're at least a little bit into the dick." When all Annie wanted was a hug, it was frustrating for Juliet's voice to be so light and teasing. "You don't want to have to bother with turkey basters and needles someday."

Rather than crossing the room and embracing Annie, Juliet fired out a breath and flopped into a chair. "God, you'd never catch me doing that."

The handbrake turn at the end was almost enough to distract Annie from what came before. She was never sure how seriously to take Juliet's running joke about her sexuality. The more she protested about it, the more Juliet doubled down on the bi erasure.

And then Annie really considered what Juliet was saying. "What? You wouldn't consider artificial insemination?"

Was this her way of telling her she wanted Annie to be the one to carry their future children? Annie had to slap that thought down. Too many like it had been popping up in recent weeks and she was getting way too far ahead of herself. It was lockdown, sending her spiralling off into madness, creating an intimacy they hadn't reached yet. She was being suggestible, that was all. People kept saying there'd be a lockdown baby boom and Annie just wanted to join in.

Although, there was no denying that there weren't too many years left before fertility might start being a problem. She wasn't getting any younger. And if poor Paige was anything to go by, even when you had time on your side, there was no guarantee of anything. Could Annie steer this conversation into anything more serious?

And then Juliet shattered her hopes. "Oh, no. Kids. Not interested."

"You... don't want children?"

Juliet gave a patient nod, coupled with a slight roll of the eyes. The day was going from bad to worse. Annie wasn't just an unsupportive sister. She was in a relationship with a future she was going to have to think very hard about. All the hopes in her chest she'd been so busy ignoring were now withering away into nothingness.

JUNE

Paige

PAIGE STARED AT THE phone, misery and self-loathing coursing through her. It had taken so much time and energy to get the latest batch of appointments booked. Not that clinics made it difficult once you were out the other side of your funded rounds. Somehow, once you were responsible for footing your own bills, everyone wanted to hear from you.

The strain had all been mental, the blows coming thick and fast after the last failed implantation. The sheer prospect of having to go through stims again had made her cry even more than the shock to the system that the bloody pandemic had put everything on hold. In some ways, she was a stronger person than she used to be. Not a consolation for what had happened to her. It was obligatory, the only way to keep living the life she'd been handed. Paige was better at standing up for herself, calling out insensitive comments and the like. But that didn't make it any easier to get through these sorts of tasks.

Being stuck in limbo while waiting for word from on high that they could get cracking again felt like an apt metaphor for the way everything else was going. It wasn't as if there was any particular *reason* they'd ever found for Paige and Luke's ongoing infertility. If she'd been diagnosed with a dodgy uterus or Luke's swimmers weren't making it to the finish line, well, it would have been awful, but the fact that they both kept getting clean bills of health but had a fat lot of nothing to show for it was infuriating.

Deep down, she knew phoning would be pointless. There'd have been something in the news if clinics were allowed to start booking appointments again, but if she didn't keep checking it felt like that would be a prelude to giving up altogether. For once in her life, she wanted *something* to be fair. Was a dollop of justice too much to ask for?

Her phone pinged with a reminder, and it was a relief for Paige to shake herself out of her funk. No time to call now. She'd do it tomorrow, probably. As the *tech-savviest* member of the council, also known as one of the few below retirement age, she'd been designated meeting master general. The veiled secrets of Zoom were far beyond the capabilities of poor Frank. It would be a miracle if he had both camera and microphone on from the start of the meeting.

In a horrible way, the pandemic was proving to be a real boost for Paige's other agenda. Somehow, not being able to meet anyone indoors for the foreseeable placed something of an emphasis on making the outside world as nice as possible. The wildflower verges had proven to be such a hit that she was almost certain she could push the communal garden through without too much strain. At least she was able to get *some* stuff achieved in her life.

She hit the meeting link and texted Jamil to place a bet on how long it would take Quentin to realise proceedings had been underway without him noticing. He didn't seem to understand that wearing the headphones he permanently had around his neck might help. Jamil was reigning champ at their little game and Paige was determined to beat him. You had to find your fun somewhere in the middle of all the unprecedented times that kept piling up.

JULY

Annie

GETTING JULIET TO MOVE in had been such a mistake. Not just because it felt like Annie had been rushing things. Or even forcing a level of intimacy they hadn't earned yet. As much as anything else, it left Annie wondering what came next, if she should leave things for longer rather than accelerate them along the timeline. She had no idea, never having made it past this point before.

Living with a girlfriend was her dead end. Idle conversations about the future – marriage, kids, a joint account – never became serious. How did other people manage it? Paige and Luke had got engaged after Russell's wedding. In contemplative moments, Annie found herself scheming to get Margaret down the aisle to see if that would work some magic in her own love life.

Confidence came so easily at work. Even at a Covid-imposed distance, Annie was killing it. People trapped in their own houses were a boon for extension planning and the like. And staring out the window at the blank-faced monstrosities they were putting up over the road and calling new-builds was feeding her creativity. An excellent example of what not to do. She could take her opportunities to enhance and update and take confidence in a job well done.

At work, she knew everything she had to do down to the smallest detail, her grasp of what she wanted to get done and how to make it happen was clear. But in relationships… things became so much blurrier. Partners refused to stay in their neat little boxes, defying classification and maintaining an annoying level of free will.

Having forced her hand early on, she felt like her problem was trying to pin things down. One of her problems. Juliet was with her, what Annie ought to have been doing was to continue to try and enjoy the moment rather than worry about the future. It wasn't as if her girlfriend was the type to instigate deep meaningful conversations about where they were heading. The children question kept plaguing her, making Annie so many kinds of unsure about what she wanted.

The extraordinary times they were mired in weren't helping, they made her all types of insecure about what else might be coming. Living in the horrible moment, that was all she could do. But the paranoia wouldn't shift, her sense that something was wrong wouldn't go away.

She was becoming someone she didn't recognise. An ugly person, driven by mistrust and jealousy to the brink of outright insanity. Everything tipped over into the black waters when Annie found herself checking Juliet's phone. She had to know, that was all, if there was anything to justify her suspicions.

When she found it, an odd sense of calm descended. She drifted towards the kitchen, where Juliet was halfway through a bowl of cereal, as if it were any other morning. If she didn't ask the question burning in her chest, she'd implode. The calm seemed to have left in quite the hurry.

"Who's Nikki?"

"Oh, someone I've been texting. Think we might even meet face to face." Juliet smirked. "To start with."

So matter of fact. So… callous. As if Annie had asked something innocuous, rather than levelling an accusation. It was impossible for her to get the words out, but the devastation on her face was writ large enough to do the talking for her.

Juliet had the grace to look somewhat surprised in response. Her raised eyebrows drove slivers of icy doubt under Annie's skin. Was her righteous indignation misplaced? Juliet… she *had* been hiding it, hadn't she? Annie didn't know what to believe anymore.

"We never said we were exclusive, love."

Clinging to the word love like a life raft, Annie scrambled for compelling arguments. They'd never said it to each other, but did they really have to? It was everywhere in… in all the…. In everything.

"You're my girlfriend. We… we live together. I've never felt like this before." The last sentence was a whisper unbearable in its feebleness to her ears. If she'd thought the weakness in her tone was hard to stomach, the melting sympathy on Juliet's face plumbed new depths of insufferable.

"You are such a kind, sweet thing." With a condescending giggle, she shook her head. "Silly. That was to stop me from going stir crazy, you said so. And you're the one who promised me we'd just be flatmates." That annoying, sexy little smile that made Annie's heart do a belly flop crept across Juliet's face. She still had all the power. "The best kind of flatmates. Ones with benefits. Why would you want to stick another label on it?"

"But—"

It was almost a blessing that Juliet laughed and shook her head in disbelief before Annie could figure out how to finish her sentence. "I don't know why you're making such a big deal out of this. You didn't seem to mind that I was going out with someone else when we met."

Annie's eyebrows furled together as she puzzled out what Juliet was saying. When the penny dropped, having taken far longer than it should have, her eyes widened. "You and Kitty? You weren't, I mean… you said you were hanging out."

And that was all it took for the pity to return to Juliet's expression. Annie was the lowest of the low, not a partner in a relationship, but a desperate supplicant crawling at Juliet's feet.

"Exactly, hon. Casual. Not getting too hung up on anything. That's how these things are supposed to go. I thought you and I were on the same page about this. I'd never have…"

There was a crack in Juliet's composure as she pushed a hand through her hair. Maybe she wasn't being quite as cruel as it seemed. The fissures in Annie's heart yawned open. Giving the woman who was ripping it out the benefit of the doubt was debilitating.

"I don't want to settle. Settle down, I mean. Not yet. Maybe not ever."

Whether it was a Freudian slip or the plain truth, Annie knew in that moment that whatever it was she and Juliet had, an arrangement, a relationship, something a heartbeat away from a sugar mummy-baby setup, it was over. Unsalvageable. Dead. The pandemic had created an artificial extension of what they had. A chance for Annie to cling onto someone determined not to be pinned down. It had always been a matter of time before Juliet pulled away altogether. And, deep down, Annie had known that. There was a reason browsing for engagement rings online had never turned into an actual purchase.

"I want someone who thinks that being with me, just me, isn't settling."

It was Annie's turn to be the one to stop the other from speaking. Before Juliet could offer anything in her defence, Annie shook her head. "Lockdown's over. For now. I think you should take advantage of this window of opportunity and go."

It wasn't Juliet's fault that she was more than happy to follow Annie's advice.

All along, Juliet made Annie feel breathless, daring. She'd wanted more of that sensation in her life, forever. Translating it into the everyday was so much trickier than she'd expected. It took hours, minutes even, for her to crave Juliet's company. It was the most obvious thing in the world to Annie for her to try and get more Juliet into her life. But having to consciously catch your breath all the time could be exhausting.

*

Annie couldn't bring herself to hate Juliet for how everything had panned out. Not truly. Yes, she'd lied to Annie, by omission. Maybe what Juliet did had only morphed into outright deception because Annie had been so keen to look the other way, to convince herself she was in something far more real than it was. It was for the best that she hadn't told her family about any of it.

At the end of the day, Juliet had used Annie for her home and her heart and even her body. She'd been much too accessible to someone prepared to take advantage of what she was offering. But when Annie took the time to think about it, she couldn't claim that the level of deceit had been anything other than skin deep. She had been so desperate for something serious that she'd latched onto the first good thing that came along, convincing herself she could force the pieces to fit if she was prepared to try hard enough.

She'd been downright giddy about exploiting a global pandemic, looking past all the lives lost and vulnerable people blighted, to try and keep her and Juliet together. Juliet wasn't innocent. She deserved some of the blame for what had happened between them, but the real loathing was something Annie had to reserve for herself. It was all her fault.

SEPTEMBER

Annie

ANNIE WAS LONG ENOUGH in the tooth to know that believing she'd never love again was a little juvenile. Teenage angst and heartbreak didn't suit someone approaching forty in a hurry. She couldn't afford to go to pieces over the break-up. What she hadn't expected post-Juliet was an utter fixation with sex. Juliet had got her hooked and whisked away the supply. Withdrawal hurt.

All Annie could do was redirect her focus. She used to think her crushes came at random, a lucky dip across the sexual spectrum. But she'd developed an appreciation for the way her libido, now raging, seemed to respond to her emotional needs. At least something within her had some semblance of emotional intelligence. Couldn't hang onto a girlfriend, but her rampant longing didn't have to satisfy itself by zeroing in on lookalikes.

After Juliet, the idea of being with another woman any time soon was draining, debilitating. To the point of actual nausea. So, Annie's subconscious was doing its level best to help by serving up imaginary beefcakes on a platter. They were diversions from her Juliet-less misery, uncomplicated departures from memories of lithe beauty. Which explained why Annie's male fantasies weren't trending along their usual

Matt Smith slash Cumberbatch tendencies, nerdy whippets and their ilk. It had all gone in a young Nathan Fillion direction of late — strictly his turn in *Firefly* rather than *Buffy* — a vision of manhood with a touch more muscle than Annie was used to, but far more than she could ever imagine on her ex.

Being with women always felt like… home. It was enough that, every now and then, she had to question if she was kidding herself about her bisexuality. Juliet poking her fingers into the cracks hadn't helped. Many a lesbian had rolled their eyes at Annie for voicing such thoughts, waiting for her to wake up and smell the power tools.

But it was just a different experience when she was with a man. Less complex. More in the moment. And sometimes that was what a heartbroken girl needed. Wanting something casual was unlikely to be a problem with guys. She'd never had any problems with that sort of thing.

It was only a matter of time before she acted on her new feelings.

*

Mere weeks later, Annie lay back on the bed with John – Hugh? No, Kyle. Matt, definitely Matt. Something monosyllabic and a little predictable – sliding his knee between her thighs. As he did so, she became aware of something else in the room.

An imaginary Juliet sat in the corner, her legs tucked underneath her in a way that shouldn't have been possible with the stack of rejected outfits piled high on top of the chair she was on. Annie hadn't been confident enough in her ability to pull to tidy up before she'd headed out for the night. Juliet was looking distractingly sexy in a lab coat and glasses, taking notes, criticising poor Matt's technique even though the man hadn't had anything like a decent chance to get going.

You were always the one obsessed with this possibility, Annie thought to the vision. Where else would Juliet, or at least a version of her, be when Annie was finally getting ready to dick down? It was too distracting. She was almost laughing in the middle of supposed passion, not the most effective of aphrodisiacs when the other person in the room wasn't in on the joke, and she could tell that whatever this was with poor Chris or whoever wasn't going to work.

By the time she made her excuses to a baffled and disappointed mystery man, Juliet's grin had grown to Cheshire cat proportions while she furiously scribbled down reams of supporting evidence for her Annie-isn't-really-bi hypothesis.

But Juliet wasn't the only one who could indulge in the scientific method. If at first you don't succeed, change a control factor or three. Annie's solution for the next night was to get blackout drunk before getting her back-to-boys cherry popped. Such a role model for the children.

More than anything, she understood why she wanted men right now. With them, she could be in charge. So much less uncertainty in the transaction between them. Annie was the one setting the terms and those didn't have to go any deeper than the surface level. There was a certain irony to the new arrangement. Wasn't this the precise sort of thing Juliet had wanted? It was easier to get where she was coming from, without worrying about the future. Annie was finding it far easier to have the kind of authority over men that Juliet had wielded over her with such ease.

She didn't remember much the next morning, but there'd been a sexy little masculine grunt from her chosen partner for the evening as he plunged into her. His face might remain a mystery until morning, but that noise was enough for Annie to know that she was back in business. From then on, the sky was the limit.

NOVEMBER

Annie

HER PHONE DINGED. YOUR period may start today. It was almost enough to make her growl. The stupid thing was such a tease. She'd had the same notification for the past four days and did she have the smallest spot of blood in her knickers to show for it? Of course not. It was odd though, the last time she'd been this late it had been thanks to that working hours nightmare at the office when Oscar had taken on one too many new clients and made the whole team suffer for it.

Oh god. She was an idiot. A ridiculous cliché of a blithering simpleton not in command of her reproductive functions. In her eagerness to get over Juliet, Annie had forgotten her pre-GCSE biology. What happened when a mummy and a daddy loved each other very much or a heartsick bisexual downed too much Sambuca, engaged in several weeks' worth of athletic sex, and got a bit sloppy with the old protection?

She couldn't be pregnant.

One test could be a false positive. Or faulty. Two, even, could be chalked up to a weird fluke that could be laughed about later. But Annie was leaning hard into the romcom trope of a clueless woman as she stared at the five test strips. All positive. Ten stark lines peering up at her.

What would Juliet make of this development? Annie tried to imagine what it would be like with Juliet crammed in the bathroom with her, leaning against the bath as Annie hunched on top of the toilet, lid down, staring at the positive pregnancy tests resting on the windowsill like live grenades. If Juliet were here, would that turn this moment of bewilderment into one of joy?

Annie looked away from the test strips, tears in her eyes. It hurt to realise how much she thought about her ex, how much she still cared about Juliet's opinions and judgements about her life. Children were one of the many things that had split them apart, after all. Well, it was one of the reasons Annie knew they'd never make it long term, even without the cheating. As much as anything else, she had picked a future with potential babies in it rather than chase after Juliet.

As she washed her hands, Annie tried to get a handle on her breathing. It was all coming on much too fast. She fought the urge to sweep all five sticks into the bin, pretend she'd never seen them, never had the realisation. But she knew she had to hang onto at least one, prove that this was really happening.

By all rights, Annie should have been thinking about the baby themselves. Wow, baby. Weird. Or the father. She was almost certain she knew which of her assorted conquests had hit the jackpot. With any luck, which seemed to have deserted her altogether, she could prevent this from morphing into a *Jeremy Kyle* scenario.

But the moment she stopped thinking about Juliet, she was consumed by thoughts of her sister. Would Paige ever forgive her for getting pregnant? At all, let alone like this? Every time she had talked to Paige about her romantic woes, which in all fairness hadn't happened much of late what with the delicacy of the Juliet situation, she couldn't miss the small flare of relief in her sister's eyes.

Paige's logic wasn't difficult to decipher. In her mind, a stable partnership meant it was only a matter of time before the question of babies reared its head. An uncoupled Annie meant she was in a safe box, not getting pregnant any time soon, not betraying Paige and blindsiding her with a baby from unexpected quarters.

The intrusive thoughts of her little sister served as a distraction for Annie from the biggest question of them all. She was clutching the surviving test strip in her hand, almost afraid to let it go. Did she *want* this baby in the first place? Maybe she could take care of this problem without ever having to tell anyone about it, Paige included?

But then, it couldn't be a secret forever, could it? If Annie had an abortion, it would come to light someday. That was how these things worked. Forget romcoms, this was telenovela logic. And when the truth came out, which treachery – the pregnancy or the lie about the way it ended – would be deemed greater by a wounded Paige?

What if… it was madness. One sister desperately wanted a baby and the other…

It wasn't the most conventional of routes to surrogacy, but was it totally out of the question? Annie would never need to go Christmas or birthday present shopping for Paige ever again. It was everything Paige had spent the past few years tearing herself apart for. Annie's son or daughter could become her nephew or niece. Someone else's problem when it came to all the sticky issues.

This way, Annie would get to be the fun auntie she'd been denied the chance to be for so long. They would stay close, this baby. And she would get all the good stuff, the newborn snuggles, chances to stroke that downy soft skin, see those gummy smiles.

She could be there for all of those and still be able to hand the baby back when they wailed, pooed, or got bored. Someone else would be responsible. There was a reason why you wanted two parents at a minimum for the raising of a baby. If possible. It wasn't as if Annie had much of a village at her disposal. Being a mum was such a massive thing.

She could do it. Her phone was in her pocket. It would take next to nothing for her to pluck it out and tell Paige the good news. For half a heartbeat, Annie almost had herself convinced that it was the answer. Until she noticed where her hand was. The one not still holding the test strip. It was rested on her stomach, thumb stroking back and forth. Her body had done this and now it knew what it wanted.

This baby wasn't some bargaining chip, or even a doll that two sisters could share if they were prepared to play nicely. Bit like Luke. Between them, Annie and Paige had everything, but not in a way you could split down the middle. With careful reverence, she went and placed the positive test on top of her chest of drawers. Pride of place.

What if she lost this baby the way Paige had lost hers? The thought was a shower of icy water down the back of Annie's neck. Babies died every single day. The womb was supposed to be the safest place in the world, and they died in there all the time. How could the outside world, with all its sharp corners and incompetent parenting, be any better? They were much too fragile, too many rules involved in the everyday activities of keeping them fed and cleaned.

Why had no one invested time and research into the kangaroo system? Birth them when they're the size of a jellybean, let them crawl up your belly and into a safe warm pouch. Much less trauma for the mother and that way they're out and safe but still with some level of protection. You didn't see kangaroo mothers contorting themselves into pretzels just to get the teat into a joey's stubborn mouth.

When was the earliest opportunity she could book a scan? Just to make sure everything was alright. No sense in letting the cat out of the bag until things were certain. Annie dug out her phone, not to dial her sister, but to find any clinic nearby that would be prepared to give her uterus a once-over before the official NHS scan at twelve weeks.

DECEMBER

Paige

THERE WAS ONE PERSON Paige knew she could rely on no matter what. Her partner in complicity, aiding and abetting her failure to provide Margaret or Russell with any grandchildren. Not to discount Luke's place in the picture, of course. But while Paige's childlessness was down to mysterious biological issues – multiple fertility specialists had failed to identify the root cause of her continued non-pregnant state – Annie's was by choice. It all panned out to the same result though: no babies. And then Annie swanned into Paige's living room with an uneasy look on her face.

"Annie, what's wrong?"

Her mouth twisting into a twinge of something guilty, Annie flopped into a chair. "What makes you think something's wrong?"

Because it was beyond painful how obvious it was. This wasn't a social call, another visit where Annie was just popping by to see how her sister was. Those had dwindled over the years, and, overall, Paige was glad for it. Made her feel like less of a basket case.

Right now, there was news in the offing. And there was no getting around the fact that, by the dull sheen of Annie's face, what she had to say wasn't going to be anything welcome. Was she heading off to join Margaret's escape-from-reality troupe?

"Because I've known you for more than five minutes. Anyone could tell that something's up with you. Spill."

"I'm having a baby."

Thrown by the unexpected declaration, Paige almost jolted out of her chair. Where had this come from? "You're adopting?"

"No. I have a womb of my own, actually. Turns out it works."

"But…" It was so many stripes of unexpected news that Paige didn't have the first clue how to handle Annie's revelation. All her conversations with her sister regarding fertility had been so focused on her own lack of it that she had almost forgotten Annie had the same reproductive equipment she did. In better nick apparently.

"Are you telling me it was immaculate conception or something, Oakley?"

It wasn't a fair question. Annie had always been clear that she was bisexual, rather than an all-out lesbian. When she broke the news, Paige was almost sure she'd heard Margaret mutter something about already having one daughter parading a Sapphic haircut and now this. In practice, Annie only ever seemed to take women home. The serious partners, those Paige had met, Hallie, Beth and Freya, hadn't done much to confound her assumptions either.

Paige had to play nice. "You've got a boyfriend then?"

"Not as such."

Why the hell was Annie being so cagey about all this? It was getting on Paige's nerves. On her own, Annie didn't have everything required to make a baby. Wasn't Paige living proof that even when you had all the constituent ingredients at your command, it could be a lot more complicated than you'd think to conceive?

She sighed. It wasn't as if she'd been the most attentive sibling of late, but it felt now as if she'd missed vast swathes of Annie's life. "So, it's a new girlfriend? This is a huge step though. I'm... I'm missing something, right?"

Sod's law made it possible that Paige could have been experiencing a massive enough lapse in concentration to have ignored a whole burgeoning relationship of Annie's. But for it to have progressed to the point of pursuing artificial insemination together?

Maybe it made sense. Annie knew Paige was having such trouble conceiving the old-fashioned way. And the expensive, high-tech way. Considerate of her not to rub such fecundity in her sister's barren face.

Annie broke Paige out of her thought churn. "No, I mean, yes. You're right. I haven't got a partner of any description now."

"Help me out then. Feels like we're going in circles. Wait, you said now?" Her forehead crumpled and Paige felt like a monster. How much TLC had Annie sent her way in recent years? Why couldn't Paige have given her sister the space to meander to the point in her own time? It seemed that nothing about this conversation was conforming to expectations.

"I... er. Well. I haven't been seeing anyone for a while. And this wasn't planned or anything. There was someone I was with a few months ago. Juliet. And... and I was starting to think that maybe she was, well, the one. But it turns out that was somewhat premature. I don't know why I even went there. It's not like I introduced her to you or Dad or whoever."

It would be cruel not to try and help her along. But with a little bit more gentleness than Paige had been deploying. "I'm guessing this story doesn't come with an especially happy ending?"

"Juliet and I... I guess we wanted different things."

"Children?"

Nibbling her lip, Annie shook her head. "Not as such. I mean, we didn't get into those sorts of conversations. Just wanted to... explain where my headspace was at. I'm not sure I'd have made kids a dealbreaker anyway. I'd never made up my mind when it comes to sprogs." She sighed and rubbed her face. "For her, what she didn't want was monogamy. Commitment to me."

So, Annie had managed to find an Owen of her very own. Someone else who wasn't into "labels". Paige could still remember the moment they'd met, the sheer electricity running through her veins as soon as she'd clocked him at the bar. Every sensible fibre of her being had told her there was no such thing as love at first sight, but something momentous, something immediate and chemical had been going on behind her belly button, drawing her to him.

A swell of sympathy knocked the baby revelation out of her head. How much had she put herself through at Owen's hands for the sake of that instant connection with him? How long would he have strung her along if he'd felt like it? How many years would she have let him?

"Oh, I'm so sorry. That sucks, no two ways about it." And then her thought train caught up with her. "But that still doesn't explain how you're..." she trailed off, unwilling to say the word out loud.

"I, well, I went out a few times to, er, drown the sorrows." There was a distinct amount of uncomfortable shifting going on in Annie's chair.

Raising an eyebrow, Paige dared her sister to continue.

Annie swallowed. "I'm thirty-eight and I got pregnant from a one-night stand."

Jealousy cracked Paige's skull in two with a lightning strike. Briefly, Annie wasn't her sister, her dearest friend. She was a stranger, one of those infuriating women she heard about all too often, those who fell on a penis, almost by accident, and found themselves unexpectedly with child. As if more confirmation were needed that the universe was crammed with random shards of cruel unfairness.

Nothing in life could be expected to be fair, of course, but this snatched every biscuit in the tin. One sister had nothing to show for years of sex timed to within an inch of its life, a raft of expensive vitamins, extensive fertility treatments, and several doctors' worth of opinions, and the other went out and got up the duff with the first stranger she could find. Paige hated herself for the way her thoughts were so wrapped up in what *she* didn't have and how the world was screwing *her* over.

Every pregnancy announcement was a brutal reminder of what she wanted with every fibre of her being. And for this to have come from Annie… it was so much more painful than Paige could have expected. Mainly because she'd never seen this coming.

From somewhere below her diaphragm, she tried to winkle out the last few vestiges of sisterly support she could muster. Just because Paige was the baby of the family, that didn't mean that Annie wasn't deserving of some small return on the extensive emotional buttressing she'd sent Paige's way all her life.

After far too long a silence, she managed to pipe up. "Congratulations, Annie." She was making an assumption, but she didn't think that Annie would have gone about telling her this way if she wasn't intending to keep her surprise bundle.

"Thanks, lovey. I'm… I'm so sorry."

"No," Paige crooned. Her heart was ripping in half, not least because she could see how much hardship she was causing her beloved sister. "Not everything has to be about me, I swear. This is wonderful news. I get to be a proper aunt for once."

The first time a friend had casually referred to her as Auntie Paige had been cute. It didn't take too many repetitions for the novelty to wear thin, for it to feel like an affectation, a consolation prize, rather than something meaningful. But this was a world away from that. A far more genuine connection.

Annie seemed unconvinced by Paige's breeziness.

"Does the father know? I mean... do you, um?"

Maybe there wasn't going to be one. Did Annie even have his number? There was an agonising moment before Annie took pity on her. "Yes, I know who he is. We've... talked. I made it clear I didn't need anything from him, but that I was still planning to go ahead with it."

"Wow." If Paige hadn't already had the greatest respect for Annie, her sister would have it now. She was a badass. "And what did he say?"

Shrugging, Annie leaned back in her seat, one hand unconsciously creeping towards her still-flat stomach. With a twinge in her heart, Paige could remember the way she did the same thing from the moment she'd learned she was pregnant with Button. The knowledge that something was in there acted like a magnet, the urge to protect them strong and immediate.

"I guess I can't blame him for taking me at my word." Annie sighed. "He doesn't want to take any responsibility."

"Oh, Oakley."

"Look, I know it's asking heaps, after everything you've gone through..." Annie took a shuddering gasp. "But it would mean the world to me if I knew that I wasn't alone."

"You're not. Not ever."

"You know what I mean, Peep."

Paige sighed. "I'd be lying if I said I wasn't jealous of you right now. But you're my family. I'll be there for you, every step of the way, whenever you want me. And there's nothing wrong with getting a bit of parenting practice in before I have my own kid."

If she stopped saying things like that, promises about a future where she was going to be a mum, she knew it would be giving the hope up altogether. And she'd developed quite the talent for spotting micro expressions as her limitations at baby making had begun to make themselves apparent to the world. Enough to know that Annie didn't think her sister was going to have a baby of her own anytime soon, if her fleeting wince was anything to go by. But you let things slide for the sake of love.

*

As she so often did in fertility-related matters – or pretty much anything else liable to send her spinning off her axis – Paige went to see Celeste. It was a blessing that Annie had already spilled the beans by text to Russell. Paige could get straight down to unloading what was in her head to a sympathetic audience.

While Russell's head was still spinning, Celeste had been expecting a visit from her younger stepdaughter, no explanations required. The safe harbour was still open for business.

Paige sighed. "She's a *Grey's Anatomy* storyline in the flesh."

"Minus the scalpel?" Celeste quipped.

That made Paige giggle, the first crack of sorely needed levity. "Minus the scalpel," she agreed. "And I don't know which part I'm meant to be playing."

"The supportive sister, or the jealous one?"

Lip quivering, she nodded. "I *want* to forgive her." She groaned and rubbed her cheek. "No, I want to feel like she doesn't even need forgiving in the first place. She didn't do anything wrong. It wasn't even *about* me, or I really hope it wasn't. Pretty inappropriate way for one's sister to get her kicks."

Even though Paige knew she was rambling, she also knew that was alright. In Celeste's presence, it was a relief to feel that it hardly mattered. She'd heard it all before and then some.

Taking a deep, shuddering breath, Paige had to get to the core of what was bothering her. "It's just… after all this, it's as if I don't even believe that pregnancies can really *be* unplanned. My horrible jealous lizard brain keeps whispering that she did this on purpose. Just to hurt me. To… to rub it in my face."

It was a blessed relief when she saw understanding in Celeste's patient smile. She reached out to pat Paige gently on the hand. "It takes a certain set of experiences to make you quite so incredibly aware of your fertile days. The thought that others might get there by winging it when you've put in so much effort is so unfair that you push it all the way out of your mind."

For someone who'd never been through that kind of infertility, Celeste was excellent at putting herself into the mindset. Wasn't much of a leap, Paige supposed. She shouldn't have been at all surprised at Celeste's capacity for empathy. Her days of underestimating her stepmother weren't over. She found herself smiling back at Celeste.

"I do know. Button wasn't. You know. Planned."

"Oh, love."

"I couldn't remember if I'd told you that. I've… I've tried to put it all out of my head. To put it back in the hands of the universe or… or what have you." Paige did her best to keep the eye roll out of her words, knowing how much all that stuff meant to Celeste. It was less than successful. "But it doesn't work."

To her credit, she didn't take the bait. Over the years, as hard as Paige had tried to respect Celeste's assorted woo-woo beliefs, she had in turn been restrained about pressing them on Paige, whose scepticism was obvious.

"When it's all you want, it's hard to make yourself ignore what you know. Like trying not to think about an elephant."

"How do I…" Paige's voice was strangled as she forced the words out. "How do I do this? It's not like she's the first person in my life to get pregnant, but how do I do this when it's so close to home? Did you… have you ever had to go through this?"

Celeste's lips quirked to one side. "I don't have any siblings, so I've never gone through *this* particular scenario, but people do keep on having babies and it's a matter of time until someone close to you ends up pregnant. It's so unfair that this is yet another of the things one has to go through after baby loss. There's no silver bullet to make it all more bearable, I'm afraid."

Disappointed but unsurprised, Paige nodded and waited for Celeste to continue. She looked as if her thoughts needed careful mulling to reach the kind of conclusion Paige needed.

"You take the time to think about what you need from her and ask for it. If it's lots of updates to make sure everyone's still alive, that's fine. Or if it's being there for her by discussing everything but the pregnancy. What is it they say these days? You do you. Anyway, that's plan A. If that arrangement doesn't or can't work, you set your boundaries and go from there."

It was a lot to process. Paige gave a slow nod. "I am worried about her. I can't help it." She sighed. "It's got a bit better, but every time I hear that someone's pregnant, it's like I'm waiting for the other shoe to drop. Even after I've got over the impulse to punch them and say that I hope it's got two heads, I can't settle, can't shake the anxiety until they haven't lost it. Every nine months is so long, and it's not even me."

"After what you've been through, it's natural to have such thoughts."

"Do you have them?"

Celeste laughed. "There have been times when it's felt like I'll always have someone tucked at the back of my mind, a pregnant woman I have to mind for three endless trimesters. Cousins, friends, colleagues, neighbours. There's always someone somewhere expecting a baby. And it's hardest to cope with when they're close."

With her head and her heart as clouded as they were, Paige couldn't stop herself from confessing her next thought. "Someone tells me they're pregnant and I get trapped by all these awful thoughts. It happened to me. Why *wouldn't* it happen to them? Why did it have to be me?" Paige paused, remembering who she was talking to. "Us?"

"Being on the wrong side of statistics hurts. It's understandable to feel hard done by. It's not fair. Nothing will ever make it so."

Being seen wasn't making Paige feel better in the way it normally did. "I don't want to feel that way about my own sister. She's older than me, it's not like I was expecting her to wait until I was there before having children of her own. I… I just…" Her chest was heaving. Paige wasn't sure if she was holding tears back, afraid of how much they were going to hurt, or if this was the start of an unquenchable wave.

"You weren't expecting this. You're married, she isn't. You've been trying so hard, and this was…" Celeste paused, and Paige wondered how her stepmother was going to euphemism her way out of this one. "This wasn't planned." She took a breath before repeating herself. "It isn't fair."

"Preach."

"Are you still thinking about another IVF cycle?"

Mired in despair, Paige couldn't find the words. She knew Celeste's feeling and outlook. The quest for the alternative, the unproven. She'd always sensed a level of resistance from

Celeste about the IVF plans. Not that Celeste ever ventured a negative opinion about it – more like she'd never expected it to work.

Trusting science got more and more difficult as it kept letting Paige down. But she didn't want to give up. Women deserved better testing, earlier, to get more potential answers. And not just because the continued failures were starting to make Celeste's way of seeing the world seem even more tempting.

Without breathing a word of it to her stepmother, Paige had gone to a womb healing session before the last implantation. Just in case. And it still hadn't worked. Went to show that it really was all nonsense. More science, not less, that was the way to make it harder for folk of Celeste's ilk to get a toehold in the same space.

That was the intellectual answer, the one that didn't explain why Paige still couldn't face picking up the phone to the fertility clinic. She couldn't shake the feeling that she'd run out of road. Luke was supportive as always and made it clear that he would follow whatever she wanted, but she could sense the same reluctance in him. Would either of them ever be brave enough to call time?

"I... I want to do another cycle, start over. But I also don't. All this stuff with Annie, it feels like it's... it's like... A sign? A signal? That this is it for me. I don't know if that makes any sense?"

"Keep going." Celeste had her counsellor hat on.

"There's more than one way to have a family. It's a thing people say. It's even something *I've* said more than once." Paige stared down at her fingertips, wiping a phantom stain off her jeans. Anything to keep her eyes away from the burning compassion on Celeste's face. Confessing things to her stepmother helped, but they also made the thoughts inside so much more real. There was also a compelling argument that Luke should be involved in one or two of these conversations.

But her husband wasn't in front of her, and Celeste was there to spill everything to. "Almost in the same breath as hearing that I'm having fertility issues, people raise the subject of adoption, as if it's a new concept to me. But for it to be... for it to work, for them to accept us, you have to believe it. It's... so hard to close the door on trying. Even if there are windows or, or other routes to what we want, it's... we have all the equipment between us. It worked once. After all those tests and so much money, there's nothing wrong with either of us, no reason why trying naturally or the transfers wouldn't work, but there's been *nothing*."

"It isn't fair." Celeste would never be able to say it enough times.

There was nothing else to say. "You're telling me. I... I know why you didn't try again... after Stephen. But do you ever wonder what might have happened if you did?"

"Of course I do. But the what ifs will always find a way to torture you, no matter what path you choose. Never trying again, that was a definite end to everything for me. A guillotine slice to all those dreams I held so dear. But what I can also say is from that moment on, there was a settled sense of expectation to all my tomorrows. Your road... well, that's been another layer of torture on top."

"Just... different, I guess." Paige sighed. "It's the hope that gets you."

"It took the longest time, far more than I ever expected, but in time different forms of what I longed for came to me."

Celeste's meaning slid into place and Paige almost felt like laughing. "That's a terrible lesson. That it took a man to provide you with what you'd always wanted. Getting dangerously close to everything happens for a reason territory.

That if... if it hadn't happened, then you and Stephen might never have—"

"Oh, I didn't say anything like that. Don't you think it's more than clear from the way Stephen and I parted that our marriage wasn't long for the world anyway? He'd have found some excuse to make whatever happened my fault. Getting pregnant. Not getting pregnant. The children falling short of whatever expectations he had. And I didn't fall in love with your father because of his daughters."

"Well good, because that would be creepy."

That earned Paige a conspiratorial smile from Celeste. "If that were the case, you'd have to admire my perseverance."

Paige had the grace to look embarrassed. She'd treated Celeste terribly.

"I think we're past all that. Look, sleep on it. On everything. It's still early days for Annie, plenty of time to adapt to what's happening. And as for trying, you don't have to make any decisions right now."

Her fingers playing with the fabric of the arm of the sofa, Paige could feel her lip trembling. "What if I'm ruining her experience of pregnancy already? Who can relax with their own personal doom fairy hovering in the corner? Hungry-eyed ghost at the feast."

Celeste shrugged. "A small reality check can be helpful. It's not always smooth sailing and knowing how bad it can be lets you know you're not alone when anything happens that isn't textbook. And it's not compensation for not getting to take Rebecca home, but I do like to think I'm an excellent advocate for anyone with doubts about movement or anything requiring medical attention. The worst thing that can happen by a false alarm is that you waste a hospital's time and that's not something you should care too much about. Not when considering the alternative."

Before Paige could think too hard about what Celeste had said, there was a shout from the hall. "We have another visitor."

Please don't be Annie, I can't cope with her yet.

But it wasn't her sister. Russell shuffled into the room with Luke behind him. "Hi, Celeste." He turned to Paige. "You weren't at home, it felt like it was worth checking here before I got too worried. Is everything alright?"

Paige blessed Luke and his radar for trouble. They'd been living this life for long enough that he could detect an emergency Celeste therapy session. She gave a small nod to confirm his suspicions that something was indeed amiss. "Annie's pregnant."

For a horrible moment, she wondered if she should have laid a bit more groundwork, preparing Luke before dumping the news on him. If someone had slapped her in the face with an unexpected pregnancy announcement, it would be enough to trigger a panic attack. But she and Luke didn't have the same reactions to things like that. News of someone else's impending baby wasn't as much of a knife to his heart.

"That's," his face took a while to land on a definite emotion; the fleeting uncertainty and concern were eventually replaced with a hesitant smile, "that's great for her. Right?"

And another trial for us. The guilt of blighting Luke's life like this – not that he'd ever let her frame it that way out loud – prickled at the back of Paige's neck. *This shouldn't be how this is happening. I should have got there first, be able to reassure Annie, lend her a small person to practice her parenting skills on.* It wasn't fair. No matter how many times it was said, it wouldn't be enough.

"I think so. She wants to keep it, anyway."

Luke came to sit down next to her. With a brief sideways glance towards Celeste, he stroked Paige's lower back. "How are you doing?"

"Rather badly, I fear." She sighed. "I'll have a look at eco baby things and get a present for her, vote of solidarity."

"Won't that be hard?"

"It's all hard." Rather than sigh again, she shrugged before leaning into Luke's gentle touch. "We knew at some point there'd be a pregnancy I couldn't get away from. Lucky I've been able to dodge them for this long. I want to do my best for her."

Luke kissed her hair. "We will."

2021

MARCH

Annie

I N SOME WAYS, THE renewed lockdowns had felt like a reprieve from having to face the rest of the world. The November one had given her an excuse to delay announcing the pregnancy by a precious month. At the time, it had felt like a face-to-face conversation, even though she knew Paige's preference for that kind of thing was a text. Gave her a chance to have her reaction in private. Technically, as a single-person household, Annie was within her rights to bubble with someone else. But no time like the present to get in the habit of independence.

New Year had felt so different to 2020 and spending time alone with her painful memories had been a refreshing distraction from her pregnancy concerns. The latest worry was that she wasn't in decent shape. The frown from the midwife when Annie weighed herself at the last appointment was a reminder that while Juliet had darted out for lengthy walks at the drop of a hat, Annie had opted to stay inside and eat crisps.

She didn't want to draw too much attention to why she'd suddenly felt the need to improve her fitness. Rubbing any of the pregnancy stuff in Paige's face felt cruel, but it had started to feel like her sister was always there. Maybe Annie had been hoping that mentioning she needed to go out for a walk would be a good way to escape Paige's company for a while. Instead, they were stomping down the streets together.

"So, you're past the halfway mark. Have you signed up for classes or anything like that yet?"

"You don't really want to talk about this, do you?"

Paige looked surprised. "Who other than my sister can I live through vicariously when it comes to my frustrated dreams of pregnancy?"

Questions batted back and forth. Was Annie making it worse because she couldn't share all the details, gory or otherwise? It wasn't that she was trying to shut Paige out. Everything felt as if it was teetering on a knife edge, not quite real. All she wanted was for the world to leave her alone for this bit. Maybe this was a primal version of nesting, wanting to retreat into a darkened cave while in this vulnerable state.

"Just wanted to wait for a while."

"Fair enough."

She could sense Paige itching to ask more questions. Probably wanting to know when the next appointment was and if she could come. Annie knew she wasn't being fair to her sister. Still, there was a certain level of... not ownership, but something like it from Paige. No, she was making the best of a crappy situation, being as supportive as possible, and Annie couldn't even give her the credit for it. Another surge of guilt lapping through her gut.

And then Paige's attention was somewhere else. For a moment, Annie could have sworn she heard her whisper something to a cat watching them from across the road. Strange, Annie was sure her sister had never been much of a fan of cats before.

It didn't take much to provoke one of Paige's ever-so-fun lectures about how bad for the environment pets could be, especially cats, what with their all-meat diets and predilections for murdering unsuspecting birdlife. In a way, Annie was grateful. Paige was the one thing standing in the way of her loneliness turning her into a hermit cat lady – having a baby was the more eco-conscious way to behave in that respect, right? But did the girl protest too much? Was Paige trying to hide a soft spot the size of Wales for cats?

They didn't talk much more for the rest of the walk, but after Paige deposited Annie back at the flat, she paused before taking her leave. Her smile was gentle, giving.

"You *can* be happy about this." She was almost whispering, but Annie could hear the giveaway crack in her sister's voice, a sign of how much it was costing Paige to say the words. "You don't have to hide it from me. I know, I know how hard it can be for pregnant women around me or I can see what it can do to them. I..." she was blushing a little, "I know I go all yearning – Luke's told me it's almost cartoonish – and it makes them maybe a tiny bit uncomfortable."

She shrugged. "I didn't know what I had until it was gone, and it took me so long to get back to a place where I was ready to start trying again and I didn't see what I'd done until it was too late. God, I'm rambling." She swallowed. "My point is, no one else's pregnancy should be about me. I hate ruining people's buzzes by being a reminder of how easily it can all go away and never come back for no bloody reason."

Annie had to interject. "You're not—"

But Paige was having none of it. She shook her head. "What I'm trying to say is that you can be happy and confident and ready to take motherhood by the balls, because it's coming for you, Oakley. You've only got so much time left to prepare and the last thing I want you to do is have any awkwardness about it because of me. Maybe I'm being a bit self-centred. But I should also tell you that Celeste and I have had words about this and we're doing our best to guarantee that nothing untoward happens to that baby of yours with whatever higher power Celeste's into this week."

A surprised laugh burst out of Annie's mouth as Paige rolled her eyes. On a certain level, Celeste and Paige's relationship these days made all kinds of sense, given what they'd both been through. She was a heartbeat away from being the surrogate daughter Celeste had never been granted. But their friendship was still plagued by that utter personality imbalance. Bonded through loss though they were, it was still amazing that they could cope with so much time together without killing each other. Well, without Paige getting violent at any rate.

Before Annie really thought about what it meant, she was almost jealous. She and Celeste got along fine, always had. Once upon a time they were far closer than Celeste and Paige, but there was an invisible wall between them. One of a different kind than the one between Annie and her actual mother. But she knew she didn't want to join the club Celeste and Paige were in.

After Paige left, Annie stroked the little bump she'd soon be unable to hide. Once spring had sprung, she'd have to put the bulky coats and chunky knitwear away. Wouldn't be too long before this pregnancy had to go public. For now, she could still get away with asserting that the growing belly was just thanks to chips.

JUNE – JULY

Paige

EVERY TIME PAIGE MET up with her sister, she couldn't help giving the growing bump a quick once-over. That was all she allowed herself, training her eyes on Annie's face the rest of the time.

It was an unconscious effort, the way that she automatically knew which week they were in, which milestones they were sailing past. Annie and her baby, vaulting all of them with ease. The first trimester had posed all sorts of anxiety for Paige, so it was quite the relief when Annie reached the "safer" bits of pregnancy. She and Celeste had found week thirty-one especially intense, but even that was fine.

With grim determination, Paige pushed all thoughts of barrenness and infertility out of her skull. This ugly habit of comparing notes wasn't going to do much but drive a wedge between her and her sister. One day, she would have her own baby, by hook or by crook. Going down the adoption route would mean giving up trying the old-fashioned way, but her continued failures in that area were making the prospect of packing it in more appealing.

When her time came, she could be the one in the hot seat, making all the tough decisions. Still, she couldn't quite understand why Annie insisted she didn't want to know the sex. Why wouldn't she want every possible scrap of information as soon as it was available?

There were other things to ask in the meantime. "Who are you thinking you want with you for the birth?"

Annie looked hesitant. "I... I didn't know who to ask. You, you don't have to, I swear."

"Oakley." Paige's voice was firm, keeping out as much reproach as she could. She was being bolstered by her own righteousness, almost sure she could perform this service for her sister. "I'll do whatever you want."

It wasn't as if Margaret would be able to find time in her busy schedule to step up to the plate, not now she'd finally inherited the crown of director. And, in the absence of a firm father figure for Annie Junior, there was an obvious vacancy for Paige to step into.

In the end, she was spared. By promising to do it, she secured a win-win when Annie changed her mind. At the eleventh hour, she'd decided she wanted to do this bit on her own with the medical staff. Maybe she just didn't want anyone who knew her to have to watch her poo on the floor.

Paige had known all along that she'd have to meet a baby she was related to at some point. And that at the rate she and Luke were going, it wasn't going to be one of hers. But none of that knowledge meant that she was ready to meet her niece.

As she strolled along the hospital corridor, not capable of moving at a quicker pace, it felt like she was missing a layer of skin. Everything was too much, too raw. A flood of sensations was ready to engulf her, hurl Paige over the edge, banish her forever from the realm of sanity.

Ultimately though, she knew she'd never be able to forgive herself for shirking her duty towards her sister. It was hard enough that Annie had decided after all that she didn't want her there for the actual birth. If it had been anyone else in the world, Paige might have been able to find some reason to put off this already delayed meeting. But this was a time for family, especially since Annie was insistent that she could handle all of this without a partner by her side.

Not that she'd been left with an abundance of choice in that department. While Mike was on the scene every now and then, a little bit more present than his initial reaction to the news had indicated, sightings of him were the exception rather than the rule. And Annie had been resistant to the idea of dating for the time being. Not in her condition.

Maybe she'd meet another single mum. Somehow, even though Paige knew how this baby had come about, she couldn't picture her sister settling down with a man. With a sigh, she realised she had to face up to the fact that she was trying to distract herself from what was lying in wait for her at the end of the ward. She clutched the teddy bear in her arms tighter.

Shivering with a wave of nausea that had nothing whatsoever to do with pregnancy – impossible at this point in her cycle – Paige commanded herself to get a grip. Once this was over with, the next time would be easier. Her niece would be more than a baby to Paige then. She would be herself. A little human growing up in the world.

When Paige crept into the room, she almost turned right back out again. They were both sleeping. Annie looked so exhausted that all Paige's thoughts about her own pain were chased away. It had been such a long, hard labour, with an epidural that hadn't worked and a tear extensive enough to make anyone wince.

But there she was, nestled in her little box, worth all the struggle to get her there. Libby. Paige was already in love with the name, not least because it had never been on her own list.

"Hello, beautiful."

Even though she had whispered, it was enough to disturb her sister. Paige heard Annie shifting in the bed and turned to meet her sister's dog-tired expression.

"Are you alright?"

Paige's heart twisted. Labour-exhausted Annie was still trying to look out for her. A mother to the core, preoccupied with doing her most to mind the first person she'd had to be responsible for. Even though she should now be so much more concerned about the baby snuggled in the plastic cot next to her bed.

"Shouldn't I be the one asking you that, Oakley?"

"Doesn't have to be a limit on such questions. We can ask each other, can't we?"

"Yeah, but you've got someone else to worry about now. I'm fine." Paige sighed. "I mean, I will be. I've got a niece now, a perfect, scrummy little angel. She's gorgeous."

She meant it. As much as she desperately wanted a baby of her own, looking at Libby didn't inspire the same raging level of jealousy that Annie's pregnancy announcement had. Libby was her own person now, not some totem of the life Paige craved. Being an aunt was going to be fun. Not some consolation prize. Very much its own distinct experience.

"Your time will come."

"I wish I felt so sure."

"There's more than one way to make a family, Peep. Maybe it's time to start looking into other options?"

It was as if Annie could see into her head. They'd talk about the realities of adoption soon, she was sure. It was such a relief to see that layer of tension had sloughed off Annie. She'd been almost brittle for the bulk of the pregnancy. The safe and sound arrival of little Libby had to have been a balm for all involved.

"You mean I should go out to a nightclub, bang a stranger and cross my fingers that something takes?"

"Oh, have some originality. Loses a bit of impact if it's part of a trend. Folk might object, Luke, for instance."

"You might have a point there. Baby timeshare?"

"Get your own."

"I will." Paige leaned over and scooped Libby into her arms, marvelling at the weight of her baby niece. "Can't be so hard if you've done it."

JULY

Annie

THE DOCTORS HAD LET them go home. For the first time since the baby was born, Annie was without any kind of supervision. Sure, health visitors and midwives and, most daunting of all, family members would be stopping by. But for the most part, Annie was on her own with a brand-new whole other human being she was responsible for keeping alive.

No need to get bogged down by all the... everything. One step at a time. First things first. The baby needed somewhere to sleep. Annie had been waiting for the famous nesting instincts everyone had assured her would come to set up the nursery. A sign that the baby was on her way.

But labour had come early, and Annie had missed her moment to make her home welcoming for a new life. It had been difficult enough to stuff everything into the hospital bag in time and even then, she'd made a few glaring omissions. Nappies had been easy enough to get her hands on, a nightie without a massive rip somewhere unfortunate was trickier.

There was so much to do. And Annie wasn't sure how she felt about having to put the baby down to wrestle with flatpacks. Except, it wasn't necessary. Someone had come and assembled everything, folded, tidied, and cleaned, even spirited away the packaging.

She didn't know what to do with her feelings. It was a relief for the job to be done. While she knew she should appreciate, at a minimum, the kind gesture someone had made for her, Annie couldn't help but wonder if her nearest and dearest had just decided she couldn't put a cot together. And she wouldn't have even thought to put it there. She'd been picturing it against the far wall, but under the window, with the sunlight streaming down onto it, looked perfect. Why was it so much better than her plan?

She was besieged by waves of helplessness, each one slamming her back down before she could scramble to her feet after the last. She didn't know what to *do* with the baby. Her judgement was so shaky and unsound. Before she'd even been born, Annie was so busy making all the wrong decisions. The last thing she'd been sure about was Juliet and look how that panned out.

So much of the pregnancy had felt like some weird simulation, as if it were happening to someone else or in a different dimension. It was so much easier to avoid preparations. And now Annie wasn't sure how to get through all the hours before the next visit from someone who knew what they were doing.

When she looked down at that tiny, wrinkled face, a far cry from what "newborns" looked like on telly, Annie didn't feel that rush she'd been promised. If love was lurking somewhere at the bottom of her heart, it was drowned out by too many other emotions.

What had she been thinking? Annie wasn't cut out to be a mother. There was a reason she'd been so drawn to Juliet, someone who didn't want children at all. If Annie deserved motherhood, then someone else would have come along to share the experience with her. If her baby could have two parents, two mothers, it wouldn't matter so much if one of them was deficient.

She'd been so selfish, so... so up herself. Run away with the romantic idea of being a single parent. Why had she talked herself out of giving the baby to Paige? Her sister was the one who deserved a baby. Or Celeste. Not Annie.

The full truth slammed into her with the wet thud of a sodden sandbag. An accident. Libby wasn't meant to be here. Paige had lost her child. Wouldn't the world have been so much simpler if Libby had gone the same way? If Annie had found a different way to salve her heartbreak, puzzles or something, then a whole entire person wouldn't have been created. It wasn't meant to happen. How could she have done this? How could she ever explain it to Libby?

Food. That might help. Maybe the same nursery-assembling fairy had been kind enough to stock the fridge.

Day one home alone was off to a flying start.

*

The baby was crying. Again. Was it colic? No, didn't fit the criteria according to Google. Not yet. This time, Libby was the one having some feelings and nothing Annie could do seemed to soothe her. One of the forums suggested skin-to-skin contact might help. Something else she hadn't thought of.

She had zero instincts for any of this. It felt like she was spending half her day on the internet, scouring it for advice because none of her impulses were the least bit helpful. Maybe she should call Paige? Oh, that would go down well. New mother wants to complain to her barren sister that things are difficult with an infant.

She had *chosen* this. She deserved every blistering moment of motherhood because she was waving it in the faces of the bereaved parents in her life, those with aching arms that hadn't been filled even after years of trying. It was blind luck that Annie had blundered her way into this situation.

Everything she did was wrong, and people didn't think she was trying hard enough. The health visitor's disapproving face the other day had made it pretty obvious that Annie was clueless. Not enough to be dangerous, or the health visitor wouldn't have left, or she would have done and someone else would have been round to confiscate Libby, but it was obvious that she was making such a mess of this.

Her eyes flicked towards the clock, and she felt like sobbing. It took nothing at all to make her cry these days – this was a household of copious tears – but this took the biscuit. Libby was straining to feed, and Annie's concentration was splintering. The realisation that it was 9 a.m. and not p.m. was crushing. How was it that there was still so much day to get through?

This was fine. It had to be normal. It would pass, right? Even though it felt endless? This was how it was supposed to be.

By lunchtime, her tiny vestiges of energy were sapped. Cooking was beyond her, and she'd run out of ready meals. Even though she knew she was going to make one or other of them ill with her new weakness for Haribo, she broke open a new packet for the sake of something to do, stuffing it into her face one-handed with Libby draped across her other arm.

Annie missed work so much. It was so silly, so childish, as if she were wishing to sit and draw make-believe houses, scribble and colour in, rather than doing the vital work of raising her own daughter. Maternity leave seemed like such a long interminable stretch ahead of her and when she got to the end of it, what if she couldn't afford childcare? What if she could never go back to work?

Bad mother. That was what she was for wishing this time away. What if a sinister genie could hear her thoughts and decided to take her seriously? She had to get a grip. Annie was good at her work. It made sense she'd hanker after it. How many years of hard graft had she put into becoming an architect? And now she didn't know for sure when she was going to get back to it.

It had taken over a year and a handful of huge life changes, but she was finally beginning to understand Juliet's frustrations when she was isolated from her old life, locked up with only Annie for company. Everyone left her at the first opportunity. What if Libby did the same thing?

Was that what it all kept coming back to? It was the trifecta. Celeste had lost a baby early and a baby late. Paige had lost one early and now didn't seem to be able to make another. There was no earthly reason why Annie should be allowed to have all the luck her sister and her stepmother had been denied. Why hadn't she realised that clearing all the early hurdles meant that something else had to be going on? She'd just been setting herself up for greater pain later in the day.

The universe, big salty expanse of boundless cruelty, craved novelty in its repetitive patterns. Libby, sweet, innocent baby girl who hadn't had a chance to do anything to anyone at this point, was destined to die to close the loop. How had Annie not seen it before? What would she do if Paige worked it all out? Was that why she hadn't already tried to snatch Libby for herself? Was her sister waiting for her niece to die so she could have a chance to have her own baby?

Breathing shouldn't be this difficult.

AUGUST

Annie

I T WASN'T MEANT TO be like this, was it? Libby smiled at Annie for the first time. Not trapped wind, not a tentative testing out of the muscles. A genuine smile. Where she'd learned to do that trick, Annie had no clue. With such a dull, joyless mother plagued by all these doubts and anxieties, Libby was bound to be at risk for all sorts of developmental delays. And yet, a smile. Bang on schedule.

These thoughts couldn't be normal. The joy was supposed to have arrived by now. Something was wrong. Some terrible sense of foreboding weighed down, so heavy that Annie had to keep reminding herself to breathe.

This had to stop. She couldn't keep feeling like this. The one thing standing in the way was that she couldn't figure out what to do about it. She could never hurt Libby, not on purpose, no matter how much she was afraid that she was going to. Her mind wouldn't switch off, wouldn't let her rest, wouldn't let things ease off for even a second and allow normality to trickle back in.

She needed to talk to someone. Someone who'd been through all this. Well, maybe not *this*, but something similar. A mother. Mara had been her port of call in Paige's time of need, but Annie didn't want to bother her now. About a week after Libby was born, Mara's father had collapsed in the middle of the supermarket and now she was buried in probate. The inevitable fate of an only child.

And talking to Mara would make all this real. She was too… too close. Too able to swoop in if she felt the need. And if Mara felt the need to take command, what did that mean about the trouble Annie was in?

So, in the absence of any other contactable mothers she could come up with, hers would have to do. There was no way Margaret was going to do any swooping anytime soon. She hadn't even been to visit. Rehearsals were far more pressing than the arrival of her first living grandchild.

"Annie, how lovely to hear from you. I'm a little bit busy now, but I'm sure you must be too. We can make this a quick one, can't we? So, how are you getting on, darling?"

"It's… hard." The words were impossible to get out.

"Oh, well. Anyone who ever told you this would be easy was either lying or selling you something. All you can do is keep calm and carry on until nap time." She tittered, pleased with herself.

Margaret wasn't understanding her. For all that she'd been afraid of the idea of someone intervening, what if… what if that was what she needed? "Mum, I'm scared. I… I don't know what to do. I keep picturing awful things. Like her drowning in the bath or, or…" She choked back a sob.

But Margaret cut through the tearful confession before Annie could give away any more of the secret feelings she'd been clinging onto. "That's perfectly normal, sweetheart, nothing unusual there. We've all been there. Protection mechanism. It would be more worrisome if you *weren't* a little concerned about that sort of thing. Everything gets a bit desperate for a while, but it will settle. Let her cry it out for a bit, have a nap yourself, and everything will look much better afterwards. Of course, in an ideal world, you could hand her off to the father – not that yours ever really pitched in back in the day, but these are more modern times. Anyway, I'm sure you can make do."

She could hear what Margaret wasn't saying, loud and clear. She'd chosen this. Against all advice and better judgement, Annie had opted to become a single mother. She'd gone ahead and had a baby all on her own, sacrificing the luxury of being able to complain about the consequences of her decision-making. Rather than whinge on the phone to her mother, Annie was supposed to be pulling up her big-girl pants and making do with what she had.

At least the dreaded intervention wouldn't be coming. Maybe the second true smile would inspire some of that motherhood glow. This couldn't be depression. It was normal. Why did no one talk about any of these awful bits of trying to have children? Probably because if everyone knew it was nothing but death and disaster, no one would go through with it.

AUGUST

Paige

"YOU ALRIGHT?"

The tossing and turning had to be a bit of a giveaway. Especially if it had bothered Luke enough for him to ask. Paige sighed. "Just... worried about her."

"Which her?"

In the darkness, she paused, considering the question. Not that it needed much thought. A lot of the anxiety about Libby had receded after the birth. Now Paige was worried about her sister. Annie was shutting her out.

"Annie. Definitely Annie. Libby's got enough people in her corner. She... she doesn't seem like herself. I know that motherhood changes you, but this feels like something a bit more... serious? I don't know."

"Go and check on her then."

"What, right now?"

"Yeah, roll out of bed and storm over to your sister's in the middle of the night, wake them both up and demand to know if it's baby blues."

Baby blues? Paige's worries about Annie had been pretty non-specific until that moment. Now she had to wonder why she hadn't considered the possibility of postpartum depression. Luke had done his homework. The thought of it gave her a small twinge of regret. But now wasn't the time to address it.

"I don't want to interfere." The excuse sounded pathetic. "You're not helping."

Luke cuddled Paige closer under the covers. "Course I am. You're just not sure what advice you want to hear. Seems like someone telling you what to do isn't what you're angling for."

Why did he have to keep making such good points? Wonderful, practical man. It was like when they were dropping off all that food at Annie's and Luke spotted the still boxed-up nursery furniture. He was like a kid on Christmas morning, getting to use his pocket screwdriver.

"It's more like… well, after we lost Button, Annie knew exactly what to do. What would help. I don't know where to start here." The distance between Paige and the mothers of living children in her life stretched like a yawning gulf. She didn't have a Mara she could appeal to for wisdom.

"Tell you what, we'll pop round to Annie's in the morning. See if there's anything either of us can do to help."

"I love you."

Luke kissed the back of Paige's head. "Damn right."

AUGUST

Annie

ANNIE WANDERED OUT OF the doctor's surgery trying to feel relieved. How did she keep getting away with this? Somehow, she'd managed to convince Paige and Luke that everything was alright, she had a check-up to get to, so would they please let her get to it? Everything was fine. The baby was healthy. Annie's stitches were looking good. There were zero causes for concern, so what else could she have said when the GP asked if there was anything more?

Why did everyone feel the need to congratulate her on having such an easy baby, smiling down at Libby as she cooed contentedly in the carrier? None of it seemed easy to Annie. Here she was, on the lowest difficulty setting, it seemed, and she was still drowning. It was like this for everyone, right?

All the conflicting advice rolling in didn't help. The GP had promised a referral regarding breastfeeding, somehow ignoring the pleading look in Annie's eyes. Breastfeeding seemed to hurt her and Libby both so much that she was desperate for someone to tell her that she could stop. Supplementing with formula could just turn into a full-time thing.

It was her fault. Her mother had told her as much. She had insisted she could do it all alone, there was no need for her to depend on any opinion other than hers. Women all over the world did it all the time.

But Annie couldn't. She resented the baby. Everyone was obsessed with her and barely cared about Annie's needs at all. Even the doctor. All those questions about Libby and by the time they asked anything about Annie, she'd lost her nerve to say anything about the heaving mass of dark thoughts lurking in her brain. They'd take Libby away, and Annie was afraid that she almost wanted that to happen.

What if they were going to take Libby anyway? That had to be Paige's plan. She'd only offered to watch Libby so Annie could have a bath, or whatever bit of supposed self-care she'd suggested, because she wanted to have the baby all to herself. She was so desperate for a baby of her own that she could have so easily decided to take her sister's. They were family already. Who would notice the substitution of mothers?

The ragged breaths firing themselves out of Annie's chest added to her panic. She had to hide. People on the street might be watching this breakdown. Couldn't give them any more ammunition, to compel them to move faster in snatching her child away.

*

It was like a bad dream. She kept coming back. With reinforcements. First with Luke and now with their father and Celeste.

As Celeste guided her towards the sofa, Annie wanted to scream. What made it worse was watching, helpless, as Paige scooped Libby out of the carrycot. She looked so natural. Heart heavy and head fuzzy, Annie tried to focus on what her stepmother was saying.

"We're concerned about you."

Annie waited for her to say something else. Something she could deny. But the patient sympathy in Celeste's eyes was close to unbearable.

"It's… it's fine. We're getting by. Doctor says everything is fine. My daughter is healthy."

"It's not a judgement on anything you're doing, love. I know that this is a difficult time, especially when you're doing it all on your own. There's a difference between coping by the skin of your teeth, holding it all together until something cracks and it's too late to ask for help, and taking my hand now because you know it's what you and Libby need."

How could Annie admit that she just wanted it all to stop? Her treacherous eyes were already welling up, betraying how close to the mark Celeste was getting.

She hesitated before speaking again. "I… I remember what it's like not to want to live. Not to die. But if there'd been something more passive than that, it would have been so tempting. To have a chance to be with my babies again… that was everything. Having to carry on in a life where they weren't was hard, but…" Celeste trailed off, eyes wet. "Depression doesn't need an excuse to come and bite you. It can come for anyone in this position."

A surge of something bitter sank its teeth into Annie's throat. This was torture. "J-just because you've had it worse than me, just because you didn't get your chance, that doesn't mean you know what's happening here. If it was possible to guilt me into responsible parenting, don't you think it would have happened by now?"

Annie was tired, that was all. That was why she was being quite so awful to Celeste. She didn't mean what she was saying. But she didn't have the energy to say so.

Maybe Celeste could tell. Her expression hardened, but not by much. "No, it has nothing to do with a guilt trip. Listen to someone who's been there before—"

The next words were out of Annie's mouth before she could help it. Celeste's experiences, though terrible, had no relevancy to her situation. "You haven't—"

"No, I haven't." Celeste agreed. "I've done the postpartum bit though, without the baby. I didn't have anyone to worry about but me. And I had to go through this without a partner either. There might be more of an overlap than you might think. I had to keep an eye out for the signs of depression all on my own."

When Annie burst into tears, she knew it was over. Celeste would turn her in to whatever authorities had jurisdiction, get them to take the baby away, maybe even give Libby to Paige and have done with it. They were a club, Celeste and Paige. And yet her stepmother was here with her arms around Annie. It was all so confusing.

"We need to get you some help, my love. Are you ready for that?"

Miserably, Annie nodded. There was no point in fighting it anymore.

"It's all going to be okay. Libby isn't going anywhere. We'll make sure she stays with you no matter what."

Maybe all those crystals had power after all. Celeste was a witch. Mind reader.

After that, there was a lot of talking in hushed whispers, excluding Annie from the decisions everyone else was making. She sat in a sad little huddle, hoping it would all go away, even though it was what she'd wanted.

She became aware of Paige's hand resting lightly on her shoulder.

"Why did you do this?"

There wasn't a shadow of doubt in her mind that this was all happening because of her sister. Paige refused to take her word for it that she was alright and now she'd gone and got more people involved. Annie's only confusion was whether she was grateful or resentful of Paige's behaviour.

"Oakley, you came and sat with me in the hole when that was what I needed. It was *everything*. Will you let me do that for you?"

"What? That's... I mean, it's not, like... you *told*."

Paige's eyes were swimming. "We want to help. That's all. I swear," she whispered.

If only Annie could believe that. "You're trying to take her away from me." More than anything else, she wished she hadn't made it so easy for Paige to get what she wanted.

An expression of horror stemmed the tide of tears. "I know whose daughter Libby is. Even if I wanted her to replace B..." her chest was heaving, "that would never happen."

"Just get out!" Annie couldn't bear for her younger sister to see her like this. The tide of tears surged over her. She was certain they'd never stop now they'd started.

AUGUST

Paige

SINCE ANNIE STILL DIDN'T trust Paige and was worse when they were in a room together, a divide and conquer approach was devised. Celeste, having handed over the shop keys to her assistant manager, moved into Annie's flat to give more day-to-day support and dragged her back to the GP to talk about treatment options.

It killed Paige to have to keep her distance, but she had to respect her sister's wishes. Since sleep was part of Annie's prescription, there were opportunities to help with the baby while Annie was out of it. While Paige appreciated getting more time with her niece, her sister's health was a terrible trade.

"Is it harder for you with girls?"

Celeste looked up at her. Libby raised her chubby fist and Celeste smiled down at the baby in her arms. "I suppose it used to be. Well, in so many ways it still is. The fellow loss parent friends I made were kind enough to have boys at first. By the time Hannah had Bethany, it was all a little bit easier to cope with girls. Or at least I'd had some extra time to process. But with any baby I hold, every single one since Rebecca left my arms, I know they're not her. The tiny little pieces of her that I remember, the things I'm sure about, they're reinforced whenever I hold another baby. None of them are her. Even the girls."

What Celeste was saying hit home. Babies didn't replace babies, Paige knew that. Her expression must have said as much as Celeste gave her a lopsided smile.

"Maybe it's because I've never held another dead baby. It's a very different experience when they wriggle around. Even sleeping, there's no mixing them up. And the curve of little Libby's nose, hugely different to Becky's. She looked like Stephen when he was asleep. Really, I should thank him for leaving me. I didn't have to see her face in his ever again, stirring up all those memories."

Paige looked at her niece. "Whatever else we can say about her appearance, we can count our blessings that Libby doesn't resemble a middle-aged man."

"No." The smile on Celeste's face shrank. After a cautious pause, she locked eyes with Paige. "She looks quite a lot like you, or at least that's what I think. Makes me think of that picture of you girls that your father has in the guest bedroom."

"The one from Christmas where I'm trying to pretend that I'm not on the verge of throwing a strop because Mum bought me the wrong Beanie Baby? Not at all a spoilt high-maintenance child."

"Of course not." Celeste paused. "How is it for you, looking at her?"

"Well, I know Libby's not Button either. We'd have to hope that they got a bigger share of Luke's genes. I... I suppose it's nice that there's a baby in the world who takes after me."

Celeste draped an arm around Paige. "I'm not going to say don't give up. I'm just going to reaffirm quite how unfair this all is on you. You're being very brave, my girl."

Resting her head on Celeste's shoulder, Paige did her best to hold the tears back. "Did we do this?"

"What do you mean?"

She wondered if she should even be saying this out loud, let alone if Celeste was the right person to voice these thoughts to. The guilt was weighing her down too much not to talk about it though. "Were we both so focused on what can go wrong before birth that we completely overlooked this kind of scenario?"

"Heavy use of this 'we' word, dear. But while it's getting bandied around, we both know that parenting isn't the easiest thing in the world even when you've been blessed with a living child." Celeste's smile was wry. "It's hardly a surprise for us to jam someone else's situation through our own warped lens. You saw something, you said something."

"I just, I was so worried about getting her through the pregnancy. It's like I made a wish and didn't think about any of the ways it could backfire."

"For someone who believes in *nothing* spiritual, you have quite the level of confidence in your manifesting abilities."

Paige was almost sure Celeste was joking. With all the nonsense she *was* into, manifesting or whatever wasn't part of that, surely? Did Paige even want to ask?

"I'm overthinking it, aren't I?"

"Maybe a smidge."

"Have I earned a Libby cuddle?"

Celeste laughed and deposited the baby into Paige's waiting arms.

SEPTEMBER

Paige

SOME SUNSHINE WAS IN order. Everyone needed a break, so Celeste and Paige stepped out with the pram while Luke stayed with Annie in the flat and tried not to call too much attention to the fact that they were all still a little bit too nervous to leave her on her own. Not that Annie had ever tried to hurt herself, but the doctors had made it clear that it wasn't a total impossibility.

Paige stopped and smiled. Celeste followed the line of sight and gave a knowing little nod.

"Is it Button?"

Glancing back over at the black cat wedged against a row of iron railings – comfort was such a relative quality – Paige laughed. "No, that's just tabbies. I'd spend all day saying hello to Button if it was all cats. You know how it is."

A long time ago, Celeste had told her about the significance of magpies with regards to Rebecca – and deer for Hart – that they were her children's way of checking in on her. Maybe that was all Paige had needed, permission, to begin thinking the same way. She was never going to subscribe to half the woo-woo stuff that Celeste was into, but even before that conversation, she'd made an independent start on associating Button with cats.

Once she'd allowed for the possibility, there was no turning back. Cats, who somehow didn't seem half so hostile as they used to, were Button's way of making a connection in real life. It didn't matter if there was any truth to it, the association had already been made in her head.

"Course."

"I mean, the fact that I even started to interpret cats as the universe's way of putting me in touch with my lost child is about the closest I'll ever get to accepting that there might be a little bit of something to *some* of the stuff you believe in."

A smug smile spilled across Celeste's face. "Then I will take that as a win."

"Please stop sending me reflexology vouchers though."

"If I refer people, I get a discount."

"That's how all the cults get started."

"Slow moving cult." Celeste grinned.

When they got back to the flat, Paige had been expecting to find Luke pretending to read a magazine or something while he kept a not-so-subtle eye on Annie. Instead, she could hear their voices before she even opened the door. Was it a heated debate?

"…just wouldn't take too much to make them look a bit more interesting, that's all. I mean, maybe if it was all social housing and doing it on the cheap was more important than aesthetics there might be some kind of argument in favour of those blank-faced slabs, but even then, it seems unfair." Annie sighed dramatically. "I guess people get charged through the nose for those horrible characterless boxes to increase profits for those poor beleaguered house builders, but enough folk seem prepared to pay the price. What I wouldn't give for a little asymmetry, maybe a curved fascia or two."

Paige and Celeste smiled at each other. If Annie was breaking out the modern-architecture-is-dire rant, that had to be a good sign. At least she was beginning to care about things again.

"I think she might be getting better," Celeste whispered.

They stood and continued to listen at the door. "Luke can be the same. To be honest, I'm surprised at how restrained he's being not chipping in. There's a very similar diatribe he's got locked and loaded about how hench cars are getting."

"Next time, I'm sure." Leaning down, Celeste smoothed the blanket in Libby's pram. "Shall we take you in to see Mama?"

Paige hung back, knowing it still wasn't time for her and Annie. It had been better, the last time they were in a room together. But it was still difficult for Annie. She didn't quite trust Paige, couldn't settle in her company. It was better not to force the matter.

If Paige could have some idea of how long she was going to be… not punished, but something like it, that would go some way to soothing the hurt raging in her heart. But she could understand that what was going on didn't have to be rational. How long had she held Kelly at arm's length for something that wasn't really her fault? She could do her time here. At least she managed to share a smile with Luke before backing away and heading home.

*

A soft clearing of the throat yanked Paige's attention towards the doorway. A tentative, ashen-faced Margaret had arrived. To save the day?

It was hard not to be shocked that she was actually here. While it had felt like the decent thing to do, to get Russell to notify Margaret that their daughter was in quite so much trouble, Paige hadn't expected anything to come of it. She could count on the fingers of one hand all the events that had drawn Margaret away from Dorset in the past decade and none of them were anything to do with either of her daughters.

Why was she here? Shouldn't Margaret have turned up on Annie's doorstep rather than Paige's? "Mum?"

"I…" if Margaret could ever find a way to recapture the delicate agony on her face and put it on the stage, she'd make an amazing actor after all, "she confided in me. And I," she sucked in a half sob, "I dismissed it. I mean, there are always times when new motherhood feels like it's all getting a bit much, but I thought she needed to pull herself together. Tough love and all that. You know what I mean? I'll never do it again, I swear. If either of you girls need me, I will be there. I will listen to whatever you want to say."

Maybe the next time one of your children tries to confide in you, you'll remember this moment. Not that Paige was still sore about Margaret's disappointing efforts after the miscarriage. But she didn't want to leave Margaret struggling on the hook. It looked as if her mother had spent the whole journey up pulling at the threads of her cardigan to the point that it was on the verge of disintegrating.

"She's alright, Mum. Annie's going to be okay. She kind of already is. We're out of the woods. She's in regular counselling. We've worked out a support schedule and everything."

Margaret's timing was impeccable. She'd missed all the scariest moments. If she was here to plunge in and save the day, it was a bit late. There was a lot more that Paige wanted to say. That Annie still didn't seem to trust her. That she had never felt further from a motherhood of her own. That knowing you did the right thing and believing it were two separate matters.

But Margaret was already moving on, her guilt neatly bundled up and stuffed out of sight. "Oh, how marvellous. Well done you. Your father made it sound so doom and gloom, but I was sure that couldn't be right."

"No, it was… I mean… doesn't matter."

There was zero chance that Margaret would be able to learn from this episode and not wait until the next mental breakdown before she decided to visit again. But she'd come now. That probably had to count for something.

"So, are you going to pop by and see Annie? Meet the baby?"

For a moment, there was a sliver of something genuine on Margaret's face. A hesitation that suggested she knew she had something to make up for. "Well, I don't know. Wouldn't want to stick my nose anywhere it's unwelcome."

The best thing to do would be to run it by Celeste. She was the most plugged in to how Annie was thinking and feeling. But Paige knew her mother well enough to predict how she would take the suggestion that she needed a go-between like her husband's second wife when it came to visiting her own daughter.

"Maybe you and Dad could go together?"

"It would be a shame to come all this way and miss out on saying my hellos. Of course, there's nothing stopping all of you from popping down to see us. I'll make sure the spring production is something suitable for the little one."

It was the closest they were going to get to a concession. Paige grinned. She and Annie could take bets on how inappropriate the Durdle Door Players' take on family friendly would be. If Annie was talking to her by then. Missing Annie was almost worse than tearing herself apart with anxiety over how she was doing. Of all the sacrifices Paige had been forced to make, not seeing Annie was one of the hardest.

"And how are you, darling?"

Paige heaved a sigh out of her cheeks. How honest to go? As far as she was aware, Margaret didn't know about the failed IVF cycles, let alone the fact that she was on the verge of giving up on the entire process altogether. "Broken, a bit hopeless. You?"

"Well, if you're just going to be silly."

She should have known her mother's pledge to listen was destined to be short-lived. It would have been unsettling, really, for Margaret to change at this point in her life. Reassuring to see that she didn't have it in her. She couldn't have chosen to do it before now. At least Paige got another Margaret-special hug out of the visit. That was something.

*

"Mum stopped by."

One of Celeste's eyebrows quirked upwards. It didn't take much time in Margaret's company to get a decent measure of the woman. And even though he was a gentleman through and through, Russell had to have talked at least a little about his ex-wife. There was bound to be quite a lot that Celeste knew about Margaret. "Oh. How did that go?"

"Predictable, really. I think she wanted some kind of absolution." Paige sighed. "She's not much of a mother these days. I know how much she wanted to make it clear that she didn't want to pressurise me or Annie to have kids. Possible that she went a bit too far off the other end."

She didn't even ask whether Margaret had been to Russell about seeing Annie and Libby. At the end of the day, it didn't matter. There was something more important that Paige wanted to talk about.

"You're, well, I mean..." She sifted through her brain, trying to summon up the right words to capture what she wanted to tell Celeste. Maybe Margaret's drive by had been good for something after all. Painted quite the contrast between her and certain other mothers. The work of parenting didn't come to an end even when your child went into the ground. Celeste qualified for the title, no matter what anyone else might think.

"You don't have to say it."

Bless that woman. Even more reason why Paige had to try and put her thoughts into words. "I want to, though. You've done a lot more mothering, to me and Annie, than Mum's bothered with in such a long time. I'm... I'm really glad you're in our lives. As Libby's grandma as much as anything else."

Celeste's eyes were shining.

Heart wrenching as she continued, Paige met Celeste's kind gaze. "I'm... I'm glad Annie could give that to you."

Reaching out her hand, Celeste gave Paige a reassuring squeeze on the arm. "I was that for Button long before Libby. I do believe that."

"And even though I didn't know it for a long time, when you and Dad got married, I got an extra stepsister. And Hart. I'll always wish I could have met them."

She wondered if she was taking things too far with the present she'd brought round for Celeste. But it was an idea that, once she'd had it, Paige couldn't get away from. Though she couldn't be sure, she didn't think it was overstepping as such. She was more afraid that she was pushing something that might hurt Celeste a lot more than it would help.

Too late now for second thoughts. Not that Russell would give her away. More that his blessing had been enough of a spur to follow through on her initial impulse.

"I, um, I had a thought about something."

"What was that?"

"Well, because I get the most depressing pop-up ads these days – hot doctors in your area seeking infertile women and whatnot – I found this company who do birth-size pillows. Very social media, oh look how tiny they were compared to how much they've grown."

They both took a moment to exchange sad smiles. Both women knew what it was to have children who would never grow up. The dark side of wishful statements that babies would remain the same forever. Celeste was the only one who'd had something to hold though.

"I… I asked Dad if you knew how big Rebecca was. Her length and weight. And well, I mean, they don't come weighted, so it was a bit of a makeshift job." Almost guiltily, she produced a lumpy parcel. "You don't have to open it in front of me or anything. I… I just. You deserve to get to hold her again. Even if it's only pretend."

Celeste made no response, not that Paige had been expecting one. The tears that had been threatening to spill trickled down her cheeks. After Paige got to her feet, she pressed a kiss into Celeste's hair and squeezed back when her stepmother flung her arms around her waist.

SEPTEMBER

Celeste

WHEN SHE WAS ALONE, Celeste opened her memory box, something she did so rarely these days. It wasn't really where her memories were. She could have added to it, she supposed. But she had her trips to the woods and her tattoo. And candles she lit whenever she felt the urge. Those were more fitting, and it was important to honour those sorts of impulses, she'd learned.

Most often, the box served to highlight all those empty spaces. She should have pictures, other ways to preserve those few precious memories. She should have felt brave enough to display the footprints, rather than lock them away for fear they'd disappear too.

She scooped out the tiny wristband. The one Russell must have studied to provide Paige with the information she needed. Baby Hartman. Two pounds, twelve and a half ounces. Sixteen inches long. Every now and then, Celeste considered updating the label to say Rebecca, but she always stopped herself. There were no do-overs, and she didn't want to ruin what she already had by attempting to edit.

She held the package Paige had given her. Something new. With shaking hands, she discarded the wrapping. She eased the cushion out of its bag and stared at it. A black outline on the front curled into the image of a sleeping baby. She knew people who did this sort of thing, got weighted teddies to represent their lost babies, but Celeste had always found that a little bit strange. Rebecca wasn't a bear, with a glassy smile and beady black eyes. Her eyelids had been closed to the world forever.

Some instinct took over and Celeste gathered the cushion into her arms. A tangible piece of her child. Something inside her remembered the weight of Rebecca, even this many years later. She cradled the pillow in the crook of her elbow, tears trickling down her face, closed her eyes, and slid back into that darkened room in her mind.

There was no way to change the mistakes she'd made at the time, but she could imagine the opportunity to do things differently. To lay that cold skin next to her own warmth. To commemorate every inch of delicate flesh. Every dainty toe and tiny finger. The curve of her eyebrows, the button nose, the shape of her mouth. To have brought something with her to the hospital so Rebecca could have kept a little piece of Mummy.

Why hadn't Celeste thought of stripping off her top so Rebecca would be left with her scent? It didn't matter that Rebecca had been dead, couldn't smell even if she wanted to. Her whole life had been spent inside Celeste. The last sound she would have heard would have been her mother's heartbeat.

Celeste was human. Mistakes were inevitable. But there were tiny remedies that could push some of the darkness back. She cuddled the cushion close, not caring what anyone else might think of what she was doing. Bless Paige for thinking of this. They'd never be mother and daughter, no matter how close they became. They were family though and that was something. Rebecca would always be Celeste's baby. It was nice really, even so many years later for her ways of holding Rebecca close to evolve.

Since she'd had to say goodbye, Celeste had held so many little ones. Maggie's Nico and Hannah's Zane, born a handful of months apart, were some of the first. And a little while after, Bethany. But the experience of holding a living child who wasn't yours was such a different experience to holding a dead one, especially your own.

Rebecca would always be with Celeste. Nothing could or would change that. And this wasn't the same, not by a long shot, but this was a way for her to share her baby with others too. Her husband, her stepdaughters, they could all have some idea of what it was like to hold her daughter.

OCTOBER

Paige

THERE HAD TO BE a way to dress up this proposal. Make it, well, a bit sexier. Anything to make Frank go for it. Paige had read about a local community initiative to set up and run a scrap shop. If she could convince local businesses to donate their waste and surplus stock, she could sell it all as craft supplies and the like. Provided she could find premises. And staff. All on a shoestring budget.

The slim silver lining of her work situation was that Paige could make the numbers dance. Far too many years spent as a wayward accountant had lent her a certain set of skills that were coming in very handy. It was hard not to slip into the fantasy of managing the shop, using it to promote environmentally responsible crafting and such. She sighed. Her dreams used to be so much bigger. And maybe if she kept ignoring it, the idea at the back of her head, the other one, would keep on blooming until she was ready to acknowledge it.

An irritated rap at the door broke her out of her train of thought. It would seem she'd been ignoring something else.

"Coming!" she yelled out. Hauling herself to her feet, she tried not to huff with disappointment at the interruption. But she'd been so close to a breakthrough. She was sure of it. Nothing she did was going to stem the tide of climate change, but it wasn't nothing and any win, no matter how small, was progress.

All annoyance was forgotten when Paige opened the door. "Peep?"

"Annie! You look great! Sorry, that was really patronising, wasn't it?"

"Just a tad."

It was nothing but the truth though. Her heart was fluttering with relief. Not only was Annie here, talking to her, but also looking happier and healthier than she'd seemed since, well, since before the pandemic if Paige were being honest. It was more than the fact that her hair was washed, and her clothes were clean, even though those facts alone were impressive from the single mother of a three-month-old. With Libby strapped to Annie's chest, gurgling, it was clear they were finally the package deal they should have been all along.

"Can I come in?"

"Of course. Sorry. Tea? Or, or something stronger?" In her surprise at the complete reversal in Annie's attitude towards her, Paige had forgotten how to behave in her sister's company.

"Tea would be lovely. And I'm the one who's sorry."

"No!" Paige had to find a way to stop shrieking. Communicating in exclamation marks wasn't her usual style.

Annie flapped a hand. "Stop that. I just… I got so lost, and it was," she gulped, "it was easier to blame you than get to grips with whatever was going on."

It was clear this was a speech that she'd been rehearsing. In the nicest way possible, Paige didn't care. The last thing she needed from Annie was an apology. Having her sister back, her old self shining through all the gloom that had settled on her since Libby was born, maybe before that, Paige couldn't ask for anything else.

"Seriously, you don't have to do this." She reached over to squeeze Annie close in a hug, careful not to squish the baby. "You're my big sister, you were due a freakout. Biding your time after the Monopoly incident, right?"

Annie giggled. "Right." They'd have this out, eventually, but this wasn't the time. She deposited a sleepy Libby onto Paige's lap, smiling.

Even though her sister was doing so much better, Paige couldn't help being a little surprised by the kind gesture. After a surprised pause, she held the baby closer and felt herself relaxing into her chair.

Over tea, Annie confessed. "The antidepressants are helping. It's hard to remember everything that happened, to be honest."

"Probably for the best."

"What if it happens again?" Paige smiled sympathetically. "If I've learned anything over the past few years—"

"And you probably haven't." Annie put in. They grinned at each other.

"It's that no matter how isolated you're feeling, someone, somewhere, has had to deal with the exact same feelings as you. Someone will have had to cope with circumstances like yours and felt the same way. Everything else just has the annoying effect of drowning them out, too many normal people separating everyone into their private hells, feeling like no one else will understand."

For a long few seconds, Paige stared out of the window. Something brought her back to herself and she ploughed on. "So, because your comrades take a bit of finding, it's easy to make the mistake of believing they don't exist in the first place. Way too much doesn't get talked about. Everything gets crammed through the lens of ordinary, the most common experience, what everyone ought to expect.

That way, anything that doesn't quite fit spills out into the fringes, creating misfits and outcasts of those who didn't get the memo. No one wants to worry the pregnant women, so they don't talk about the realities of baby loss or postpartum depression."

She drew to a halt, a little surprised at the length of the speech she'd made. Then her lips quirked to one side at the thought that Annie probably wasn't the one who needed lecturing at this point. "All you can do is keep talking about what's happening in your head. A problem shared is a problem that much closer to being identified."

Rather than make outright fun of the earnestness, Annie was kind enough to meet Paige with gentle teasing. "You're going to start dragging me along to support groups, aren't you?"

"Nah, mate. Internet forums. Find your tribe from the comfort of your very own home. And if that fails, we'll get you sectioned again."

"Ha-ha."

"If people talked about this kind of thing more, it would all be so much easier. For years, I had no idea that Pippa, my boss, well, her brother and his wife went through recurrent loss. I only found that out a little while ago. It does explain why she upgraded my medical leave without me knowing about it. I always thought that she'd decided I was a total basket case who couldn't be trusted around the office, but no, it was informed empathy."

"It's a small world."

"Yeah." Paige felt her face falling.

"But not small enough?"

She nodded. "Too many people getting their happy endings while I'm still out in the cold."

Annie waited.

"Pippa only brought it up because she was overcome with joy about her beautiful little nephew. The rainbow at the end of way too many storms."

"It's not fair."

People did keep saying that to Paige. But it was the kind of thing she'd always take from Celeste and Annie. She nodded. "You're telling me."

It was nice to have a chance to talk about her own problems with Annie again, rather than having to worry so much about her. A relief to see her sister wasn't made of glass. Then again, they could stand to spend a little bit more time discussing Annie and her situation, rather than reverting to form and making everything about the state of Paige's infertility.

"You're not on your own. Two parents — the whole nuclear standard — it's just one kind of family. But we're all here for you to put us to use. I don't know if you've noticed, but Luke's love language is taking care of people. He'd do anything for you guys."

"That's right, rub it in that you've found the perfect partner."

"I won't be all condescending and tell you to keep looking or whatever." Maybe infertility wasn't the only predicament that came with trite sentiments about what you wanted happening when you weren't expecting it. She had to tell Annie something that was going to make it sound even more like she was bragging about her amazing husband. Maybe she was. "He's building a doll's house for Libby's birthday. We really need to give him a bit more parenting experience so he can figure out when that sort of thing might be age appropriate—"

"Might just be giving himself a realistic deadline." Annie chipped in. "Time for him to master woodworking while she works on fine motor skills. They might be evenly matched by the time she starts school."

"True. He's got the idea from somewhere that it needs to

have interesting bay windows and asymmetrical flourishes. The point is, we all love you both and want to do our bit. We're *gagging* to barge in. Even Mum, well, that might just be the guilt talking. She's coming round from the attitude that she had to suffer through it without much support, so she didn't see why everyone else doesn't have to. The rest of us have fewer strings involved when it comes to our offers of help."

"I should have let you all in."

"Oh, no recriminations. It's not like that. I'm just going to keep reminding you of how much you're loved. Both of you."

Annie looked like she was going to cry again. But in a good way.

OCTOBER

Annie

"HAS THIS WHOLE BREAKDOWN of yours been your elaborate way of sending me the message that having a baby isn't all it's cracked up to be?"

Annie gave a small, cautious smile. "Did it work?"

"Nope. Baby crazier than ever."

They laughed together. "Damn."

"No going full psychosis or whatever." Paige was doing her best to sound stern. "It's not going to put me off."

Annie sighed. "Fiiine." She cracked a smile, what felt like the first she'd managed in years.

They didn't have to dig any deeper, but she knew there was a true kernel of warning lurking behind Paige's light tone. If they lived another fifty years, would Annie ever be able to pay her family back for what they'd done for her? She was a single mother, she shouldn't have had the freedom to break down, to sink to the bottom of that black well for such a long time, not while she had a mouth to feed. But they'd looked after both her and the baby.

Even with the meds sanding off all the rough edges, there was plenty of hurt still to process. Annie was grateful for the way the drugs turned down the volume of some of it, helping her to function. There was a lot to get through.

"I kept wishing I'd given Libby to you," she whispered. If she didn't make this confession now, she probably never would, and in that moment, she wanted her sister to know. If she could, she wanted to give Paige some insight into the thoughts that had twisted her around so much.

"Like turned it into a surrogacy arrangement or something. It's not fair that I'm the mum and you're not. And then when you were trying to help, I almost thought you were trying to take her away. I know," she almost choked on her words in her hurry to reassure Paige, "I know you wouldn't. But it was all so mixed up in my head."

"Libby's not mine." Paige's eyes were full of warmth. "I can hold her and love her, care for her because it's what she needs. But I know she isn't mine. Can't be."

Before Annie could find the words, Paige shook her head. "I mean, she's not the one I lost. There's no replacement. Couldn't be one if I tried." Her smile was rueful. "And lord how we've been trying."

"I know. I'm so sorry."

"No, Oakley. Listen to me. This isn't about you, or your gorgeous little daughter who's all yours and has been from day one. I mean, I've been trying so hard to get back to where we were and that's never going to happen."

Paige swallowed. "One way or another, I'd have learned this for myself. We'd have had another one and I'd have seen how they weren't Button. We'll never know Button, but they had a specific themness that will never be substituted by anyone else. And they'll always have been the one that made me a mum. I always will be. But," she swallowed and gave a nervous smile, "I think I'm finally ready to give my heart to adoption. Find another way. Don't get me wrong, I'm still angry as all hell about the unfairness of it all, but that doesn't get me any closer to what I need."

She crossed the room and with tender care deposited the baby into her sister's waiting arms. Once Libby was settled and content, she placed a hand on Annie's shoulder.

"Don't give me more credit than I deserve. Celeste did all the big stuff. But there were a few times when I looked after her." She took a deep breath. "And when it was just her and me, Libby and I got on great. I know we are blood and it's thicker than water or whatever, but now I know I can happily parent someone I didn't give birth to. Didn't even mind when she pooed all over me."

"Any time." Annie lifted the baby and gave her nappy a sniff. "Give it five minutes and we'll see if she's got anything brewing."

Paige poked her tongue out. "I think I'll live. Seriously though, I hope it never gets half so bad again, but you know I'll come running if you ever need me. Nice to be the one in demand for once, to be honest. But you got this now. I need to go and try and find my own kids. Really, it's by far the eco-friendliest path to parenthood."

"I want it for you. You deserve it so much."

For a moment, Paige looked as if she was struggling with what she wanted to say next. When she spoke, it was with a cautious tone. "You'll find what you're looking for too, you know. Love. You deserve it. I know Juliet did a real number on you. I don't know if you remember my last boyfriend before Luke—"

"Shitbag Owen?"

Paige cracked a smile. "That's the one. Well, I'm not saying there's any guarantees, but once you've gone through a bit of romantic shit, you can believe you're owed something downright excellent."

"Right back at you, sis. On the baby front, that is."

"Thank you. I'm not being… I mean," Paige gulped. "I don't know what I'm saying."

"Yes, you do."

"It's not some storybook ending, adoption, riding off into the sunset together. None of these decisions are easy. And you don't just get handed some little blank slate, someone ready for you to fill up with your personality. We'll... we'll miss the baby stage. But it's more than that, while you're missing your kid's months of being a baby, something terrible is happening to them. Something bad enough to mean they need new parents."

Annie's heart hurt so much. For Paige, and the child that was hers but didn't know it yet. She was beyond grateful for the little person sleeping in her lap. Her luck didn't make up for the lack of Paige's. But the way that Libby had come about didn't really have anything much to do with Paige's loss, not in the grand scheme of things. Annie reached out to touch Paige's knee.

"You're going to make up for the fact that your child, who-ever they turn out to be, wasn't lucky enough to have an Auntie Paige to hold everything together while things were trying to fall apart."

"I didn't mean it like that."

"I know." Annie didn't want to traipse further down that line of thought. If she hadn't had a sister and a stepmother who could come and take the baby when she hadn't been capable of looking after her... she held her daughter that little bit closer, felt Libby's soft skin under her fingertips. The possibility of losing her was smaller than it had ever been, but Annie didn't want to take anything for granted.

As she held Libby, Annie took her in, this chubby stranger who was so much bigger and more solid now than the ghost girl who'd haunted her dreams. This baby was sturdy, sub-stantial, far less breakable than she had imagined. Her Libby. Her love.

It was there. Her feelings had taken a little excavating, scraping away all that excess before they could breathe. There was love. Relief radiated throughout Annie's body, tingling its way from the top of her head through to the tips of her toes and fingers. It turned out that she *could* be a mother, after all. And she was going to help her sister get to the next step of building her family. Least she could do.

A NOTE FROM THE AUTHOR

MY STORY ISN'T FINISHED yet. At the time of writing, I'm still in the trenches, holding onto hope and trying everything in my power to bring home that longed-for first living child. However, one of the major reasons for writing this book was to tell the world about what it's like to love and lose children before they have a chance to make it to birth. I wanted to share my experiences in the hope that they'll chime with someone else having their own hard time.

After almost a year of trying, I was delighted to finally get that big fat positive in July 2020. We'd made a Goughling and all we had to do was wait for March to roll around and we could meet our baby. At seven weeks, I began bleeding and miscarried before I could make it to a scan at the early pregnancy unit.

As we mourned Goughling, my husband and I started trying again. It was a huge relief that it took us less time to get back to that positive pregnancy test. By January 2021, I had another baby in my belly. In an act of hope, we named this pregnancy Sticky, a promise that this one would be sticking around. After two and a half smooth trimesters and three joyful ultrasounds with no warning signs, no one was able to find a heartbeat at the thirty-one-week appointment. We'd lost another one.

Still not knowing whether the baby was a boy or a girl, I went for my induction and on 29th July 2021 at 6:52pm, I gave birth to my son. Sticky became Samuel James. We were able to spend time with him, introduce him to my mother, take pictures, wash him, dress him, read to him, and do everything we could to cram a lifetime of parenting into less than twenty-four hours.

We took a break from trying after that, but we both knew this was a temporary situation. None of the testing on me or Sam had revealed any reason we wouldn't meet with success further down the road.

At the end of April 2022, there was a faint second line on the pregnancy test. A squinter. But despite my already-strong pregnancy symptoms, that line never darkened. My husband nicknamed this one Poppy Seed and that's as big as they ever got. My chemical. I started bleeding a few days later and that was that.

Even though we tried during the next cycle, I thought it hadn't been successful. On the day my period was due, the pregnancy test was negative, and the bleed arrived bang on schedule. But after some suspicious spotting a couple of weeks later, I took another test just to rule it out as a potential cause. I hadn't seen a line that strong since January 2021.

But the impossible positive was too good to be true. My May baby whose existence was a troubling question mark, dear Maby, was ectopic. Emergency surgery to remove them and my ruptured fallopian tube meant another few months of a break in trying to conceive. And here we are again, waiting.

My babies matter. All of them. I will remember and love them for always. Here's to a happy, healthy pregnancy number five.

ACKNOWLEDGEMENTS

A HUGE THANK YOU IS owed to everyone who has worked on this book with me.

A big thank you to my amazing editor, Aimee. You took a soupy mess of grief and hypothetical plotlines and helped to craft an actual book. It has been such a privilege to work with you on this.

Thank you, Robin, my brilliant cover designer.

Thank you to everyone who agreed to beta read, especially Marianne. From Little Sam's mum to Big Sam's mum, your input has been invaluable.

Thank you to my wonderful and supportive family who've cheered me on at every step. And thanks for the bonus round of proofing, Dad.

The creation of this book has been an act of catharsis, grief, and, of course, love. It would never have been possible without so many people who have supported me through these years.

A not-exhaustive list:

Amber, there are no words, you've been everything.

Nicola, thank you for all your support, and the books.

The ladies in my WhatsApp group, thanks for creating an excellent space to vent.

First C and now S, my incredible counsellors, thank you so much.

To anyone who has listened to my story at support groups and on forums and shared theirs with me in turn, thank you.

An overwhelming thank you to the NHS and all the staff who've had to work so hard to keep me alive. The bereavement team at the John Radcliffe: Laura and Candice. Thank you to each and every midwife who cared for me in labour with my Sam, as well as the midwives who cared for him after he was born: Emily, Heidi and Sian, who made a particular fuss over his feet. And you can see why, they are gorgeous.

Jessie, you didn't sign up to be a support dog, but you've done a magnificent job, nonetheless. I hope I can pay you back in enough belly rubs and giant sausages for how much of a good girl you've been.

Thank you to my amazing family, again. Gerry, who made sure to include Sam on the family tree. Della, who told me how extra-special the timing of Sam's birth was. Thank you to everyone who has kept my little boy's name alive through their incredible fundraising efforts: Sarah, Jenn, Anne, and Rich. Thank you to everyone who loves him as a member of the family.

Mum, Dad, and Tom, I could fill so many pages with thanks for everything you've done for me. Thank you.

And last, but definitely not least, thank you to my husband, Rob, the most wonderful father to all our children, my partner in all of this. I love you so much. I feel so lucky in that all we've had to get through, I've had you with me.

RESOURCES

MY EXPERIENCES WILL NOT be a perfect match for anyone else's. These are all personal recommendations for resources that have been beneficial for my grief:

Charities:

- **Tommys**: along with incredibly moving video campaigns such as #WeSeeaMum, Tommys and their research gives me hope.
- **Sands**: along with reading their helpful literature, my husband and I have been able to attend support group meetings with fellow bereaved parents. Sharing stories helps.
- **4Louis**: waiting for us in our bereavement suite when we took Sam up was a memory box that now sits on his shelf.
- **Aching Arms**: our bear, also waiting for us with the memory box, is Reuben. If his family ever reads this, thank you. Having him to cuddle helped.
- **Petals**: I was lucky enough to be offered six sessions of free specialist baby loss counselling and have continued working with my counsellor in a private capacity ever since.

Books:

- *The Miscarriage Map* by Dr Sunita Osborn
- *An Exact Replica of a Figment of my Imagination* by Elizabeth McCracken
- *Ask Me His Name* and *A Bump in the Road* by Elle Wright
- *They Were Still Born* – a collection of essays edited by Janel C Atlas
- The book that Russell mentions during his dinner with Paige is *The Myth of the Perfect Pregnancy* by Lara Freidenfelds

Podcasts:

- *Griefcast*: covers all sorts of grief, so I'd like to highlight certain episodes in particular – Lou Conran, Sara Barron, Anna Whitehouse, Zoe Clark-Coates, Garett Millerick, Sarah Brown, Amanda Palmer, Genelle Aldred, Geoff Norcott, and Charlotte Bennett.
- *The Worst Girl Gang Ever*
- *Big Fat Negative*
- *Best Friend Therapy*
- *The Other Mothers*

Instagram: there are lots of baby loss-oriented accounts out there and incredible connections to be made. Two accounts I found in my early days on there that helped were @_thethingsiwishyouknew and @breathingafterloss.

CONTACT ROS

ros.goughpress@gmail.com
Instagram @ros.gough